A NEW LIFE IN EVERSLEY VILLAGE

VILLAGE

AN EVERSLEY VILLAGE ROMANCE

SUZANNE FOX

LITTLE ORCHARD PRESS

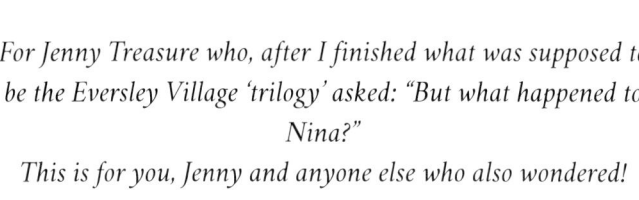

For Jenny Treasure who, after I finished what was supposed to be the Eversley Village 'trilogy' asked: "But what happened to Nina?"
This is for you, Jenny and anyone else who also wondered!

A CHILDHOOD MEMORY

Nina smiled at her mother as she tucked her in and reached to turn off the bedside lamp.

"Not yet, I'm not tired," Nina said through a yawn.

Sumitra laughed. "You're shattered. Have you enjoyed today?"

"Yes, Ma. I love swimming in the sea." They'd motored to Devon for a day at the beach. It had been glorious, involving sandcastles, ice cream and fish and chips with her mother, father and paternal grandparents.

"And now it's time to sleep, otherwise you'll be late for school tomorrow."

"Ma, tell me again about when you met Daddy," Nina said and she watched her hesitate. Her father had been called out to his shop by the security firm as his alarm had been set off. Because of this, he was unable to do his usual night-time duty of reading her a story. Her father was great at delivering a tale but Nina preferred her mother to talk about India and of when she fell in love with her father. Sumitra was better at telling real stories than reading fiction.

Sumitra smiled as she sat on the edge of her daughter's bed. Nina thought that Ma also liked telling the story; her face lit up whenever she remembered it.

"Okay, then you go to sleep."

"Yes, Ma."

"I was sitting in the university library, studying for my degree, when I saw the most handsome man in the entire world approach the table with a pile of books in his arms. He had golden hair, like an angel, and beautiful blue eyes and when he looked at me, I could see into his soul and knew he was a good man inside and out. I felt butterflies in my tummy and a voice in my head told me – we would be together forever."

Nina grinned at her mother. "Daddy does have lovely eyes. Then what happened?" she asked, although she had heard the story many times before.

"Granny was not happy. She'd already found a match for me. A doctor living one hundred miles away in a big city. I told her, no, I've found my true match in Somerset."

"Did she fall in love with Daddy when she saw his golden hair?"

Sumitra laughed. "No, not at first. I told her that it must have been Parvati the goddess of love who sent him as he was so beautiful. Granny is very traditional and she loved India. That's why she moved back when your grandfather died."

"And then what happened?" Nina asked.

"What happens next is that you, my angel, must go to sleep."

"Please tell me." She looked up at her mother.

Sumitra sighed. "Daddy asked me to marry him as he was worried I would become engaged to someone else. He sold his motorbike and bought me this diamond ring." She showed it to Nina. "He left university while I continued to study so that he could take a job to look after us. To prove to my parents he could take care of me."

"Do you think Granny will like me when she comes to see us?"

"Of course she will. She shows your picture to all of her friends. She cannot wait to visit us." She had been taking care of Nina's great grandmother in her final years which had kept her away. "She will love you. And Granny grew to love Daddy too. She's very proud of him and the life he gives us."

"Did you know as soon as you saw Daddy that you loved him?"

"It was love at first sight," she said.

"I can't wait to meet my love at first sight," Nina said.

Sumitra stroked Nina's forehead. "Not everyone has a love at first sight. And you are only six. Now, settle down." Sumitra kissed Nina on the forehead and left the room, leaving the door ajar.

As soon as she was gone, Nina slipped out of bed and went to her desk. She sat down and pulled out a piece of paper and a pen and wrote:

Dear Parvati goddess of love,

Please send me my love at first sight when I am a grown up. He has golden hair. Blue eyes. Rich and strong. I want a little girl just like me. And we will have a happy ever after. I'll be a good girl and do my very best.

Nina xx

CHAPTER 1

*N*ina sat in the quiet of her shop *Something Special,* a premier bridal boutique which attracted customers from across south west England. She was seeking solace in her shop, for it was election night and the council seat she'd held for ten years was being contested. She breathed in and out slowly as she listened to the rain bouncing off the pavement outside. The droplets were coloured with the light emitting from the yellow streetlamps. She wished Ethan was there; he always made her feel calm. She was used to not seeing him for weeks at a time. He worked away frequently but she'd never felt so vulnerable and, in that moment, a hug from him was what she longed for.

Nina jumped as she heard a rapping at the shop door. It was her friend Holly dressed in a purple raincoat, her image distorted by the water covered glass. Nina realised it was impossible to have any amount of time to herself on election night, other than a few snatched moments, and stood up to open the door.

"Everyone's looking for you," Holly said as she walked into the shop and removed her hood, droplets falling onto the doormat. "We were worried." In contrast to Nina's dark hair and eyes, Holly was willowy with blonde long wavy hair. "Are you okay? You look upset. I've never seen you like this before." She bit her lip.

"I could lose everything," Nina said, feeling her stomach lurch.

"Why are you worried this time?" Holly's blue eyes widened.

"Because this time I think I will lose." Nina reached for her handbag. She would have to return to the town hall, considering her team were on the hunt for her. At least she'd managed to grab a few moments to herself. "Dad will be mortified."

Holly gave a reassuring smile. "Of course you'll win! You've been a Wells councillor for ten years. Now come back and eat something Councillor Smith otherwise you'll faint on stage when they make the announcement."

Nina grabbed her raincoat, a stylish cream one by her favourite designer, with a belt that accentuated her curves. She knew what suited her and was always well turned out. She followed Holly out of the shop. As she closed the door behind her, she wondered whether she'd still be a councillor when she returned. She put her umbrella up and stepped out onto the wet pavement.

The town hall in Wells was situated not far from the Cathedral in the historic Somerset city. It had been a busy few weeks campaigning and a long election day as a stream of local residents turned up to place their votes. As they walked across the square, Nina felt the weather splashing up her calves. Once inside the main entrance, they removed their coats and shook the rain from them. Then made their way to the meeting room which had been designated for Nina and her team to use. As she entered, her stomach turned over at the smell of the food her mother had prepared. Nerves had got the better of her. She usually loved the snacks Sumitra made but she wasn't in the mood for them, not with worry tying her insides into knots.

"There you are," her father said, running a hand over his closely shaven head of white hair as they entered. "We were worried."

"I needed five minutes to breathe, Dad." She looked into his blue eyes, feeling a burn in her stomach. He was so proud of her, his daughter the councillor. And he'd always been her greatest cheerleader.

He gave her a fatherly hug. "I understand. I take them myself. It's good to clear the mind. And now you're refreshed, you can go out and thank the team."

"I…" Nina was feeling too distracted by her nerves to make polite conversation. She felt a lump form in her throat. Whilst she had confided in Holly, she could not bear to admit to her father that she dreaded defeat.

"Tony, Nina needs to eat something," Holly said, coming to her rescue. "All she's consumed today is half a cheese sandwich."

"In that case, stay and eat and I'll report that you've been found. They're still searching." He pulled his mobile phone from the inside pocket of his smart suit. "I'll send a text in the group chat."

Nina sighed as her father left the room. She picked up a small crispy onion bhaji. Half of the food had already been eaten and it was clear that the rest of the team had already snacked. Hopefully that would mean she could eat in peace. She slowly put the food up to her mouth and took a nibble before returning it to her plate. "I've been overeating so much these past few weeks with all the stress and now I've no appetite at all."

"It's not surprising with the nightly canvassing. I don't know how you do it. You really are a superwoman. Always have been." Holly picked up a paper plate and began loading it with snacks.

"At least Ma's not here. She would be fussing over me if she saw me like this."

"I was surprised when she left early," Holly said then bit into a small, well-done naan slathered with a garlic ghee. "She doesn't normally miss it."

"She's covering for me tomorrow at the shop. A customer's arriving at the boutique at nine for an emergency fitting."

"You seem so nervous but why? Everyone knows how much work you've done for the area. You're a well-known, respected businesswoman, and you were the youngest to ever have been voted onto the council. You're on three committees always in The Gazette being praised for the environmental initiatives you've set up. You work hard and are more present than any of the other candidates." She gestured at her with her naan. "You're a local hero for goodness' sake, they want you to be the next mayor."

"I won't be mayor if I'm not re-elected." Nina sat down. Her father had been so excited about her becoming mayor – especially with Ethan often away, as she had said he could be her stand-by plus one to the events.

"What's got into you?" Holly bit her lip.

"Everyone loves Hedgehog Sam," Nina said in a small voice. She hated mentioning the name of the man she was worried would steal her seat.

Holly finished her mouthful of bread. "Not him again? I hadn't even heard of him until today. The constituents are savvy, no-one's going to vote a man onto the council just because he saved a hedgehog." She laughed then spooned some raita onto her naan.

Nina sighed. "The main parties get their candidate voted in. They always will as people vote for the party rather than the person. I'm usually the only independent to win a seat, now I've Sam as my competition. Populism is on the rise and that video of him went viral – more people know him than they know me. Literally millions across the globe. Did you see the kids outside queuing up for his autograph?"

Holly chewed her food then spoke. "Children don't vote. For local council elections the only people who show up are those that really care about who's being elected and are aware of the local issues. And quite frankly, you're the only one out of the candidates who has anything relevant and sensible to say and who really cares. Sam has no hope. He's a fifteen-minute celebrity."

Nina took a deep breath. "It would be great if you're right. Although, I'm not so sure." Dread seeped into her gut. It seemed that whilst Holly was ignorant of who Sam Brent really was, half the world had seen the video of him stopping the traffic on the B3134 so he could rescue the helpless baby hedgehog laying next to its deceased mother. Sam then appeared in daily videos as he nursed the spiky mammal back to full health, feeding it with a syringe of milk. He finally went live on social media, releasing 'Hoggy' into his natural habitat, miles from any roads as people commented on the post that his story had brought them to tears.

"I guess I've so much to lose," Nina said after a short silence. "I've been a councillor for a large portion of my working life." She was voted in when she was twenty-seven. "Being Councillor Smith is part of my identity and I can't imagine going back to being 'Miss Smith'."

"I wish Jaz was here, she'd talk some sense into you!" Holly said.

Nina and Holly had been at sixth form together studying art and textiles, and Jaz was Holly's best friend who she met when socialising in Eversley village. She'd not liked Nina when they were in their teens, but in recent years she too had become close to her.

Nina pulled her phone from her pocket. "That reminds me, she texted me earlier." She opened up the message from Jaz and smiled. Jaz had moved that day into her new home in one of Eversley village's cul-de-sacs having relocated approximately three hundred yards from her previous home with her husband and his son. They had been living above The Eversley Arms pub. Her younger siblings also stayed with them for most of the week so they were really a family of five. Nina showed the picture to Holly of Jaz's husband, Julian, lifting her over the threshold.

Holly grinned. "It's a great cottage, I was there first thing. Mitch has been there all day helping. They're having a housewarming a week Saturday. Are you and Ethan coming?"

"Of course." Nina hoped her fiancé Ethan would be at home that weekend. She needed to sync their diaries, all she knew was that he was due back from Germany on Monday evening.

"And you'll be all smiles by then, having been re-elected as Councillor Smith. Now come along, eat up," Holly said, offering her a plate of samosas. "We can't hide in this room for much longer, your supporters are out there and want to see their woman!"

Nina took a deep breath and began eating, although found it difficult to shift the feeling of nausea. She checked her phone. She had a message from Ethan:

Good luck babe. Wish I was there to celebrate with you. Can't believe I'm missing it. Love you to the moon and back xx

"Ethan's messaged me. He wishes he was here."

"Where is he again?" Holly asked.

"In Berlin for discussions about a design he's submitted."

Ethan was a successful architect and had attended sixth form with herself and Holly. Although he'd transformed since his college days. Unlike his teenage self, the adult Ethan had ticked all of Nina's boxes. She'd waited years to meet the perfect man and now she had him as her fiancé. If only they could sync their diaries and set a date for the wedding. There always seemed to be something on the horizon which they needed to wait to pass. They'd been together for six years and engaged for three. Nina couldn't complain – his business was going from strength to strength, and he was being carried along by the momentum. She was immensely proud of him and had not protested when he said he could not make election night. She didn't want to pull him away from this potential contract – he'd been clear, if he succeeded in sealing the deal, it would be a massive step up.

"What's the big job he's bidding for?" Holly asked.

"I feel guilty... I've been so tied up with canvassing, I'm not entirely sure, other than he thinks this will open a huge door."

"He showed me a design over at the arts hub a few weeks ago. It was a huge skyscraper. I guess it's that."

"They're getting larger," Nina said, placing the remaining corner of her samosa back on the plate. "He's building a name for himself now. I know he's particularly excited about this client." She decided that as soon as the election was over and Ethan was home she would take more of an interest in his work. "Over the past few months our respective businesses have tired us out. We haven't been on a proper date since Valentine's. All we seem to do is veg out on front of the TV when our paths do cross. We've both been too shattered for anything else."

"And you need to set a date for the wedding."

"I think we'll be looking at next year."

"Even if it's over a year away, at least it'll be in the diary."

Nina nodded. "I'm looking forward to it. I've changed my mind on the dress so many times."

"Your wedding is going to be perfect, with all your contacts and experience."

"I hope so. I've a favourite venue that's perfect, next to a lake. Ethan loves it too." It seemed weird to Nina that out of everyone she was the one yet to walk down the aisle, considering she was the one with the bridal boutique.

The door opened and her father appeared with a grin on his face. "Nina, the count is in!"

"Already? That's early!"

"Yes, come along." He held out his hand eagerly, gazing at her. "I'm so proud of you, angel."

As NINA STOOD on the stage with the other nine candidates competing for the six seats in the St Cuthbert's ward of Wells, her legs trembled. Sam Brent was there wearing a t-shirt with a photograph printed on it of the famous 'Hoggy'. In the crowd were his noisy fans, with his mascot – a full-sized hedgehog wearing a green rosette with *Hoggy* printed on it. Nina knew why Sam had put himself forward as a councillor – it was because of his father. Barry Brent had one hand on the hedgehog's shoulder with the other holding an unlit cigar. He was a local businessman often running a dubious scheme with his finger in many pies. He'd also been a thorn in Nina's side, always vocal and objecting to the council's plans. Especially the ones she put forward. She was in the final stages of pushing through stricter regulations on waste management for businesses, introducing higher penalties for those that did not comply with new recycling standards. Barry Brent had argued that this would cause his off-licence business to have an increase in costs and lead to shop closures across Wells and beyond.

Barry Brent shouted across the room. "You're gonna walk it my son."

Nina cringed and shook her head. In contrast her father stood proudly at the side, quiet and dressed in a crisp suit. Everything with Tony Smith and his tailoring business was always above board. She smiled at him as he gave her the thumbs up. She had always strived for him to be proud of her and she couldn't bear to see his face if she lost. Looking back at Barry Brent she realised he was a very different type of man to her father. Although Barry attended all of the local charity events as a compère, he rarely put his hand into his own pocket. No one really liked him. He'd never have a chance getting voted onto the council himself, so it looked as if he was getting his son up there, hoping to influence the decisions. Nina felt even more nauseous. She took a deep breath but couldn't chase the sickness away as her stomach churned.

"Excuse me," Nina said before taking the short steps from the temporary stage that had been put up.

"Are you okay?" Holly asked as she met her at the foot of the steps.

"I need to visit the ladies."

Nina reached the toilet just in time.

Holly had followed her and rapped on the cubicle door. "Are you okay in there?"

"Must be the samosa," Nina groaned. "I should have avoided fried food."

"I'm fine and I've had three," Holly said. "I guess it's the stress. I'll just pop out and get you some water."

"Can you fetch my bag?" Nina called out.

Nina came out of the cubicle and checked her reflection in the mirror. The woman who looked back at her was tired. Her forehead felt clammy and she smoothed away her hair which was stuck to her face. She shut her eyes. *I'm a mess*, she thought. It had been a while since she'd been to the beautician, although had stopped using the most extreme beauty treatments. Having forgone treatments during the pandemic, everyone had commented that she looked much nicer without them. At least she'd managed to fit in an appointment at the hairdresser who had given her hair a trim. Not that it looked it's best in that moment. She also noticed she'd put a little weight on, probably from all the comfort food she'd been eating with all the worry.

Holly entered the room with a glass of chilled water in one hand and Nina's bag in the other. "They're waiting until you get back on stage to call the results." She handed her the glass and placed the bag on the sink.

After drinking the water, Nina retrieved her make-up and brush from her bag.

"In five minutes you'll be able to relax," Holly reassured her.

Nina brushed her hair and retouched her make-up. She straightened her suit and popped a mint into her mouth.

Back in the main hall, there was a small round of applause from her supporters as she headed for the stage.

"Good luck, dear," an elderly lady said to her.

"Go on Sam," Barry Brent shouted, followed by a huge round of applause and chants of "Hedgehog Sam is our man."

"His supporters are loud, but it doesn't mean the locals voted for him," Tony said into her ear as she passed him on her way to the stage.

Nina took a deep breath. *Dad's sensible and always right*, she told herself, as she climbed the steps to the stage for the final results.

Standing on the platform with the four other candidates she waited to hear the numbers. As usual they called the results for the main political parties first. She had never competed with them; her competition was always the other independents. After the main parties had been called, she took a deep breath: there were five candidates left and only one seat remained.

"Christine Allan, independent, four hundred and five votes." There followed a small applause. "Greg Beaumont, independent, three hundred and four votes." Another applause followed. "John Ludlow, independent, three hundred and fifty votes." Moderate applause followed. "Samuel Barry Brent, one thousand and twenty-five votes."

That's huge, Nina thought, as shouts from his supporters filled the room. She nervously caught her father's eye. He ran a hand over his head and lowered his eyes. That was more votes than she'd received the term before. *Maybe turnout was higher this year?* she thought in a last attempt to think positive, but deep down she knew she'd lost.

"Nina Smith, independent, seven hundred and fifty-two votes."

Nina felt dizzy as Sam's supporters went wild, lifting the life-sized hedgehog into the air. She was rooted to the spot with a fake grin frozen upon her face. She turned to Sam who appeared shocked and apologetic. She shook his hand and then stepped back while he moved forward to take his turn with the other elected candidates to give thanks. Nina's cheeks quivered and knew she would not be able to take the microphone afterwards without descending into floods of tears. Her emotions were off kilter; they had been for weeks. She had to get off the stage. As she reached the steps, Holly was there to help her down, her face a mixture of shock and concern.

Her father also approached the stage and when she had descended took her arm. His eyebrows were raised, creating creases across his brow, "It's nothing you've done wrong, angel. Let's get you home and work on your comeback plan."

"No. I'm going back to Shepton Mallet. I want to be alone." She also wanted to call Ethan, suddenly wishing he was there as she needed a hug – a big one.

"I understand. I'd want space too – to regroup."

"Are you sure, Nina?" Holly asked. "Shall I come with you?"

"She'll be fine," Tony said. "My daughter is made of strong stuff and that young man will fail miserably." He shook his head as Sam's supporters lifted him in the air. "There'll be a by-election for sure and Nina will be waiting in the wings to come back stronger." He gave her an encouraging smile but his eyes were now glassy, as if mirroring her own pain.

Nina passed her team and supporters and they offered their condolences and she smiled back, nodding, unable to speak as her throat was so constricted. As she left the main doors of the Wells town hall, Nina felt as if a part of her had died.

CHAPTER 2

*W*arren viewed the land at Booth Farm, situated about half a mile from the centre of Eversley village. The farm sprawled out from the Mendip Hills with a variety of crops and milking cows. It was a fresh morning with the sun glinting on the ground which had been drenched in rain the previous day. He owed a lot to the owner Mitch Booth for believing in him enough to allow him to use a portion of his land for the initiative which was central to his PHD. The next step was to secure funding for the lease of the field long term, and extra funding would be needed for the project to continue. It was more than a project for Warren's PHD now that the field was taking shape. It was going to be something for future generations. An initiative which would hopefully survive them all. Mitch was a lecturer at the college Warren had been studying at for some years and had encouraged him to take the PHD and suggested they applied for funding to enable him to create a silvopasture system, combining forestry and the grazing of animals.

He smiled to himself. Who would have thought that Warren Hunter the wayward lad would be months away from receiving a doctorate. *Dr Hunter,* he thought with a smile.

"Warren."

He was brought out of his thoughts by the call which was accompanied by sounds of a yapping dog.

He turned around to see Mitch's wife approaching. Holly waved at him as her small white dog with tan ears pelted towards him at top speed. He dropped his spade and strode up the slope towards Holly. She stood with her hair blowing in the wind. The dog jumped up at him and he lifted the fluffy Shih Tzu as it tried to lick his face.

"Trixy, calm down," Holly said with a laugh as he reached her. "I've never seen her so in love with someone, especially a man. She's usually not keen." Warren knew why it was that Trixy liked him – it was because he'd been feeding her treats until he found out they kept the small dog on a strict diet due to the vet's recommendation. Although that had been a few months before, the dog still made a fuss when she greeted him.

Holly gestured behind at her shiny new transit van. "I've got the saplings and a few plants from the list you gave me."

"That's great, Holly, thanks." Warren had found both Mitch and Holly to be a warm and welcoming pair. Mitch owned the farm and Holly owned the neighbouring garden nursery and attached arts hub. She ran many community art projects and Lovelands was a popular stop for school trips and adult coach parties, so his field was ideally situated for educational visits.

"The thanks go to you, Warren, for your ideas and expertise. You'll bring students far and wide to the silvopasture and that'll serve all of us here. Apart from that, I love Agroecology." She gestured over her shoulder. "Let's get the plants."

"Your new van's great," he said as they approached it.

"It cost a bomb, being electric, but I wanted to move with the times and our carbon footprint needs all the help it can get with the cows." She laughed as she nodded towards the sheds than homed the herd and their fields beyond. Warren was also pleased Holly had a new van as she'd passed him her old one. Although it was many years old, it meant he had transport.

Holly opened the van and Trixy jumped into the back. "Out," she said. "We're not going anywhere yet."

"This isn't all for me, is it?" Warren asked as he looked inside the filled transit.

"Yes, it is. But it's not just from Lovelands, I mentioned your project to my suppliers and they were happy to help. Just so long as you mention them at the end of your information leaflet."

"Of course I will." Warren felt excited as he looked inside and smelled the aromas of the plants.

"I'll email you their details," Holly said.

"These saplings are advanced," Warren said pointing to them.

"I managed to source the horse chestnut and willow you wanted. It's amazing planting things for future generations." She handed Warren a box of smaller plants. "But of course your field is going to benefit the current generations too, through the learning they'll receive."

It took some time for them to carry the plants to the field. They placed most of them into a large greenhouse Warren had built. He decided to plant the trees immediately, as he knew exactly where he wanted them to be. He was lucky that the area already had a few established trees and these two would add to the ecosystem of the field.

"Remind me how the horse chestnut helps the field," Holly said.

"Its extensive root system helps prevent soil erosion and enhances water infiltration. Then the flowers attract pollinators like bees."

"When are the bees arriving?"

"I'm still in talks with specialised beekeepers. It's not something I'll manage myself as it needs an expert hand. I've a couple interested in the project though. And you obviously know the willow is there for craft making. Mitch tells me he's excited about choosing a breed of cattle."

Holly yawned. "Yes he is." She held the sapling whilst Warren dug a hole.

Am I boring her? he thought. Sometimes he wondered if he chatted too much about his silvopasture. He didn't have much else in his life to talk about, apart from this project. "Sorry, shall we take a break?" he asked. "I'm tiring you out."

Holly laughed. "Not at all, I was brought up with physical work at the nursery." She gave another yawn, bigger this time as if he had given her permission. "I was up late last night, as in all of the night."

"Were the girls keeping you awake?" Warren asked.

Holly and Mitch had two very sweet looking but rather boisterous twins.

"No, I was with a friend of mine who stood at the council elections in Wells."

"Did it go well?" Warren asked.

"No. She's been a councillor for ten years, done so much for the area and beyond and was pushed out by some guy who apparently saved a hedgehog on the B3134."

Warren looked up. "Hedgehog Sam's a councillor?"

"You've heard of him too?" Holly asked.

"Everyone's heard of him. Not just in the UK, all over the world."

"Except me," Holly said with a laugh. "I was telling Nina all night not to be so silly, as if a guy with no experience was going to take her seat. I felt terrible when he won, and it wasn't a slim win either! He walked it. She's done so much and was supposed to be the next mayor."

"Sam seems to be a nice guy but doesn't come across as the local councillor type. He's younger than me, only twenty-six."

"Is he? Oh, no!" Holly said. "That's even worse."

"Why? What's wrong?"

"Nina carried the record of being the youngest person to have been voted onto the council. He's stolen that crown from her too." She bit her lip.

"I'm sure your friend will be back soon. I can't see Sam lasting." He straightened up, having planted the tree.

Holly picked up the watering can and watered it in. "Nina was devastated. But at least she's got *Something Special*."

"What special thing is that?"

18

"It's the name of her shop. A successful boutique and the go-to place in the whole of the county and beyond for wedding dresses. I got mine there." She looked up with the empty can in her hand. "Both of them," she said with a laugh.

"You were married before Mitch?" Warren asked.

"Briefly," she said with a smile. "I'll tell you about that another time! For now, we need to get to the farmhouse and put the kettle on because I'm in serious need of caffeine."

Warren retrieved his mobile phone from where he'd left it in the greenhouse. There was a notification of a call. He swiped his phone to find it was from an unknown number.

"I just need to check my messages. I have a few outstanding enquiries." He called his voicemail as Holly went outside.

He groaned as he listened. It was from Scottie asking him to call. He knew he'd been sent for a stretch in prison and must have been released. He'd met Scottie in one of the foster homes he'd been in as a child. They were both the same age and had become close as that set of foster parents were not doing a great job. They were separated when the couple were struck off the list but had kept in touch for the rest of their childhood and went to the same school. They'd got into a few scrapes together over the years, the last one resulting in Warren's arrest. He'd achieved nothing with Scottie that he was proud of. Since he was sixteen, Warren had been on a different path. But while Warren had moved on from his wayward days, Scottie never had and often turned to Warren when in trouble.

Warren carried on towards the farmhouse and didn't call him back. *It'll have to wait.* He'd been told by many people to cut Scottie loose. It was tough; with little family, Scottie was the longest friend he'd had and they referred to each other as brothers. But the excuse for not cutting ties with Scottie was wearing thin. Rather than getting out of trouble, Scottie seemed to get deeper in each time and Warren guessed he was ultimately heading for a longer stretch in prison, rather than months. Warren put the phone in his hoodie pocket. He knew he had a tough decision to make and yet he always put it off.

"Mitch should be back from the sheds now," Holly said. "I've a primary school class coming to the hub for a college project, so it'll be nice to have a calm cuppa before the storm."

As they entered the working kitchen of the farm, with its stone floor, they found Mitch already inside eating toast and drinking tea as he read a farming magazine. They used this kitchen during the day but there was another in the living part of the house that Mitch and Holly had refurbished for students and staff to use. They had moved out of the farmhouse themselves and lived on Holly's land in a cottage with their daughters.

"Hey, take a pew," Mitch, with his dark hair and ice blue eyes said to them in his Essex accent. "I'll make some more tea and toast. I can't believe you're still awake." He placed a hand on his wife's shoulder.

"Me neither. And it's coffee for me please, the strong stuff," Holly added as Mitch went to the sink. "I've got a second wind but I'm not sure how long it will last."

Trixy jumped up at Mitch's legs and Warren smiled as he looked at the couple. They were so comfortable in each other's company and when their girls were with them, they seemed like the perfect family.

"When are your parents coming to visit?" Holly asked him.

"Nick and Jane aren't my parents," Warren said. He knew when they'd dropped him off, the Booths guessed they were, even though he looked nothing like them. Nick was a short white man and Jane was West Indian. Not that Warren had any idea of his own ethnic origin. His skin was a light brown and his hair, which he kept short, was thick and grew into a tight curls if he left it to its own devices. He remembered his mother, but blocked out the lasting image he had of her. He knew he could sign up to a DNA site, but Jane had always taught him to look forward, not back. So he'd never had the urge to look into his roots.

"Are they relatives?" Holly asked.

When Warren arrived, he hadn't felt he wanted to talk about his past. But there, sitting in the kitchen with Mitch and Holly, who were so approachable, it seemed to be the right moment to explain. "They unofficially adopted me."

"Oh," Holly said. "Do you not get along with your own family?"

"My mother died."

"I'm so sorry," Holly said.

"And I never knew my father." The truth was he did not know the name of his father and he assumed neither did his mother as no father was named on his birth certificate. But he didn't reveal that as Mitch passed Warren a coffee. "Thanks." *Shall I tell the truth?* he asked himself, then decided he wanted no ugly secrets to present themselves. "I had so many foster homes I can't recall all of them."

"So when you say your mother died, she died when you were young?"

He nodded. "Five years old." He paused. He only had vague memories of his mother, but the vision of her laying lifeless in the small flat they'd shared was always crystal clear. And the pain hit him in his chest every time he recalled it. "I wasn't able to settle anywhere, I was always in trouble. I remember overhearing the social worker talking about me to one of the foster parents who told her I was attention-seeking." He swallowed, realising he was sharing more than he'd intended.

"It's understandable, mate," Mitch said. "You were an orphan. I can't imagine how that must have been. So were Nick and Jane foster parents?"

"No, I met them when I was sixteen. I'd found a bike. It was sticking out of a skip. The neighbour where I was living at the time was handy and helped me pull it out and bring it back to life. It gave me the freedom to go off on my own, without needing money for the bus. Then someone took it when I was in a shop. I was only gone a minute, I thought it would be fine. I saw the lad cycling off on it. I ran but wasn't quick enough. I tripped." He didn't add that he'd cried. A sixteen-year-old who'd considered himself tough. "Some other kids laughed at me. I wanted to hit out. It was the only thing that was mine, really mine. Someone had taken it and got away with it, so I decided it'd be okay for me to do the same."

Holly bit her lip as she looked at him intently. "Go on," she said when he hesitated.

"I saw this great bike in an alley next to a café. I was

already tall, and it was an adult bike. Black and red. It wasn't locked so I jumped on and rode it down the alley but when I reached the end a big guy, and I mean huge, was standing there with a chain lock in his hand, looking as if he was going to swing it at me. I screeched on the brakes. It turned out to be his bike – he'd just gone off to collect the lock."

"Did he beat you?" Mitch asked.

Warren smiled. "No, the opposite. He could tell I was scared. And calmly asked me to get off and give it back to him. I tried to dive past him and he grabbed me by the arm and told me to stop. I did as he said. Then once he locked the bike he told me to follow him into the café. I don't know why I didn't run. There was just something about him that I picked up."

"He bought you some food?" Holly asked.

Warren nodded. "It turned out he was a policeman. I thought I was in deep trouble when he showed me his badge across the table. But I think he was just showing it to me so I knew he wasn't a creep." Warren shuddered; he'd met a few creeps in his time. "He told me his name was Darius and chatted to me, asked me about myself, then told me he used to be a wild lad too. And that everyone deserves a second chance."

"What a great guy," Mitch said.

"As I chatted to him, it seemed as if he was the first person to actually see me as a real person. A stranger who seemed more interested than anyone else I'd met."

Holly stood up and tore off a sheet of kitchen roll.

"Hey, sorry, I don't… I never tell people." There was also more to the story of his wayward teenage years, but he knew he wouldn't tell them all the details.

"Nothing wrong in sharing your past, mate," Mitch said. "So how did you go from bike thief to doing a PHD?"

Warren gave a nervous laugh as it wasn't just the bike he'd stolen as a kid. He'd shoplifted countless times. *Was that really me?* "It still sounds mad when I think how different my life is now. Darius, the policeman, called over the café owners and they joined us for tea. After we chatted they said if I needed space to myself or was hungry, that I could go to them for a meal every day and that they wouldn't need paying."

"So you did?" Holly asked.

"Yes. They were Nick and Jane, and Nick is Darius's brother, although they have different mothers. Nick's mum died when he was young, so he seemed to understand. He's a lot older that Darius. Nick is short for Nicolaus, they're from a Greek-Cypriot family."

"So you're still in touch with Darius too?"

Warren nodded. "He's a sergeant now." He took a gulp of his coffee. "After a couple of days, Nick and Jane said I could stay longer if I helped them clean up. Within two weeks I was working there after school every day and they started to pay me. I saved enough to buy a new bike. Then Jane helped me with my homework when we shut. It was the last year of school and I just loved learning when I was with her. I managed to scrape through maths, English and science and with a letter from my social worker, they managed to get me into college when I didn't have the highest of grades. It was like a new door had opened. As I applied myself, I discovered I was academic." He laughed. "The young me would never have believed that. I always loved being outdoors – I thought at the time it was just to get away from the foster families.

Although they weren't all bad, I just never felt I belonged. I did a rural science course and the rest is history. After college, I went to university and I guess I'm addicted to studying considering I've been doing this PHD for years."

Holly's bottom lip trembled. "What a success story, you have to tell everyone. I can write it up in the pamphlet I'm preparing at the hub, explaining all about your silvopasture."

"Hey, no. I don't think I'm ready for that," Warren said with a nervous laugh. He certainly didn't want any deeper delving into his past. Up until then, he'd kept his wayward background a secret. Whilst it felt good getting it off his chest, he wasn't ready to tell everyone, or the entire sorry story. Part of him wanted to keep it to himself because it was not something he wanted to think about. That part of him pretended that not only did he feel a different person, that he *was* a different person, erasing a chunk of his life as if it never happened. "I'd prefer it to be kept between us," he said.

"We understand," Mitch said. "Don't we Holly. No telling your friends, especially not motormouth Jaz."

Holly laughed. "Okay."

Warren liked Jaz. She was Holly's best friend and came over to the farmhouse once a week for a big family meal. Her husband didn't come as he was the licensee of The Eversley Arms, the local pub which he'd yet to visit.

"Bless Jaz," Holly said. "She's not the best at keeping secrets. Not that she does it on purpose, she just forgets what's a secret and what's not!"

"How's Nina today?" Mitch asked. "You could ask her to come to the pub on Friday with Ethan. I haven't seen them for ages."

Holly pulled her phone from her fleece pocket. "I texted her, but she's not replied. I think she wants some space. I doubt she'll be ready to face the villagers yet, she'll have to get used to losing her crown. They all called her Councillor Smith."

"I'm sure Ethan will help her put everything into perspective. She'll be back, fighting for her seat at the next local election. How long is the term?"

"Hmm," Holly said. "Five years I think, unless a seat becomes vacant. But maybe Nina and Ethan will finally set a date for their wedding as she won't be as busy now."

"Yes, she's always encouraging others to tie the knot, and there she is, still single."

Warren sat listening. This Nina sounded like a high-flyer.

"Have you got a girlfriend?" Holly asked him.

"No. I've not really met anyone I feel I'd like to be serious with. Most of the women I meet are students, too young for me and dating by app isn't my thing."

"You need to get out," Holly said. "All you see is us and the others at the farm."

"Come up to The Eversley Arms a week today," Mitch said. "Julian's putting the dart board back up and one of the locals is getting a team together. It's a friendly match. Can you play?"

Pub games like darts and pool were something Warren had played a lot of, since before he should have been in pubs. He'd been tall from a young age and started drinking and going to the pubs in his mid-teens, the publicans turning a blind eye as the regulars wanted him on the darts and pool teams. Once Nick was on the scene, he'd ended up taking him to make sure he didn't drink and get into trouble and he'd joined a darts team with him. Nick had wanted Warren to play the circuit but Jane told him he needed to focus on his studies. And she'd been right, but he did miss pub games.

"I've played a bit," he said, not wanting to say he used to play the leagues in case he'd lost his touch.

"That's you signed up then," Mitch said with relief in his voice. "I was looking for someone to replace me, I'm useless. I can be the sub."

Warren knew he should get to know the local people – after all, the project he'd started at Booth Farm was for the long term. He'd already decided to make Eversley village his home for some years to come, so it was about time he integrated.

CHAPTER 3

"*D*on't forget, the lease renews this year," Connor said to Nina as he drank a coffee from a take-out cup. "I've two people waiting for commercial properties in Wells. Your rent has been the same for years. I'll have to increase it."

"I'll need to look at comparables," Nina said, glancing around her shop.

"It has to be the going rate."

"I've been a good tenant. And I've kept the building in excellent condition."

He gestured around the room. "Everyone can see how well you've done. I can't afford to subsidise you."

"You're hardly subsiding me, Connor. And while it might look as if business is booming, there's been a slump." Nina knew what average rents were and understood prices had risen and interest rates were expected to be on their way down. She guessed Connor was worth a few million and was simply trying it on with her. "I'll go

28

over my books and do my numbers, to check the business would still be viable with an increase," she said, being non-committal. The truth was she really needed to have a plan if she wanted to turn a decent profit. She didn't want to have to live off Ethan. Yes, he'd spoiled her and she lived in his house, but she paid the utility bills and bought their food. Being independent had always been important to her. "What sort of increase are you considering?"

"I think it should be fifty percent higher."

Nina refrained from reacting. She didn't want to get into an argument with him, not when she was feeling particularly emotional. "As I said, I'll check my books." She had known he would go in hard and she would negotiate that down to what she felt she could afford.

Nina watched Connor's back as he left. It was Saturday, two days after she'd been ousted from the council. She'd spent Friday in bed feeling completely lethargic but knew she had to snap out of it. Ethan was due home Monday evening and she wanted to get back to the real world and consider her position. She couldn't languish in bed which made her feel as if she was ill – she'd even been sick again that morning. *I have to take care of myself,* she told herself planning a balanced meal that evening. Ethan was a vegan and their diet was extremely healthy but while he was away and with her canvassing, she'd been living off fast food, albeit vegetarian, often consisting of fried treats. *No wonder I'm feeling sick and drained,* she thought, assuming she was low on vitamins.

She pulled her accounting books out of the drawer and studied them. *Something Simple* had suffered during the pandemic when no one was getting married and even though she'd had a rush on when things picked up, foot-fall was down. Without profits, she'd been living off her councillor's allowance and with all the extra committees she was on, it had been more than enough to survive on. The shop had been running at a loss.

She looked up as the door chimed to find Jaz walking in. She was always dressed smartly with high heels, although she was still shorter than her as Jaz was petite. She had dark bobbed hair, big brown eyes with a fierce resting face, which came alive when she smiled. She was successful in a way Nina was not, financially successful, a millionaire with a business selling high-end motorhomes and caravans. And being a step mum and caring for her siblings, she juggled a family. *And* she'd come from humble beginnings. Yes, Jaz was the real deal – a superwoman.

"Hun," Jaz said. "I called in yesterday to see you, but Sumitra was here and said you were taking a day off. How are you?"

Nina stared at Jaz and gulped. She guessed her face said it all because Jaz turned the open sign to closed, then locked the door.

"I'm sorry, I guess I look awful," Nina said, running a hand through her long, dark brown hair.

"Awful, never, but I can see the strain on your face, hun. Come out back, let's get a cuppa."

Nina stood up and did as she was told. Jaz was well known for being bossy and at times it irritated her, but in this instance she was pleased she was taking the lead.

Jaz filled the kettle, switched it on then swung around. "Chick, you look pale, and you never look pale."

"This whole thing has left me feeling sick. I can't believe it, even if I did see it coming."

"Holly was totally shocked. I blame Barry Brent, the guy probably got a load of his mates to vote for Sam. It wouldn't surprise me if he offered free vouchers for one of his off-licences if people rocked up at the polling station. The man's a bad lot. It's him who wants to be on the council, not Sam. Mark my words it'll be a right mess and they'll have to have another election and you'll be straight back in there." She placed tea bags in two mugs. "I give him six months and he'll be running for the Mendip Hills."

"Barry was dead against my recycling initiative. I think that's what it's all about. But I've got more trouble."

"What's up?" Jaz said.

"This place. It's been making a loss for the last couple of years and now I've lost my only source of income. The lease is up for renewal in a few months and Connor wants to up the rent by fifty percent."

"Fifty?"

"That's what he said. I know he's just trying it on but it will be going up by something. He even had the cheek to say he thinks he's been subsidising my business. I know rents have increased, but not that much. I'll negotiate him down."

"I can't believe it, chick, you're the bridal boutique of the south west!"

"I know, but many others have folded, and the reason they've closed isn't because I've taken their business, the business has gone online. And this place is high-end. It's the cheaper dresses that sell now, not the bigger ticket items. People don't want to spend a couple of thousand on a dress for a day like they used to. They focus on saving money, not spending it." She picked up her smartphone, brought up a social media site and showed it to Jaz. "Look, they even brag on social media at how cheap their dresses are. Life hacks are cool! I used to sell quite a few designer handbags but those sales have also dried up in recent years, again, people choosing to buy online. I still have a couple of regular middle-aged customers who like the bags but even the most eager only buys two a year. That's hardly going to keep the business afloat."

"I don't have to tell you, chick, how to run your business. You've got an MBA – but have you thought of diversifying?"

"Yes. I get a few people coming in this time of year, buying off-the-peg bridesmaid dresses for prom. I could do a larger line on that, but I've missed the boat this year as most of the prom crowd are sorted. I'm going to try off-the-peg wedding dresses, although I won't be getting them in from China to compete as that goes entirely against my business ethos. But I'm going to visit my suppliers to discuss their more affordable lines and any discontinued stock, to see if I can place a bulk order in popular sizes. I'll have to change my methods as my model has always worked on the client paying a deposit, me ordering the dresses and then paying as soon as I've enough from the customer to cover the wholesale cost."

Jaz handed her a mug of tea. "If you put together a business plan on a new model, I can have a word with a couple of investors for you, see if I can release anything myself."

"No, I don't want to raise funds like that."

"I'm sure Ethan can help you out."

"I don't want to feel a drag on him."

"A drag? He's lucky he's got you!" Jaz had never been a fan of Ethan's and that often irritated Nina. He was her soul mate.

Nina didn't have the energy to argue with Jaz about Ethan so made no comment. "I'll have to sit down and take a long hard look, but my initial plan is to set sale prices for my entire stock. A sale will release funds which I can use to buy a stock of off-the-peg dresses. And to relaunch, in the short term, even as a general occasion dress shop to get me through."

"I knew you'd have a plan."

"Having lost my seat, there's no way I'm going to lose this place as well. I can't be a complete loser."

"Chick, you're far from a loser. And without the council, you'll have loads more time to devote to this place. You'll turn it around. I'm here, hun, if you need to go through it all."

Nina's stomach lurched. She felt weak, the slightest stress making her sick. "I just need the loo."

She shut the toilet door and tried to be as quiet as she could – she didn't want Jaz to hear. Outside of the toilet, she opened the back door and took in some gulps of fresh air as she looked into the yard. She pulled a mint from her jacket pocket before returning to the kitchen.

Jaz had already finished her cup of tea. "Give it a week and you'll see everything in a new light and probably have your head around everything. Come up to The Eversley Arms on Friday night."

"Ethan will be back, we can come together."

"Great. We're getting everyone over. Rob's starting a

darts team. The Dog and Horn are coming over for a friendly match so they need all the support they can get, although it'll be loud," she said with a laugh. The Dog and Horn pub was located in the nearby Eversley Burrows housing estate where Jaz grew up.

Nina felt happier at the thought of going with Ethan. He'd been positive about her future when she'd called him. He always boosted her confidence and cheered her on, allowing her to see the brighter side of everything. She couldn't wait for him to return, to feel his arms around her. And having him there at The Eversley Arms would be ideal as she knew she would have to face everyone at some point after losing her seat. And it would be better for her to have everyone there together, to get the commiserations over in one day with Ethan by her side. "I'd like that," she said. "I can't wallow in self-pity forever."

"That sounds more like you, hun." Jaz went on tiptoe and gave Nina a brief air kiss.

Nina followed Jaz to the exit and watched while she unlocked the door and turned the sign to open.

"See you Friday, if not before," she said with a smile.

Nina watched Jaz trot down the side of the market until she disappeared from view. She stood there for a while gazing at the world going by. Why was it that everyone else seemed to be happy without a care in the world? People laughing, haggling for their wares with the stall holders and making jokes. She knew that behind the masks everyone had their issues. She had to remember that – it wasn't only her. She'd always been fortunate, a loving family, an excellent education, a head for business.

Life had its up and downs and she had to just suck it up and deal with it.

Having given herself a good talking to, she began an inventory of her stock. She turned at the sound of the doorbell as someone opened it.

"Nina." It was her mother, Sumitra. "I brought you some food."

The smell of samosas instantly made her feel ill, reminding her of election night, and she rushed out again to the toilet.

Sumitra followed her and rapped on the closed door of the cubicle. "Are you okay?"

When she was done, Nina came out. "Sorry, Ma, my stomach is weak today."

"You should be at home if you're ill!"

"I'm not ill, it's just the stress. But I'm focussed today. Without the council allowance I need to turn the business around, so that it's making a decent profit."

"Dad and I were discussing it last night. We know you've had a couple of bad years. We've some money set aside, if you need a boost."

"No. That's your pension money and Dad will be closing his shop next year. I need to deal with this on my own and you need to keep the money in the bank. You've nearly got the retirement fund you aimed for."

"You're always so independent, Nina." She tutted. "Now do you want this food?"

"I've eaten," she lied, not wanting to tell her it was the waft of samosa that sent her running to the lavatory.

"You can take it home then. Cool it down and put it in your fridge." Sumitra walked towards the kitchen then placed the bag on the worktop. "When's Ethan back?"

"Monday evening," Nina replied.

"When are you setting the date for the wedding? With you losing your seat, there's no excuse about being busy. You'll have so much more time without those committee meetings."

As much as Nina appreciated her mother, she was not helping matters. "We'll get there. I've the business to worry about first. When I'm settled and turning a profit, we'll think about a date." She hoped that would keep her mother at bay, although she also was eager to set a date. To have something to look forward to.

"You're thirty-seven, you need to watch your biological clock."

"A lot of women are waiting these days," Nina said.

"But there's a history in the family of early menopause. You know that!"

Yes, she did know that, her mother mentioned it often. She felt a flush cover her body. *When was my last period?* she thought. It wasn't something she always kept a note of. But she knew she'd not had one for a while. And she'd been having a few hot flushes recently. *Oh no,* she thought, *am I really in early menopause?* Whilst Nina was not what others would call a baby person, having a husband and a child was always something she'd thought would happen to her. In her mind, her future included Ethan and a daughter. A family like her family with her mother and father. Of them taking holidays together, building sandcastles on the beach, playing ball games.

"I really think you should get checked out by the doctor. I'll book you in." Sumitra had a doctor friend who was a private physician. "Dr Gupta specialised in gynaecology before she became a GP." She pulled her phone from her bag. "I'll text you the date and time. Maybe that will spur you on to set a wedding date, if Dr Gupta thinks there's a danger you will hit menopause before you're forty." She gave her a kiss. "Now, cheer up and look after yourself. Are you coming for lunch tomorrow?"

"No, I want to go through the house to make sure it's clean and fresh before Ethan returns. I'll call you."

CHAPTER 4

*I*t was Monday evening and the day had been long. Nina drove up to the home she shared with Ethan. As she killed the engine she breathed out slowly, remaining in her white SUV. She was due to exchange the car, for it was nearly ten years old, but that would have to wait. It had a sticker with *Something Special* written in pink on the rear flanks of the car which had peeled away in places. It looked tatty. *Is that what I'm doing with the business? Downgrading from classy to tatty?* She sat back in the driver's seat and sighed.

Having shut the shop early, she'd visited the doctors. Her mother had fitted her in at three with Dr Gupta. The woman was great. She'd known her for as long as she could remember, with her being a family friend of her mother's. Dr Gupta had asked many questions, including whether she'd experienced any common menopause symptoms. And yes, missed periods, hot flushes and mood swings had definitely featured in recent weeks – *or was it months?* she thought with a sigh. Nina shut her eyes and swallowed. She'd beaten back the tears at the time, even when Dr Gupta passed her a tissue. But it was hard to hold back now she was alone, with the nearest neighbour half a mile away. She opened the car door as the tears streamed down her cheeks. Not only had she lost her position on the council and her dream of being the youngest mayor of Wells, it appeared she'd also lost a huge part of her life plan, to become a mother.

As she stepped out of the car she paused before the house, staring at it. She had so much to be grateful for in a world that could be indiscriminately cruel. A world where some had to fight to put food on the table, battle with their health, live through wars. Before her was a home with land, worth at least a million, probably more, which Ethan had designed. She remembered her friend Holly telling her it looked like two shoe boxes with one stacked on top of the other at an angle. Ethan certainly had an eye for design. There were floor to ceiling windows in the property which was built in an eco-friendly fashion. The sun, low in the sky, cast a pink hue on the shiny wood which clad the property. All she could hear were roosting birds and leaves rustling in the early evening breeze. It was indeed a beautiful place and tranquil. She was loved and far from hard done by.

It's merely a stumbling block, she said to herself, knowing that one of her problems was that she'd set herself such lofty goals. And she had an amazing man in her life. Whilst they spent a lot of time apart, when they were together, it was always perfect. Ethan was her partner in life, the one she wanted to be with forever and she was so pleased that he would soon be home. He had texted while she was at the doctors to say he'd landed in Bristol and would wait for his luggage and then had a car booked to bring him back. He'd already arranged his transfer thinking that Nina would be tied up at the shop or with her councillor duties.

She opened the front door and stepped over the threshold of the place she'd called home for four years. When she'd first arrived, the house had been sparsely fitted out and was very much a bachelor pad. With it being open plan, it had taken time for her to turn it into what she felt was a homely space. Softening it with large plants and different contrasting pieces of furniture, creating walkways and separate areas. Now it felt like her home, even if it was Ethan who owned it, as these days, she was there an awful lot more than he was. His work had been taking him further afield as his reputation had grown and he'd been commuting to Germany in recent years. She'd been out there at the end of the previous year, for the opening of a huge tower in Berlin.

She took a shower and let the warm water wash away her tension. She felt refreshed as she pulled on her fluffy towelling dressing gown. As she entered the master bedroom she headed for her dressing table set in front of the window with the most beautiful view of the Somerset landscape. Sitting down, she glanced at her jewellery box. It was from India and used to belong to her mother who gave it to her when she was small. *Don't,* she told herself but still, her hand shook as she pulled out a note she'd written over thirty years before.

Dear Parvati goddess of love,
Please send me my love at first sight when I am a grown up.

He has golden hair. Blue eyes. Rich and strong. I want a little girl just like me. And we will live happy ever after. I'll be a good girl and do my very best.

Nina xx

A solitary tear ran down her cheek. Ethan was that man with golden hair. Although the highlights were salon created, he had the bluest of eyes and indeed was rich. A millionaire a few times over and an avid gym goer, having lost the weight that had plagued him as a teenager which he wholly blamed on his mother who worked in a bakery. But the words *a little girl, just like me* brought a lump to her throat. She swallowed it away, fearing that would never happen. She folded the note and returned it to the small compartment of the jewellery box. *Snap out of it*, she told herself. Her mobile phone rang in the distance. She felt slightly dizzy so did not rush and by the time she was downstairs and had located it, the caller had rung off. She saw it was a missed call from the doctor. Had they found something irregular in her blood or urine? She really couldn't face any more bad news and considered leaving it, but knew she would worry about all night. She immediately returned the call.

"Dr Gupta."

"It's Nina, returning your call."

"Hello my dear. I know it's late but I just had to give you the news."

"Yes?" she asked with a gulp.

"I could tell you were worried about being infertile and the early menopause. So, I wanted to put your mind at rest. And let you know you're certainly not infertile."

"You can tell? So soon from my tests?" she asked.

"Yes."

"Are you sure?"

"Completely."

"Thank goodness for that!" she said with relief. Suddenly the whole councillor issue and her business woes seemed like smaller problems. She was sure the business was within her control, she could turn it around, unlike being in the menopause. That would have been beyond her control. "Thank you for letting me know."

"Don't go yet. There is more," she said with a laugh. "I can tell from the urine sample. I have tested it three times, just to make sure. But I am pleased to extend my congratulations to you, Nina. You are expecting a child."

Nina remained frozen. "I beg your pardon?"

"You are pregnant, my dear. Your mother will be over the moon. She has said on many occasions how she is jealous of my grandmother status."

"Oh, don't tell her," Nina said immediately as her mind raced.

"Of course not, my dear. Our service is completely confidential, whether or not Sumitra is a friend of mine. All the symptoms you have are due to the pregnancy. I will book you in for an ultrasound as soon as I can, so we can ascertain how pregnant you really are." Dr Gupta sounded incredibly pleased. "I will call you tomorrow, my dear."

"Thank you," Nina said with the phone still to her ear long after Dr Gupta had ended the call.

She placed the phone in the pocket of her towelling robe and took the stairs, holding onto the banister, unable to quite take it in. Once in the bedroom she slumped onto the bed looking out of the window with the view of Glastonbury Tor in front of the pink sky. She began to pant then ran to the ensuite to be sick.

Afterwards, she stood up and stared at her reflection in the mirror. *Maybe this is everything falling into place?* Ethan often talked about focussing on what you want and having faith that everything will come together. Maybe losing the seat on the council was a blessing. How would she have mixed the shop, a pregnancy and maternity leave with her councillor duties? This was a turning point, a new life. She looked upwards, feeling that some higher being may be able to see her life plan. She was not usually a spiritual person but if there was something out there, it seemed that it really did have her best interests at heart. After all, this was not a disruption, it was getting everything in order. *This could actually be the best day of my life,* she thought.

She left the ensuite feeling energised. She remembered Holly's wedding and how huge she was walking down the aisle only weeks before she gave birth to the twins. She turned to her side and looked at her small, yet slightly protruding stomach in the mirror, which she had thought was down to overeating and no trips to the gym. *The sooner we get married the better,* she thought. She brought to mind the dresses she had in the shop. At least she could find use for at least one of them!

She checked the time on her phone. Ethan would be there in roughly fifteen minutes. Butterflies turned over in her stomach, a feeling of excitement spreading over her whole body. She quickly dressed, and plugged in her hairdryer; her thick hair took a long time to dry. She grinned at her reflection in the mirror as she dried it, confident that everything was going to work out great.

She soon heard the car pull up outside and stood up. Ethan would be so surprised and hopefully as excited as she was. This was an amazing alternative to being 'Councillor Smith'. The title 'Ma' would surpass that.

"Babe, I'm home," Ethan called out to her, in the way he always did.

She walked to the top of the stairs and he looked up at her holding three small bouquets of flowers that she assumed he'd picked up from a petrol station on the way over. She couldn't wait to hug him, to hold him close.

"You're a sight for sore eyes," he said.

"You too. And flowers?" Nina walked down the stairs to meet him.

"I've got news!" he said. "I'm bursting to tell you."

"I've got exciting news too," she said as she reached the bottom step.

"I've missed you," he said in a low voice, and reached for her, holding her close against his body.

She wrapped her arms around him as they kissed, having missed the feeling of them being together.

He pulled away. "Well come on then," he said. "Let's have champagne, the real stuff."

"Really?" Nina said looking into his eyes. Ethan rarely drank alcohol.

He pulled her hand and led her towards the kitchen area. "I won't wait for it to chill, I'll open it now." He reached up to the wine rack in the kitchen area and pulled a bottle of Moet down, which would have been a gift from someone at some point or left over from a party.

Nina took two champagne flutes from the cupboard. Although she realised she couldn't have more than a sip, she wanted to toast their new life. She placed the glasses on the white quartz island and sat on a bar stool grinning at him, bursting to give her news.

Ethan popped the cork and poured the bubbly drink. "Tell me first, what's your cause for celebration?"

She realised that her news was too big, that it was better to hear his story as once she told him they would be talking wedding and baby names and probably ordering a delivery meal as she would be too excited to cook. Maybe they could go out to celebrate? "No, you go first," she said. "I'm excited to hear it." She'd also vowed to take a lot more of an interest in his work.

He handed her a glass. "We're moving to Qatar!"

"What?" Nina put her glass down without even taking a sip.

"It's perfect isn't it?" he said. "When you were talking the other day, about losing your seat, and the shop hadn't been turning a profit. It's everything just coming into alignment."

"Qatar?" Nina said.

"That's what the meeting was about in Germany. Remember, I told you they were considering my designs and wanted to view the building in Berlin. They want a similar design but twice the size in Qatar and then after that a sister building, as a mirror image. It's going to take at least four years, maybe five or six if we have to wait for approval. I'm not quite sure on the building regs over there."

Nina took a deep breath. "Isn't Qatar a country where there are curbs on women and what they're allowed to do?"

Ethan gestured at her. "You've nothing to worry about.

That's just the culture for locals. Plenty of westerners live there freely."

Apart from that she was pregnant, and she wanted to bring her child up where her family lived. Ethan's mother was also local. Their whole support system was in Somerset. "Why do we have to move? You didn't move to Germany?"

"It's a long way. Commuting long haul is out of the question. Germany was just a hop across the channel. Come on, babe, see it for the adventure it is. We've not seen much of each other these past few months, I don't want us to drift." He walked around the island and put his arms around her and kissed her on the lips then moved back staring into her eyes. "I want it to be just you and me."

Nina said nothing as she stared at him and the words *just you and me,* echoed in her mind because there was no longer *just you and me*, it was *us three.* With that thought, she felt her stomach churn.

He gestured towards the stairs. "I have to unpack and repack. I've got a car picking me up at six in the morning. I'm off to Qatar for my first meeting. My flight leaves Heathrow tomorrow at half eleven."

"Give me a second," she said realising she was going to be ill.

Ethan took a step away and she jumped down from the stool and ran to the downstairs bathroom.

Ethan followed and held her hair as she was ill, rubbing her back. "I'm sorry, I guess it was a bit too much of a surprise. I assumed you'd be as excited as me. I didn't consider the rules around women. Let's talk it out and I'm sure I can look into it more, whether there are specific areas we'd be best to choose to live in, which would not cause those problems."

Nina flushed the toilet then groaned, leaning against the tiled wall.

"And what was your news?" Ethan asked.

She stared at him for a long moment, then took a deep breath. "I'm pregnant."

CHAPTER 5

arren had grown to love Monday evenings at Booth Farm. As well as the current live-in staff – students Polly, Harry, and the herdsman Greg – they had extra visitors for dinner. Holly, Mitch and their twins, Jaz, her stepson and her brother and sister came over with their friends Val and Len. It was always a large and loud mealtime especially with Trixy running around excitedly. Holly had prepared a stew, which was in the centre of the long dining table with a huge pot of rice. Communal eating was something Warren had enjoyed as a lad. Eating at a table gave a family atmosphere, and reminded him of Nick and Jane. And while he was supposed to share the cooking with the other residents, none of them could manage anything that didn't involve some sort of prepared mix-in sauce, or freezer food. So he did the cooking himself. Working the land, he needed filling and hearty meals and preferred to prepare the food, leaving the others to clean up after him – which he had to admit was a job he hated. So it was nice to have his meal cooked once a week and Val always brought an amazing traditional dessert with her.

The students and Greg were at one end, Val and Len at the other with the children and he was in the middle with Holly, Mitch and Jaz. Trixy had been taken out and given her own food in the farm side of the house.

"How's the renovation of the annexe going?" Holly asked Jaz as she dished out the portions of food to be passed around the table.

"If all the tradesmen show up when they're meant to, Mum and Dad will be moving in there in a few months or so."

"How do you feel about them being there?" Mitch asked her.

"It's totally separate accommodation and me and Ju aren't there that much. It'll be better as they can keep an eye on the kids. And it's so great to be out of the pub."

"I miss it," Belle, Jaz's teenage sister grumbled. "I liked it there."

"Yes, we know, you did," Jaz said. "But we'll all be in one place so you'll have one bedroom and won't have to go back and forth to the estate."

Warren smiled at the teenager. "How's the new house?"

"It's amazing, it's a massive cottage," Mikey, Belle's brother and the younger of the two boys said. Both siblings had dark hair and eyes just like Jaz. Mikey continued, "We've got a garden. A big garden with a tree and Julian says in the summer there'll be cherries on it. Lots of cherries. I love cherries."

"Mikey, the cherries you like come out of a jar, my love. They're glacier," Val said with a laugh as she was passed a plate of food. "It's my fault, I've always got some at home."

"And we've got our own rooms," Noah said. "Me and Mikey had to share at the pub."

"You've got your own room at your mum's big fancy house," Belle said to Noah.

"Mum says you and Mikey can come with me any time you like. But you never want to."

Belle huffed and looked at her phone.

"Get off your phone," Jaz said.

Belle flashed it at Jaz. "I'm revising French on an app! Remember GCSEs?"

"Seems they do everything on their phones these days," Len said before returning to the previous conversation. "I think it's great you'll all be together and still close to us. We're only in the next road."

"And I love popping over to see you without having to go through the pub," Val added. "And then up them stairs. I don't want to get me other hip done."

"And we can keep an eye on you," Len said. "With us being just around the corner."

Jaz laughed. "It's us keeping an eye on you two, you mean."

Good-natured Val and Len were in their eighties and both appeared to Warren to be in good health.

"Are you coming to our housewarming, Warren?" Noah asked him.

"If I'm invited," he said with a smile.

"Of course you're invited, as are you three." Jaz nodded at Millie, Harry and Greg. "It's more of a family thing than a rowdy party. No need to bring anything, we've plenty of booze and we're doing snacks."

"Thanks," the three said in unison.

"When is it?" Warren asked. He removed his hoodie and put it on the back of his chair.

"This Saturday," Jaz said.

"Oh, I can't," Warren said. "My er… parents are coming. I don't see them much so I'm cooking them a meal here and we're catching up."

Holly smiled at him from across the table. He got the impression she wanted him to share something of his background, but he didn't feel comfortable enough. He was saved by Belle.

"Cool tats," the teenager said, pointing at his arm. "I like the one with the snake. I want one just like that down my back."

Warren noticed Jaz shake her head at Belle, so he focussed on his casserole which was delicious and had soft carrots and meat in a deep tasty gravy. On the side, as well as the rice, was steamed broccoli. As he ate, Warren listened to the students chatting about their home life. Mitch and Holly took it in turns to encourage the girls to eat their vegetables. He relaxed and enjoyed his food. After he took the last mouthful, he sat back feeling satisfied and homely. He felt his phone vibrate and he pulled it out of his pocket and looked at it. *Scottie calling.* He'd added the number to his contacts after receiving the previous call, although he was yet to call him back. He waited for it to stop – as he had no intention of answering him until he was ready to speak to him and had decided how he was going to deal with the man – then placed the phone on the table.

Following the main meal, Holly brought out the

dessert that Val had prepared, an apple crumble and custard which was sweet, tangy and very satisfying.

"Are we playing a game?" Mikey asked Val and Len after they had finished.

"Of course we are," Len said. "It's your turn to choose."

Mikey moved from his seat. "I'll get it." He went to the cupboard. The older couple always played a game with the boys and the twins. They started what turned into a noisy session of Snakes and Ladders. Belle sat tapping at her phone while Jaz and Holly chatted as the students and Mitch cleaned up. Greg had to leave and check on the cows.

"Will you put that down and engage in conversation," Jaz said to Belle. "Or make yourself useful."

Belle put her phone on the table.

"I don't know what's got into you these past few weeks. What's wrong?"

Belle sighed. "Nothing's wrong. I keep telling you. Stop with the beef all the time. I'm in the middle of my exams, I have a life, you know."

Warren studied Belle's face. He'd spent a lot of time with troubled kids. He'd been one himself. This one wasn't the same, she didn't have a broken sadness behind her eyes, but he could tell something was definitely bothering her. She glanced at her phone on the table.

Warren's phone began to vibrate.

"Right, that's it, I'm confiscating it." Jaz reached forward for Belle's phone.

Belle got there first and lifted it up. "It's not mine. I don't do calls!" She shook her head as if receiving an actual call was completely outdated.

"Oh, sorry," Warren said looking at his phone screen as

it buzzed on the table. *Scottie calling.* He couldn't ignore it this time. He grabbed the phone from the table. "I'll take it outside."

"Hello," he said as he walked down the passageway.

"Warren, man, glad you answered. I'm right in it." Scottie sounded hoarse down the phone, as if he had flu.

"You're out then?" Warren asked as he crossed the threshold across to the working side of the house.

"Yeah, I miss you bro. Wanted to know when you're back in Bristol so we can hook up."

Warren knew that Scottie only really called him when he wanted money. "Where are you staying?"

"They put me in a half-way house but I can't stand it. Having a house manager is like being back in care."

Warren thought that Scottie needed that level of support and rules, even if he didn't appreciate it.

"I want out of this place."

The last time Warren had travelled over to Bristol to see Scottie, it involved a loan that he knew would never be repaid. "I'm planting a field out at the moment, it's difficult to get away."

"I could try and get money for the bus and come stay with you."

"No," Warren said quickly. "There's no space here and I'll be working the whole time. There's nothing here except grass, crops and cows." He didn't want to have to bail Scottie out again. It was only six months since the last time, just before he went inside. And yes he did have a few thousand in the bank saved from jobs he'd done, but he would have nothing left if he was giving Scottie continual handouts. He heard Nick's voice in his head: *Scottie's bad news. He'll never change. Just because you lived in the same house for two years doesn't make him your brother.* He'd told him that so many times. Darius also warned him to stay away from Scottie.

"As I said, I'm in the middle of a project and can't be with you in minutes." Warren looked to his left to see Jaz come out of the house. He lowered his voice. "I'll call you next week." He ended the call before Scottie could protest. He knew if he'd continued the conversation, Scottie would only have asked for a handout. He powered off his phone and put it in his back pocket.

"Is it an emergency?" Jaz asked. "You look concerned."

"No. Just a guy I used to know trying to tap me for some money. He thinks because I went to uni I'm rich." He laughed. "Little does he know I'm still a student, all these years on."

"Hardly just a student, you're managing a huge project which will run for years."

"True, I hope it outlasts me."

"Holly was just telling me you're applying for lottery funding." She paused. "Actually, I came out to make sure I didn't scare you off about your phone ringing. Holly's convinced you left the room to get away from me."

Warren laughed. "It takes a lot to scare me." He smiled at her. "The kids are great. They're proper well behaved."

"Belle's a worry. She's keeping something from me."

"She did look worried about something. Has she fallen out with a friend?"

"I've no idea, she won't speak to me. It upsets me as I understand her not telling Mum, but I'm her sister."

"I'd have a word with her, but I don't think she'll confide in me. We haven't chatted much."

Jaz sighed. "Belle would be more likely to speak to you, she thinks you're great with your tats."

Warren ran a hand over his arm. "Sorry, they don't really fit in here. Don't you approve of tattoos?"

Jaz laughed. "I think you've got me wrong. I've my own tattoo."

"Oh yeah?" Warren just stopped himself from asking where it was.

As if she knew, she touched the back of her head. "Under this neat dark bob is a purple fire-spitting dragon!"

"No way."

"Yes. It's a reminder to me of where I came from. Now you might think everyone around here is posh, but they aren't and you'll find that out on Friday night at The Eversley Arms! I hear you're taking Mitch's place on the darts team."

"Yes, I need to get out."

"You won't have to do much for that to be a good decision. Last time he played he only hit the board a few times, let alone a double. So, tell me, can you play?"

"I used to play in the pub leagues and then Nick, my adopted dad, wanted me to enter the main circuit but Jane, that's my adopted mum, she convinced me to go to uni instead."

"She's a wise woman but that's great news for The Eversley Arms team."

"Don't tell anyone though, will you?" he put his hand to his chest. "Keep it as our secret as I don't want to raise any expectations. I might've lost my touch – it's been a while."

Jaz gave a nervous laugh. "Yes, our little secret." Then

she pulled her phone out of her pocket and frowned at the screen. "No way!"

"Bad news?"

"A friend of mine is in need, no one's died but I need to get off."

Warren grinned as he followed Jaz back inside. She made him feel a lot more comfortable and he was beginning to feel that he was fitting in.

CHAPTER 6

*N*ina leaned her back against the cool tiles of the downstairs bathroom. In her line of vision was the huge shower that at times they had shared, screened off by glass blocks. When she'd moved in with Ethan, the bathroom had been stark but she'd softened it with wooden shelves where plant pots were now perched with trailing leaves. She'd added muted colours via soft towels, folded inside a wicker shelf unit, to emulate the ambience of a boutique spa. The room always smelled of the eucalyptus shower gel she loved. Her phone dinged with a text and she glanced at it. Jaz had replied to her message.

I'm dropping the kids back home. Shall I come over?

Nina sighed then heard the sound of Ethan's car. He'd stormed off after her revelation. It wasn't exactly the response she'd hoped for and it had left her shaking. She'd called after him but he'd shouted out that he needed time alone to think. She had no idea where he'd gone but as he was back so soon, she guessed he'd simply driven off in his Maserati and parked up somewhere.

She replied to Jaz:

Ethan's back. Don't come. I'll message later.

She placed the phone on the soft rug she was sitting on and then heaved herself up from the floor and rushed for the toilet again. Afterwards, she cleaned her teeth as she watched her reflection in the mirror. Her dark hair was stuck to her tear-stained face and her eyes were blood-shot. She didn't think she'd ever looked so dreadful in her entire life. She spat out the toothpaste, pulled her hair off her face then splashed it with water. She didn't want to continue the discussion with Ethan in the bathroom and hoped a cup of tea would settle her stomach. With her head held high, she opened the bathroom door.

As she walked out, Ethan was taking the wooden slatted stairs to the upper level. She stood at the bottom and he stared down at her from mid-way up.

He took slow steps down the stairs towards her. "Look, babe, sorry to run off like that. I'm in total shock. We never talked about us having kids."

"We've spoken about the future a lot, over the years, about us getting married and having a family life." Nina felt fear seep into her veins.

"When did we discuss kids?" He reached out and took one of her hands.

"Admittedly a lot more in the early days and especially the night you proposed to me!"

"Did I?" He dropped her hand and frowned as if he was attempting to recall the memory.

Seeing him looking stressed softened her and she spoke in a steady voice. "Look, it's a real shock to me too.

But it could be a good thing." She smiled but felt her cheeks quivering. "We needed something to come along and get us to set a date for our wedding."

"I think you're jumping the gun. First, we have to discuss if this is something we both want to go ahead with. It should be a joint decision."

"How many times have you said, after an event, 'That's one to tell the grandkids'? You don't get grandkids without first becoming parents." She steadied herself against the end of the banister.

"That's just a turn of phrase!" he said. "But kids, now? I'd prefer to be mid-forties. We're still so young."

Nina turned away from him as her stomach churned. She needed something in it otherwise she would be back in the bathroom.

Ethan followed her. "Most of the guys I know in the industry aren't having kids until they're at least late-forties, even fifties. Most guys are out living the high life. With the money I've got now, we can live in a beautiful apartment block with a gym and swimming pool. I can even afford a boat. We can take trips out and explore, you love scuba diving. There's so much of the world we haven't seen."

She turned around, her mind swimming.

He gestured at her. "We can't stop now. Just when we've made it!" He lowered his voice. "I get it, you've lost your seat on the council, the shop hasn't turned a profit for a couple of years. It might seem attractive, a new era, but we've still got so much of the current era to live before we tie ourselves down."

"It's just as much of a shock to me as it is you but I'm curious, these men you know, how old are their wives?"

"Well…" He trailed off as the realisation sunk in.

"I'm guessing they're much younger," Nina said, trying to sound a lot calmer than she felt, wanting to keep the conversation level-headed, especially as Ethan was flying out of the country the following morning.

"Some women have kids later in life," Ethan said.

"It's rare for them to be in their fifties." She turned around and filled up the kettle.

"I didn't mean we'd have to be fifty, but forties. To be honest, I've never imagined kids involved with us." He approached her and held her from the back and spoke into her ear. "I love you, Nina. It's been just you and me, we're a pair. I want to be with you forever, you know that." He turned her around and looked into her eyes. "And yes, let's set the date for the wedding before we move to Qatar. And no, I'm no going to trade you in for a younger model later on, in case that's what you were thinking. I can't imagine us ever being apart. You know you're all I ever wanted and all I need." He kissed her on the forehead then held her close. "Everything is perfect in our relationship, just the way it is."

Nina shut her eyes, feeling his warm body against hers. She'd missed him so much, but at the same time, she felt sick in her stomach. "I'm not sure how I would feel about a…well…to lose it."

Ethan stepped back and wiped the solitary tear which was making its way down her cheek. "It's not a child, babe. Come on, be real, it's just a speck." He smiled at her. "A mate of mine had the same issue. See the doc as soon as possible, it could be sorted with a pill. No different to birth control."

Nina didn't tell him her expectation was that this

pregnancy was long past the time when a pill would make a difference. Ethan's phone dinged with a text which he replied to.

He looked up at her. "We'll take a holiday before we move to Qatar, you'll feel better about it. Look," he said, lifting his phone with a grin. "I've just signed the deal of my life. My advance for the job has just hit my account. It's seven figures." He showed her the screen. "Look at the bank balance." He stepped away, as if the whole pregnancy subject had been dealt with. "Thousands of people will use this building, people will work there, some will live there, some will stay there in a hotel on the sixteenth to twentieth floors. They plan to have five restaurants, one of which will be on the top with stunning views. We're a part of something big and I want us to do this together. I'm sorry you're going through this and I wish I could be with you to help you through it."

"Ethan, apart from the pregnancy, I've still got the shop. And I'm not sure I want to live in Qatar."

He took both of her hands. "Forgive me for being so focussed on this, but this is it, the contract we've been waiting for. Six years of living the life and then, yes, we'll come back here and revisit the child thing. You'll still be young enough. But right now, this year and for at least the next four, I'm committed to this project. I get why you're hesitant, but don't worry. We'll find a way. I love you, babe."

Nina felt too choked up to explain that she'd missed more than one period, the baby was not a speck. She had never imagined the missed periods were a pregnancy; it was usual for her to miss periods when she was stressed. But she could talk no longer. It would have to wait.

"Come on, you look tired," Ethan said. "Let's watch a film and it'll all be fine in the morning. Go to the doctor for that pill. I'm off for a fortnight and then when I'm away we can video chat and do a proper plan, just as you like, with a date for the wedding. It's going to be best to bring the wedding forward so our friends and family can come. And it'll be better for us in Qatar if we're married. The 2030s can be family time." He gestured around him. "And we'll need to let this place out."

Nina let him lead her away with still so much to explain. A two-week break apart would be good – at least time for her to get an ultrasound and then she could comprehend the whole situation herself. After all, it was only an hour or so since she'd found out herself. Then she could revisit the subject with Ethan. As much as he did not want to commute long-haul to Qatar, she'd have to convince him that would be exactly what he'd have to do – and she was sure he would realise that once he'd had a chance to fully understand the predicament they were in.

Later, as Ethan snored on the sofa, she covered him with a blanket and set an alarm on his phone for five a.m. then quietly went upstairs. She plonked herself on the bed and texted Jaz.

I'm fine. Ethan's booked a car at six, he's off to Qatar. I'll call you when I'm up.

NINA SLEPT SURPRISINGLY WELL. When she woke, she found a note from Ethan on the pillow beside her.

Didn't wake you. Let me know how it goes. I'll call as soon as I'm in my hotel. Love you and can't wait for our new chapter x

Nina wondered whether he had his head in the sands of a Qatar desert or whether he really was that insensitive to her feelings. The doorbell chimed. She rose from her bed and looked out of the window to see the familiar red Audi TT – it was Jaz. She glanced at her phone which she had switched to silent and saw that Jaz had been texting her.

Downstairs she opened the door.

"Hun, I was worried, I know you told me to wait."

"It's fine, come in."

"I don't believe it," Jaz said as she stepped over the threshold and followed Nina, her stilettos tapping on the wooden floors.

"I just need the bathroom," Nina said as she felt the nausea rise.

Back in the kitchen area, Nina filled the kettle. "Thanks for coming over. I had no energy to explain to Ethan that I can't simply take a tablet and make it all go away. And there's more to it. My family has a history of early menopause, it's the reason I'm an only child. This could be my one chance."

"He needs to step up!" Jaz said. "What's he doing flying off again?"

"He's got tunnel vision with this building. Once he's processed the information, I'm sure he'll see it differently. He'll know there's only one option." Nina realised she was making excuses for Ethan but her loyalty for him ran too deep to not believe in him.

"Are you sure you want to go through with it?" Jaz said.

Nina leaned against the kitchen worktop. "I really have no choice even if I wanted to. I'm too pregnant for that. I've got a scan this Thursday. They'll be able to tell me how far gone I am, but I think it's months, not weeks."

"Wow. I totally get you."

"It might not be too far gone as far as the law is concerned, but it's too far gone for me to be comfortable with. And anyway, this could really be my only chance. My mother was nagging me about starting a family and that's why I went to the doctor, because with hot flushes and a paused period, I was convinced I'd started the menopause."

"What a shocker. When was your last period?"

"I don't know, maybe as long ago as February."

Jaz plonked herself on a stool. "Wow. And you didn't know?"

"I was so busy with the run up to the election I thought it was stress. My periods often stop when I'm under pressure. They stopped during the last election."

"Don't worry, hun, Ethan will change his mind once he knows the full facts."

"I don't want to bring my child up in Qatar. I want us to be near our extended family, but I guess I might not have any choice."

"Sumitra would be upset if you left. But it wouldn't be forever."

"No, but the most important thing is that we're together." She gave a weak smile. "Ethan wants the high life. Parties, yachts and fast cars. He even came home with this!" She lifted up a Bugatti brochure that he'd left on the kitchen worktop.

"Let me do the drinks, you sit." Jaz took some cups off the side as the kettle boiled. "You've got two weeks until he's back. Hopefully he'll see sense and live between here and Qatar. What's your mum say about it?"

Nina looked up at her. "I haven't told her yet."

"That's the first conversation I'd get out of the way. The sooner the better. You know what I'm like with secrets. And Holly knows too of course, as you texted us both. She sends her love, by the way."

"I wish I could sort it with Ethan before I tell my parents, but you're right, I have to tell them, especially as she made the appointment for me at the doctor. She'll be quizzing me and I can't lie to her."

CHAPTER 7

*N*ina exhaled as she placed her mobile phone on the desk next to the cash till in *Something Simple*. She looked at the large pile of shocking pink sale tags and picked up a permanent marker to write on the new prices. *Am I going to be able to pull the business around?* she asked herself. She'd have to do that before the baby was born and until she had the scan, she wasn't quite sure how long she had. Clearly, it would be only a matter of months. If it was a regular dress shop, it would be much easier to arrange cover while she was on maternity leave. She wanted to clear the current stock as soon as possible to release the funds to buy in the new.

Having updated ten dresses with their reduced price, she heard the chime of the door as it opened and turned around to find her mother coming over the threshold.

"What's going on? Are you having a sale?" she asked, gesturing at the dress in the window which was on at half price.

"Yes, I've decided to sell the current stock and look at new affordable dresses, either bridal or occasion wear."

"Have you discussed this with Dad?"

"No." She hadn't as she'd been avoiding him. He'd looked so glum when she'd popped down to his shop in the aftermath of the election for a coffee. It was as if it was he who had lost the seat on the council, not her. She realised when she was in there how little they had to say to each other; all their previous chat was centred around her council responsibilities.

Sumitra walked up to the till and dumped the large gold handbag she carried with her everywhere on a chair. "But you're known for wedding dresses."

"I know that, but I can't keep the business as it is, without my allowance from the council it's not viable to stay here without changes. I need an income." She took a deep breath. There was obviously more to it, but she was putting off telling her.

"Have you spoken to Ethan about it? After all, you don't need to work."

"Ma, I want my own business. I can't lose this shop as well as my seat."

"I understand, you're a Smith. Ambition runs through your veins."

Nina felt a rush of emotion and blinked, attempting not to cry.

"What's wrong? Oh my dear girl." Sumitra put her arms around her.

Nina had planned on visiting her parents the following evening and telling them together in a peaceful environment about her pregnancy, not in the shop with the mid-week market outside in full swing. But now her mother was there, wanting answers as to why she was emotional, she had no choice. "Lock the door, Ma. I've something to explain."

Sumitra pulled away. "Was it to do with the trip to Dr Gupta?"

"Yes."

Sumitra swiftly locked the door and turned the sign to closed. "My darling, there's not something wrong is there? My poor angel."

Nina didn't quite know how to answer her. It wasn't wrong that she was pregnant, how could it be? By this time of her life she'd always imagined she would be a mother. It was a life goal. "Come and sit down, Ma."

"You're not seriously ill, are you?" she whispered.

"No, no, of course not."

"You're worrying me, tell me, what is it?" she asked, her warm brown eyes wide open.

Now that Nina was backed into a corner, she cast aside the long-winded explanation. "I'm pregnant."

"Ah." Sumitra dumped herself down in the chair. "Thank the Gods. I thought you were going to tell me some bad news." She sat up in her seat. "And I was worried you were menopausal. This is most brilliant news. Maybe this is a sign that you should close the shop. Ethan can support you and you can enjoy motherhood as I did – as a stay-at-home mother." Sumitra pulled out her handkerchief. "I'm so pleased, I really am." She wiped her eyes and then studied Nina's face. "What's wrong, are you worried? You don't look happy." She touched her hand. "Is the baby okay?"

"I don't know yet. Ethan is a bit shocked about my news and he wants us to move to Qatar."

"Qatar?" Sumitra took in a sharp breath and her eyes shot open wide. "You tell me that at last I will be a grandmother and you're moving thousands of miles away so I will be unable to bond with the baby?"

"Hopefully, I'm not moving. Ethan said he didn't want children until we were much older."

Sumitra shook her head. "It's a bit late for that! Where is he?"

"He left within a day of being home, for Qatar. He's already accepted a contract for a huge skyscraper."

"He can travel between here and there. He's always done that before. I'm here to help." She stood up and gave Nina a hug. "It's just the shock, dear. He'll come around once the realisation has sunk in. He's a good man. He's always stood by you."

Nina swallowed hard, not wanting to admit that Ethan thought she was having a termination.

"I bet Christine is over the moon!"

Nina didn't want Sumitra to tell Ethan's mother. "He's not spoken to her yet. He'll be back in two weeks and then we can have a proper chat about our future plans. We're keeping it to ourselves at the moment and so must you and Dad. I'm having the scan tomorrow. I want to make sure everything is as it should be, before I move forward. It's a shock to me too. I have to get used to the idea as well as Ethan."

"Of course, and I will come to the scan with you. I can't have you going alone." She took Nina's hand in hers.

"I'm taking Jaz."

"Jasmine Swift? She's not even a mother!"

"She is a mother, a stepmother. And a good one as

69

well." She pulled her hand away. "You can come to a later one."

Sumitra nodded. "Well, hopefully Ethan will be here to go, but yes, if you have already said to Jaz, I accept that. Now, I take it you will tell Dad? I can't keep it from him."

"I was planning on telling you both together, but now that you know, it's probably best that you tell him, but make sure he doesn't worry about me. I've been given this child and I intend to do the best I can for it."

"That's my strong and perfect daughter. I am so proud of you." Sumitra smiled. "It will all work out in the end; Ethan will come around to staying in the UK. And we will at last be able to spend the wedding fund we've been saving up." She hugged her. "I'm so happy I could burst. I have to go as I have an appointment. I'll see you soon."

Nina exhaled slowly as her mother changed the sign to open and unlocked the door which chimed as she left. She knew she'd played down Ethan's reaction, but she hoped with all her heart he would come around to the idea. She couldn't imagine a life without him.

CHAPTER 8

ina had placed an advert on social media for her upcoming sale. She did not want mayhem in the shop so had led those who clicked on her advert to the appointment page on her website. Slots began to fill up over the day, thirty minutes apart. She listed all the stock and sizes on the page explaining that she would pass customers on to her seamstress for any alterations. Luckily, she had the more common sizes in the shop and her seamstress could do wonders. She knew the next couple of weeks would be extremely busy but up until then, she would take it easy, rearrange the shop and set up a spreadsheet to manage what was still in, so that she could simply add 'sold' to the listings on her site. She was only in for half of the day as Jaz was picking her up to take her to Bristol for the ultrasound. She was booked into a private hospital in the Clifton area of Bristol, which Dr Gupta suggested and her mother had insisted on paying for when she had been to her parents for dinner, saying

she was a mature mother and would need the best possible care.

There was no market that day. The council had pedestrianised the market square so it was quiet and she could no longer park outside her shop. While it was inconvenient, she had promoted it to be a traffic-free zone herself and suggested the measure. It meant that she'd arranged to meet Jaz at a nearby car park. As she reached the agreed meeting place, she spotted Jaz's car and got inside.

"I'm looking forward to this, hun," Jaz said. "Have you heard from Ethan?"

"I've not taken his calls as I don't want to discuss the baby and let him know that it's here to stay, until I have the full facts. He sent me a text saying he assumes I want to have space, realising how difficult these situations can be for a woman and that when I'm ready to talk about it, to give him a call."

"That's good of him," Jaz said sarcastically and put the car into gear and slowly drove towards the car park exit.

"I feel awful not being honest with him."

"He'll come around. He'll have to."

"I hope so. The only relationship strain we've had before is when we're too busy, not being able to see much of each other. We've always been so good together, I can't even remember us arguing."

Jaz laughed. "Sounds a lot tamer than our household!"

Nina smiled. "Everyone knows you and Julian love each other." She looked out of the window as Jaz queued at the light. "I'm fine with Ethan being away. I know he's committed to this job in Qatar. I'm happy to do most of the childcare and we can have quality time as a family when he's back."

"It's all going to work out fine, hun," Jaz said. "Everyone can see Ethan adores you. He was just shocked."

Nina smiled and felt much better discussing it with Jaz. She was always clear and to the point. "I'm sure we can work through it."

"He'll feel differently once he's had time to get his head around it. As you know, I always shied away from kids. I ran away and left Julian and Noah, and now look at me, I'm a full-time step mum and do most of the parenting of Belle and Mikey. If I can have a change of heart, I'm sure Ethan can!"

Nina laughed. "You've done well, Jaz."

Jaz sighed. "I'm having issues with Belle, though. Something's bothering her and she won't tell me what it is."

"Do you want me to have a word with her?" Nina asked. She always got on well with the girl and Belle often chattered away to her.

"It would be great if you could come to darts tomorrow at the pub. I'll bring Belle, it's not really for kids but she's bound to ask if she can tag along. And it'll get her away from Mikey and Noah. It could be them getting on her nerves, she stayed at Mum's for an extra day last week."

"Of course I'll chat to her," Nina said. "But I don't want to mention my pregnancy to the villagers, not until I know what the situation is with Ethan. No one knows do they?"

"Only if they've overheard me and Julian, I haven't told anyone else." She paused. "I don't think!"

"Don't worry, Jaz, it'll be out soon enough but I'd like

to keep it quiet at least until Ethan realises I'm keeping the baby." Nina smiled at Jaz. She knew she had a problem keeping secrets which was amusing because Jaz hated gossip and didn't gossip at all, but she blurted things out by mistake. They chatted about Nina's planned dress sale as they headed for the Bristol-based clinic and Nina began to relax.

Jaz parked up and they went to the reception and after a short wait were directed to the consulting room. After completing a questionnaire about her medical history and her last remembered period, she was asked to lay on the examination bed. Nina felt the cool gel being applied to her stomach and watched the monitor as the black and white image of her child came into view.

"It's moving!" Jaz said as she put her hand to her mouth. "Oh, hun. It's so cute."

Nina smiled. "Hello little one," she said to the screen as the doctor used the equipment to take measurements. She felt a solitary tear run from the corner of her eye. *It's really happening,* she thought, knowing that having seen her child on the screen, there was no way she would consider being parted from it. She was looking at a new member of her family.

Back in a chair at the doctor's desk, she stared at the scan pictures she was given.

"Everything is as it should be," the doctor said. "I've given a rough due date of the twenty-ninth of October, although as we're not entirely sure of the last period, it could be two weeks before or after that date. I've booked your second scan in July by which time we should be able to tell you the sex as well, if you'd like to know."

"Of course, and yes I probably would like to know so I

can think of names." Nina also thought of nursery decoration. *Will my baby have a nursery in Shepton Mallet?* They had two spare rooms, one of which was ideal and her mind brought up pictures of it decked out with baby-related furniture. She was excited for Ethan to return. Although her future was still uncertain, she knew he would be moved by the scan pictures, when he saw his own child.

Nina arrived home two hours later as she had popped into the shop then driven home in her own car. She wanted to shower and change before going to her parents for tea. She could not wait to show them the scan picture. Her phone rang, notifying her that she had a video call. Looking at the screen she saw it was coming in from Ethan. She hesitated; she couldn't let him go any longer thinking she'd had a termination. What if their mothers bumped into each other and Sumitra told Christine? And she missed him terribly. He'd always been the person she confided in when she had a problem. She wanted the caring Ethan back, the one she laughed with. The one she loved. He'd been her world for years, her best friend. *I can't do this without him.*

When she answered the call, it was to see Ethan on the screen, standing before a huge window. She realised he must have his phone at arm's length. "I'm so pleased you answered," he said and his voice had a slight echo to it. "I've found us the perfect apartment." He moved the phone around the large open-plan space. "You'll love it. Can you see the views?"

She gulped, not being able to really make anything out.

Especially not the view which looked white on the phone. The picture settled, with his face filling the screen.

"It's been a tough week for you. And I'm an idiot and was harsh the other day. I'm so sorry. It was insensitive of me. You'd lost your seat, your business is in trouble at an emotional time for a woman, having to deal with an unwanted pregnancy – alone." He looked to the side. "With me out here, so many miles away." He turned back and closer to the screen of his phone, so she could see his blue eyes. "Babe. I'm so sorry. I'll make it up to you, I promise. And the good news is, this apartment is in a gated community and I've spoken to some of the residents and you won't be bothered at all. Why don't you fly out and I can spoil you. There are multiple flights here a day from Heathrow."

Nina gave a weak smile. "I'm glad you've calmed down." Although she had more to say of course. She took a deep breath. "I went to a private clinic today."

"A clinic? You couldn't take a pill?"

This wasn't going to be easy. "No, the pills are for women who are a couple of weeks pregnant." She swallowed hard. "I'm a lot more pregnant than that."

"What, so they haven't been able to do it yet? You're still waiting for the procedure? They should do these things straight away."

Her throat constricted. She wanted to discuss this in person. But at least he knew she was still pregnant.

"When can they do it?" he asked.

"I've another appointment," she said. Not wanting to lie.

"Babe, look work's so busy out here. But I'll come back early, as soon as I can and give you the biggest hug."

"Thanks," she said longing for him to be home, so she could feel his arms around her and explain face-to-face the reality of the situation.

CHAPTER 9

*W*arren added a little butter and salt to the potatoes as he mashed them.

"Dinner smells amazing, as per usual," Millie said.

"Sorry about the mess. I've used a lot of pots and pans for this one. It's chicken and leek pie."

Harry entered the kitchen during the tail end of his sentence. "I can't wait."

Greg was already in the dining room. He was a lot older and they didn't see much of him. He kept himself to himself and often went to bed after the meal as he rose early. They carried the food in and were soon sitting and eating. They enjoyed their food in silence for a few minutes. Warren had to admit the pie was tasty and he was grateful for the ready-made pastry. It cut down on the preparation time and he didn't have time to make puff pastry from scratch.

"Are you two coming up to the pub tonight?" he asked the students.

"I'm too whacked out, we were up at dawn," Harry

said. "We were let down by a couple of the casual workers on the veg box filling.

"I'll have to give it a miss too," Millie said. "I've got a video call with my parents at eight. They've been to Greece and want to tell me all about it."

Warren looked at Greg. "I don't suppose?"

"Mitch already tried to recruit me for the darts team," he replied in a monotone voice. "It's not for me."

Warren was a bit disappointed; he would have preferred to walk in with someone. Holly and Mitch were going up but they lived closer and he didn't want to sound like an idiot, asking them if he could go in with them. Still, they said everyone was friendly. He would arrive a little behind schedule, just to make sure they were already there.

He freshened up and, not knowing what to wear, put on a black t-shirt over jeans and carried a clean black hoodie. He walked down the stairs and into the kitchen where Millie and Harry had just finished cleaning.

"Wow, you look dressed to impress!" Millie said.

"Really?"

She laughed. "I guess I'm just used to seeing you in cargos and the farm polo shirt."

"You do look different, mate," Harry said.

"I've only put on a t-shirt and jeans," Warren said with a nervous laugh.

"You look good," Millie said. "For an older guy!"

"I'm only twenty-eight," Warren said with a laugh. "I'll see you two tomorrow."

"Looking forward to an update. We'll come to your next game, won't we Harry."

"Sure," Harry said with a yawn. "I'm going up now. Have a great night."

Outside, Warren found it was a clear evening and quite still. He walked towards the village. The first part of the journey he took across the field towards Lovelands Nursery. He could have walked along the road but there was no footpath that way and there was always the chance he would bump into Mitch on the way if he went by their cottage. He reached the permanently open gate between the two properties and then cut through Lovelands' car park and whilst he spotted the cottage, there was no sign of Mitch. He reached the pedestrian entrance which brought him out on the path towards the village. First, he went past the quaint stone-built church which had the last remnants of blossom on a few trees. He then reached the village green. He noticed that the small grocery store was open and headed for it then went inside.

"Hello," he said to the young woman serving and placed a pack of mints on the counter.

"I haven't seen you before," she said with a smile.

"I'm new to the village, I'm based at Booth Farm."

"I'm new too," she said. "I've been closing later to try to entice customers. I'm Katie."

Warren gestured in the direction of The Eversley Arms. "I'm off to the pub."

"On a date?"

"No, I've been asked to join the darts team."

"I love darts," she said eagerly.

Warren paid for the mints. "Nice meeting you."

She smiled back at him and called as he left the shop. "I might pop in later."

Warren wondered whether Katie was flirting with

him. He always erred on the side of caution where women were concerned, not to assume they fancied him unless they explicitly said so. He popped a mint in his mouth as he walked past the auction house. He saw the next auction was in two week's time. It was all a bit too middle class he thought. He felt out of place. He passed the bistro. He'd eaten mainly at cafés and not the posh type – the greasy spoon type like the one he'd lived in for a few years with Nick and Jane which had mostly been used by construction workers away from home wanting a decent home-cooked meal or a massive fry up for breakfast. He looked at the menu. *Today's Menu: Braised Lamb Shank with Rosemary and Red Wine Jus.* He had to admit, the smells coming from the place were enticing. The door opened and he stepped aside, not wanting to get in the way. He realised he was delaying his entrance to the pub and took a deep breath, deciding to get his entrance over and done with. He reached the large wooden door to The Eversley Arms, which was open, and then he walked inside.

"There he is," Mitch called from the far end of the room.

Warren was relieved that he was already there until her heard the whoops as he walked in, as if it was his birthday party.

"Here comes our star player," a guy shouted. He had a broken nose and looked vaguely familiar to him.

There was a round of applause. Mitch approached and shook Warren's hand then put his arm around him. "You're a dark horse, not telling us you were good enough to play pro."

Jaz appeared at Mitch's side, chewing her knuckle. "Sorry, Warren. I forgot it was a secret until they all started making a fuss. Then I realised you told me not to mention it!"

Warren laughed. "No worries, but I haven't played for years. Sorry to disappoint you guys, but I'm bound to be rusty. I don't even have my own darts with me. They're back in Bristol."

"Rusty is better than Mitch," Holly called from a nearby table with a laugh.

"I'll get you a drink, then introduce you to the team," Mitch said. "What are you having?"

"Any lager is fine. Thanks." He grinned as he looked around. Everyone seemed friendly but he still wondered where he'd seen the guy with the busted nose. He was older, about late thirties, with a face that told a story of many fights. Warren followed Mitch to the bar. Maybe he'd been over to the farm.

"Simon, a Hunky Pig ale and the best lager you have on tap and a Pinot – a large one."

Warren watched as Simon made the drinks and he and Mitch chatted like old friends. The pub did have a homely feel to it. A large guy with a red beard came from the door and looked at Mitch then him.

"You must be Warren," he said in a deep voice.

Jaz appeared. "This is my better half, Julian."

"Half?" Mitch said. "Julian's more like eighty percent."

"Tell your husband to cool it," Jaz said to Holly. "He's already on his way and he's only had one pint."

"I meant in size," Mitch said with a laugh. "Not as in better percentage."

Holly collected her white wine from the bar. "It's my fault, I don't let him out much these days." She gave Mitch a kiss on the cheek.

Julian grinned and outstretched his hand to Warren. "You'll have to excuse this lot." He gave his hand a firm handshake. "Glad to meet you at last, you can't hide in that field forever."

"I weren't expecting this," he said gesturing around. "I thought it was going to be quiet in here."

Julian gave a deep laugh. "This place is always busy and noisy. I hear you're going to be the hero of the night!"

"I may be a disappointment." He took the lager that Mitch handed him. "Thanks."

"Come on. Let's get the introductions done," Mitch said.

Warren followed him across the room and he first stopped at the guy who looked familiar.

"This is Rob Bird."

"Ah," Warren said. "I thought I'd seen you somewhere before. I watched a few of your fights!" Warren recognised him as a boxer he used to watch on TV when he was a lad.

"Nice one!" Rob said lifting his pint to him.

"Rob's our team manager," Mitch said.

"It was the lot from The Dog and Horn that roped us into it," Rob said. "They wanted to set up a league around here for pubs within three miles of their boozer, as they were fed up of travelling into Wells for their games."

"Are they here?" Warren asked.

"No, but you'll know when they arrive," Mitch said with a chuckle.

"And this is Carl, he *was* the best player we had until you rocked up. He used to play for The Dog and Horn."

"I was their worst player, though." Carl said. "We're expecting to get slaughtered by the Dogs but at least we might be able to take one or two games off them. This is our first friendly, the league starts in two weeks." He looked past Warren. "Oh, here they come."

Some of the guys rapped on the table as the men and a couple of women filed in. Warren stepped back and watched the good-natured banter and Jaz laughed with the women and took them to the bar. These people reminded him more of those back home. He was pleased he'd come.

"Hope I'm not late," a well spoken dark-haired man, said. He wore a patterned jumper.

"Reverend Stephens, you made it," Rob said, plastering on what looked to Warren like a fake grin. It was far too wide.

The reverend adjusted his jumper and Warren noticed his collar confirming this was a man of the church.

"Hey Rob what you doing?" one of the players from The Dog and Horn asked. "Arranging your last rights before your team gets slaughtered?" He followed with a hacking laugh.

"Reverend Stephens is our secret weapon," Rob said although sounded far from convinced but the reverend descended into laughter.

"You need all the help you can get," one of the Eversley Burrows women said with a laugh as she approached with Jaz.

Warren practised at the board and while he was a bit rusty, having watched the others throw a few practice shots, he guessed he was by far the best player The Eversley Arms had. He relaxed knowing that with his skill at darts, he had a better chance of being accepted into this tight-knit community.

"Where's the food?" Carl shouted out to Simon.

"It's bangers and chips. I'm cooking so it's nothing fancy," Simon said from behind the bar. "It'll come out after the games,"

"That's a shame, Rob could do with something to soak up the drink." Carl looked at their team manager with a frown.

Warren stood by the bar, watching the busy room and wondered how well Rob would manage the team, as he appeared to be well on his way to being drunk. Warren's attention was diverted when a woman entered the pub. She had long dark glossy hair and beautiful warm brown eyes. He remained where he was as if rooted to the spot as she walked through the pub. She reached Jaz who leaned up and gave her a hug.

"Got your eye on someone have you?" Rob dug him in the ribs.

"Me?" *Is it that obvious?* he thought, but he wasn't going to admit. "No, I haven't. I'm just surprised at how many people drink here."

"Why don't you go over and chat her up?" Rob slapped him on the back, ignoring his denial.

Warren wasn't used to approaching women. He watched as she approached the bar, soon close to them and about to order a drink.

"Go on, now's your chance," Rob said and pushed him, resulting in his lager splashing her.

She turned around, her eyes narrowed. "Thank you!" She looked down at her red dress which now had a patch where his drink had landed.

"I'm so sorry," Warren said.

Rob burst out laughing.

She shook her head giving Rob a disapproving look and flounced away.

"I wouldn't worry about it, mate," Rob slurred. "Nina's as stuck up as they get. Lives with a millionaire and loves herself. What you drinking?" Rob grabbed his now empty glass. "I'll replace this one."

Nina? Warren thought as he watched the woman walk towards the exit. *Is that Holly's friend?* He groaned, realising he'd upset the woman who was going through a hellish time.

CHAPTER 10

"*N*ina!"

Nina reached the end of the bar and turned around to check who'd called her name.

"I'm sorry about splashing you." The guy who had been with Rob Bird had caught her up.

As he approached, her she frowned. He clearly knew her name but she knew she hadn't seen this guy before. He was young, a lot younger than her. He stopped as her eyes met his. They were warm eyes and he was tall with light brown skin. He continued to gaze at her and she wondered whether he had her mixed up with someone else as he was staring so intently.

"Please don't leave," he said, retaining eye contact.

She kept looking into his eyes. He appeared incredibly worried. "I'm not leaving. I was going to wipe myself down." She pointed to the sign leading to the toilets.

"Oh, yes…sorry," he stuttered and broke the eye contact.

"Have we met before?" She knew they hadn't but he'd called her by name.

"No. I er…Rob said…"

"It's fine, it was only a splash." As nervous as he seemed, he appeared sincere and incredibly worried. She didn't want to make him feel bad about it. She turned and continued to the toilet.

Inside she glanced in the mirror, noticing how flushed her face was. No wonder he thought she was angry. She realised she'd not retouched her make up before she had come out. *Must be stress,* she thought. She never left the house without a thick covering of foundation. Yet she quite liked the way she looked. *Maybe this is what they mean about pregnant women blooming?* She grabbed a few sheets of hand towel and wiped the lager from her dress. She decided she would not let a spilled drink ruin her evening. She'd far too much to worry about without getting upset over damp clothing.

She came out of the toilets to find the guy who spilled his drink was still there, waiting.

"Can I buy you a drink to say sorry?" he asked.

She crossed her arms. "So is that your pick up line, spill your lager over a woman so you can ask to buy her a drink?" Nina was feeling a bit of her old self coming through. She was never timid.

"I…er. No." The guy looked mortified. "It's…I'm…"

Nina smiled at him. "I'm only joking." Her attempt at putting him at ease had the opposite effect. *Surely he isn't chatting me up?* She'd only said it as a joke as he was clearly way too young for her. "I'm only drinking iced water."

"Are you driving?" he asked.

"I am," she said. "And pregnant!" *What did I say that for?*

She'd decided not to announce it yet and she'd not told anyone other than immediate friends.

"Oh," he said. "Right, I'll get you the water."

She relaxed. At least she'd made it crystal clear that she wasn't available, in case he really was hitting on her. *But surely not,* she thought. Still, it would have been awkward to explain after a while that she was engaged, if he'd started chatting her up. She took a deep breath and scanned the room. She saw Rob Bird at the end of the bar. What was he going to say when he found out she was pregnant? *Oh, no,* she thought, realising she would have to ask this young man to keep what she'd told him to himself. She'd forgotten he was one of Rob's friends.

"One iced water," he said, handing her a glass as he held a half-filled large bottle of mineral water in the other.

"Tap would have been fine," she said with a smile. She looked over the room as Rob burst out laughing again. "Can we have a quick chat?"

The guy visibly gulped.

Nina laughed. "Don't worry. Look let's go outside, it's quite mild this evening and maybe my dress will dry off." She went through the door. A couple of groups were already sat on benches which were on the village green.

She sat down and he sat opposite her.

She took a deep breath. "I shouldn't have told you I was pregnant. I just said it because…" She didn't want to say it was because she thought he was hitting on her. "I haven't officially announced it yet. Could you keep it a secret? The thing is, it was a bit of a surprise, to me and the father. I don't relish the thought of Rob Bird finding out yet. I can see you're friends with him."

"Of course, I won't say a word. I've only just met Rob. By the way, I'm Warren, I work over at Booth Farm, with Mitch."

"You're one of the students?" she asked, guessing he must be even younger than she thought.

"I'm doing a PHD and creating a silvopasture. It's a field that–"

"Ah, yes of course. I've heard about it, the self-sufficient field. It sounds amazing. I'd love to see it. I was on the council until recently, pushing through some environmental policies."

"You can visit it any time," he said.

"You seem to be fitting in well in there." Nina gestured to the pub door.

"It's my first time here. Rob's a bit of a wind-up."

"You're a good judge of character," she said with a laugh as she took a sip of her cool water. "So how are you finding it?"

"I was only in the pub about twenty minutes before you got here. And I'm not staying long. My parents, well that's my adoptive parents, are coming over tonight." He looked at his watch. "They'll be here at about ten."

"I bet they're proud of you." Nina took a sip of her drink. There was something calming about talking to Warren, someone that hadn't known her as Councillor Smith. It was nice to chat with someone new.

"Yes, they're getting married soon."

"They left it late then?" she said.

"Well, when I said adoptive parents, it's unofficial...they've only known me since I was sixteen. They own a café I used to go to a lot and we became close. I wasn't that keen on the foster parents I had. Not them as such, I was hitting back at the system."

This guy seemed really interesting and she was dying to ask more, but it was a personal topic for someone she'd only just met. "When are your parents getting married?" she asked,

"Early August. Jane's in a stress over it. Said she can't find a dress."

"I've a bridal boutique."

"Oh yes, Holly told me you had a shop."

"She did? She spoke about me?" Nina frowned.

His eyes widened as if he should not have mentioned it. "Friday, she was yawning in the field and I asked her why she was tired."

"Ah," Nina said. "Because she was up with me when I lost my seat." She shook her head.

"I can't see Hedgehog Sam being any good at that job."

She looked down at her stomach. "Everything happens for a reason." She looked back up and smiled at him. For a young man, he seemed quite mature, more mature than Rob and his crowd that was for sure.

"Warren. There you are," Jaz called from the door. "And you, Nina, Holly's looking for you. She's worried."

"I came out for some air." She lifted her glass which jangled with the ice inside.

"It's my fault, sort of. Rob pushed me and my lager ended up all over Nina."

"He's already drunk." Jaz gestured towards the door. "Warren, you're on next! And don't let me down, we've lost everything so far! They made mincemeat of the reverend."

Nina laughed at Jaz. "Don't tell me you're the darts team manager?"

"No, I'm not. But I should be. Rob doesn't know what he's doing!"

"You'd better go in," Nina said to Warren who was still sitting where he was, gazing at her.

"Right, yeah. And sorry, again." He stood up and passed Jaz who stared at him with her eyebrows raised.

Jaz came over to the bench and sat down. "He's totally smitten with you, must like the older woman."

"Of course he's not. I told him I'm pregnant. And I'm sure he would have noticed my ring." She played with the huge diamond ring Ethan had bought for their engagement.

"Ah! So you picked up that he liked you too! Otherwise you wouldn't have told him."

Nina blushed. "It was just in case. But he's way too young!"

"But really good looking," Jaz said.

"Who's good looking?" Julian said as he appeared behind his wife.

Jaz looked up and laughed at him. "I have eyes for no one but you, my Viking beast."

Nina laughed as Julian gazed down at Jaz and it was then she recognised the look in his eyes. It was the exact same look that Warren had given her. *Surely not!*

CHAPTER 11

*W*arren was in a daze as he walked through the pub. Nina was stunning, absolutely beautiful. *She's engaged and pregnant,* he reminded himself, having noticed the massive diamond ring on her left hand. *Calm down.* Family was important, he knew that. and he would never come between a couple, even if he had a chance. He shook himself out as he stood by the board.

"Hey, he's limbering up," Rob called out. "We thought you'd done a runner." Rob approached him then lowered his voice. "I saw you chatting Nina up at the bar. You're punching there, mate. Her bloke's a flash git with a Maserati." He held out his hand. "Anyway, here's the darts. You'll need your own for the league, though."

Warren took the darts with Rob's words milling around his head. Even if Nina was single, she would still be out of reach. But maybe this encounter was for a reason. *Perhaps it's a sign I should find a girlfriend?* He pushed the thought from his mind as he threw his first dart, straight in the triple twenty.

"Oi! Where'd you get him from?" his opponent said. "Is he a ringer?"

"Calm down, Digger," Carl said. "He works for Booth, over at the farm."

"Right," the guy said as Warren's second dart also went in the triple twenty.

They cheered and Warren paused, losing his concentration. The remainder of the triple twenty was obscured so he went for triple nineteen but only managed the single. He retrieved the darts and stood behind the oche, as Digger took his throw.

Rob slapped him on the back. "You've got this, mate."

Warren was surprised at how well the darts glided in and he sealed his win with a double ten.

Jaz approached him with a huge grin. "Well done, Warren, you're even better than I imagined." She turned around. "Right, Carl, you're on next! Don't let me down."

"Who am I playing?" Carl asked.

"My Dad!"

"Hey, love. Aren't you going to support me?" the short man beside her said. He shared Jaz's brown eyes and dark hair, albeit with flecks of grey.

"You could have played for The Eversley! You had your chance!" Her hands were on her hips.

"I didn't know you were the manager!" her father said.

"She's not," Rob slurred from a table as he stared into his pint. "I am."

"Our Daz ain't defecting," Digger shouted.

Jaz laughed as she nudged her dad then turned to Carl. "Thrash him!"

Warren laughed at the good nature of the place. He felt warmth envelop him. *Can I really fit in here?* he asked himself as he watched Jaz's dad make mincemeat of Carl, the noisy Dog and Horn team supporting him.

The Eversley Arms lost the match, having only won two games out of the seven, both of which involved Warren. After playing the singles, he had teamed up with Carl to play in the doubles match. The room quietened as they ate their sausage and chips and Jaz called the team together at a long table.

"It was a good effort guys, we expected to get beaten." She turned to Warren. "What's your honest opinion of our team?"

He finished the hot dog he had made up with the rolls provided and wiped his hands on a napkin. "It's a bit small – if someone's sick you might have to throw a game."

"I'll try to drum up interest at my Sunday service," Reverend Stephens said.

"What do you think we need skills-wise?" Jaz said.

"Practice," Warren said. "A lot of it."

"Right, Monday night is practice night," Jaz said gesturing at Warren. "Is that okay with you?"

"He's always free," Mitch said.

"Great, you're our trainer," Jaz said.

"Oh, okay, yeah," Warren said, hoping Jaz didn't have too high expectations of the team.

"And I'm the new manager," Jaz said looking at everyone as if ready to beat off an objection.

Rob raised his hand from the end of the table. "Oi, I founded the team."

"And were too drunk to play!" She stood up, went to the end of the table and picked up his pint. "No drink for you on a Monday or a Friday before ten. I need you on the team."

Rob puffed out and sat back in his chair but did not protest.

Warren smiled. Even though Jaz was a small woman, it would appear no one wanted to cross her, not even a champion boxer.

Everyone dispersed and he stood up and turned around to find Nina there. He'd thought she'd left as he'd not seen her.

"I watched your game. You're brilliant at it!"

"I had a lot of practice as a teenager. I spent more time in the pubs than at school." As she was out of his league, he didn't bother to try to impress her. The truth was easier.

"I was just thinking, I'm having a sale at my boutique in Wells." Nina took in a deep breath. "So if you bring your mum over to the shop tomorrow morning between nine and half past, I've plenty of dresses. It's called *Something Special* and it's on the market square."

"I'll bring her over." Warren smiled at her, hoping Jane had not managed to sort a dress and at the same time feeling terrible for looking forward to seeing some other guy's fiancée. *She's just being friendly.*

"I'm off home now," Nina said. "I might see you tomorrow." She gave him a smile which made him wish he could go with her, but he knew that even if she didn't have the fiancé she was starting a family with, he'd still have no chance.

"Warren!" Jaz waved at him from a table and beckoned him over.

He sat at the table with Holly, Jaz and Belle who was glued to her smartphone.

"I saw you chatting to Nina!" Jaz said.

"She said she might have a dress for Jane, my adoptive mother."

"Do you like the older woman?" Jaz asked.

"Jaz, leave him alone," Holly said.

Warren laughed. "She's engaged, but I was surprised, she looks a lot younger than her age."

"You mean a lot younger than us?" Jaz asked, suddenly looking quite annoyed.

"I…er…"

Holly laughed. "She's winding you up."

"It'll be the Botox," Jaz said.

Holly shook her head. "Jaz, don't be unkind."

"Sorry, I sometimes lose my filter when I've had a couple of drinks," she said then took a sip of her cider.

"What filter?" Holly said. "You've never had one!"

"Jaz," a woman called out who had been supporting 'the Dogs' as they were being called. "We're going now."

Jaz tapped Holly on the arm. "Let's have a quick chat with Mel and Sian. I want to speak to them about that idea you had for the PTA, now it's a bit quieter." Jaz and Holly were on the parent-teacher association at Eversley Village Primary School. They'd mentioned it a few times at the weekly family meals. Holly stood up and Jaz followed.

Warren found himself sitting opposite Belle, still staring at her phone. She frowned.

"Is something wrong?" he asked her.

Belle shook her head and didn't look up.

He felt there was a conversation to be had but left it for another time. He knew if there was something up, she was unlikely to tell him straight away. *Better to build her trust slowly*, he thought.

Mitch came to the table and placed another pint in front of him.

"Hey thanks," Warren said. "It must be my round by now."

"It's a thank you, for coming. If you hadn't been here, I don't think they'd be bothering with the team."

"Or without Jaz." Warren looked at Rob as he staggered past their table.

"Rob needs to clean himself up. Jaz said she's going to be on his case. Since she moved out of here to Ashbury Gardens, he's got worse."

They sat in thoughtful silence for a while.

"This better be my last," Warren said, "as I've got to get back for Nick and Jane."

"What time are they arriving?"

"They're going to text me when they leave Bristol, so I can head back, but I think I'll go earlier, otherwise I'll be dozing off."

Mitch grinned at him. "I'm pleased you were playing instead of me. And it's great you'll be up here on Mondays. Do you think the team have any hope?"

"They might have. A lot of it is mindset. Once they gain confidence it could make all the difference. Carl said that when Rob's sober, he can throw a dart."

"That's the thing, you don't often see him sober."

They continued to chat until Holly and Jaz returned to the table and Warren decided it was a good time for him to call it a night.

As he walked home his thoughts returned to Nina and he conjured up an image of her in his mind. *Why can't I find someone like that, but single?*

CHAPTER 12

*S*aturday was market day so Nina drove to Wells early. It was a fresh but sunny morning as she walked up the High Street towards *Something Special*. As she passed her father's shop, she noticed he was already inside arranging a tie display. After spotting her, he rushed to the door. He'd been uncharacteristically quiet when she'd gone home for dinner earlier in the week. She knew he'd disapproved of Ethan when she'd said he'd been shocked at her news and not keen on becoming a father. Tony thought every man should worship Nina and had certainly been hard on her past boyfriends, if he'd considered they'd not treated her well. Her father thought she was a princess, and that any man in her life should regard her as such. And whilst she agreed that it would be ideal if Ethan was there supporting her, she also appreciated that he'd received a down payment of over a million on his current contract and couldn't cry off.

Tony opened the door. "Have you got time for a quick coffee?"

"If you have decaf."

"I do." He stepped aside to let her pass, then locked the door behind her.

"Have you heard from Ethan?" he asked.

"Not today, but I'm not telling him about the scan until I see him face to face. It's not fair to discuss something this important on a video call."

"I'd never have thought he'd act like this."

"He's doesn't know the full facts, Dad. Hopefully when we look at it calmly together, he'll come around."

"He should still be here. By your side."

"He's committed to the building. It's worth millions."

Tony poured coffee for them. "I hope you don't have to move to Qatar, but we understand if you do. Ma is planning a visit to India and can combine that with your due date and be with you when you have the baby. I'm retiring next year so we can visit you for weeks at a time. I don't want you dragging the poor child back and forth, because of us." Tony shut his eyes as if composing himself before reopening them. "If you have to live there. We have to accept it."

It was clear to Nina that her parents had been discussing her possible move to Qatar in depth. She sighed. "I hope it won't come to that. Although I know I may have to make compromises. But if we did move, I'd insist we returned before the child started school."

"So, you're considering it?" he asked, taking a sip of his coffee.

"Dad, my mind is jumbled with so many different scenarios. But I have an unknown factor to consider – Ethan. It's so difficult, sitting and waiting calmly for him to come home."

Tony gave her a hug. "You're under intense pressure, angel. I hope you're taking care of yourself."

She squeezed her father back and then released him. "Of course. It's just that I like to plan for my future. And I need to know if I have to turn the shop around – because if I'm staying in Wells, I'd hate to lose it. Having lost my council seat as well, I'm feeling such a failure."

"Don't worry about the seat. If you do stay here, then once you've had the baby and are settled, you can get back on the council when that ridiculous offspring of Barry Brent is kicked off!"

Nina laughed. "Now I've left, I'm not that eager to return, especially as I've motherhood on the horizon. You should run for the council yourself if you miss it so much."

"Ma would hate it," he said wistfully. "And just to clarify, you'll always have a place with us. There's plenty of room at our house, you'd have your own bathroom and can have the back room as a nursery and space for yourself."

"Thanks," Nina said, clearly her parents had discussed every eventuality. But going back home would not be ideal. *I hope it doesn't come to that,* she thought. But at least she had somewhere to go if the worst happened and Ethan ended it. She gulped. "I'd better get to the shop, I have a big day." She smiled at her father but also felt her lip quiver.

"Hey," Tony said. "I've upset you, haven't I!"

She wiped her eyes. "Sorry, it's not you, I keep blubbing at the drop of a hat. Ignore me."

Nina gave her father another hug before leaving his shop. She continued the last stretch up the High Street towards her shop. The cathedral loomed before her, dwarfing the market traders setting up their stalls.

She unlocked the shop door and went inside. Being faced with the sale stock, the tears returned. *Something Special* meant so much to her and she'd hate to lose it. But she gave her eyes a quick wipe and brushed the sadness aside. She needed to think positive. It had to go well.

Inside, she sorted through dresses to ensure they were in size order. Her phone dinged with a text. She picked it up from the countertop and quickly clicked on it. It was from Ethan.

Hope they've sorted everything for you. Thinking of you babe and don't worry, this will pass and we'll be living a top life. Can't wait to spoil you. Miss you, love you xx

She felt a glimmer of hope. She knew Ethan loved her, she'd never doubted that. It was going to be difficult having a long-distance relationship with a child, but she had faith in their bond. The sooner he came home so they could discuss the future, the better. When he had the full facts, he would come around, she was convinced of that. *Love always finds a way*, she told herself as she texted back that she missed him as well. She placed her phone back on the counter.

She stared into space and then jumped when she heard a rap at the door. In all the discussion with her father, she had clean forgotten the reason she'd arrived early. Warren grinned at her through the window. She smiled at the woman standing beside him with dark brown skin and plaited hair, tied back in a ponytail. Beside her was a short man, with a full head of grey hair, which he had styled into a quiff, like a rockabilly. The three people looked so different from each other.

Nina unlocked and opened the door. "You must be Jane." Nina stepped aside so she they could enter. Jane looked younger than she'd imagined her to be.

"I am, and this is my other half, Nick."

"We're Warren's parents," Nick said.

"Although we don't look alike, as we adopted him," Jane added.

Nick gestured at his fiancée. "She's a bit nervous."

Warren gave Nina a huge smile as he followed them in. "I've told her how nice you are."

Jane looked up at Warren with much affection.

"You're getting emotional, again," Warren said to Jane with a laugh.

"Getting married is an emotional business, I see many tears when brides try dresses on. Now, I have a few dresses I'm sure you'll love." She gestured at Warren and Nick. "I suggest you two get yourselves a coffee as you won't be seeing it until the day."

"Oh, right," Warren said as he turned to leave the shop.

"You can stay here and have one. There's a small utility area at the back. And a table and chairs just outside the back door in the yard if you want to sit. It's forecast to be a warm day."

"Great, thanks," Warren said.

"I've a large variety of soft drinks in the fridge if you prefer. And some snacks – help yourselves."

Once they were out of sight, Nina showed Jane a couple of dresses and one in particular fitted wonderfully.

"You can ask a seamstress in Bristol to adjust it if you feel you need anything done, but it looks amazing on you. I'd say it was a perfect fit."

"And such a good price," Jane said.

Nina had taken more off the sale price. Jane was so nice and knowing they had taken Warren in, she felt this was a woman with a huge heart. Nina realised she could not afford to be so generous for the rest of the day. She had to strike the right balance between a cost that would sell the dresses fast, while still making enough money to buy new stock. She'd spent the evenings researching and had made a couple of appointments with her suppliers who were sending reps to visit her during the next week.

Nina packed the dress away in a suit bag, hung it up and checked her watch. "I still have fifteen minutes before my next appointment if you want a coffee?"

"That would be lovely." Jane followed her to the kitchen.

"Do you have any more children?" Nina asked.

"No, we have no natural children. That's why our lives were enriched when Warren came to us. Poor kid, he just needed to be loved. After he moved in with us, his whole world turned around." She smiled at her. "He's my biggest achievement in life. I just wish he'd call me Mum."

"Aww, have you asked him to?"

She nodded. "He still has a wall. He's allowed us in and he'll let me hug him, but he always keeps something of himself back." She smiled at her. "You're a lovely girl. Are you single?"

Nina blushed, realising Jane was attempting to match-make. She showed Jane her left hand. At the centre of her ring setting was a large diamond. Everyone had called it a rock after Ethan had proposed and slipped it onto her finger. "I'm engaged, although it's complicated," she added.

"If it's complicated, he's probably not right for you.

You know when it's the right person, when it feels natural, like when I met Nicolaus."

"Sorted?" Nick asked Jane as they reached the yard with their drinks.

"She looks beautiful," Nina said. "You'll have your breath taken away."

"I have my breath taken away every time she walks into the room." He lifted up his hand.

Jane took it. "He smiled at me when I walked into his café. And I knew, immediately."

"I burnt the toast."

"It was on fire, I rushed around the counter and put it out!"

"I offered her a job right there and then."

Jane laughed. "I was there for the job, anyway. Not lunch."

"And she never left the premises."

"I moved straight in that night." She looked at Nina. "That was fifteen years ago and he's only just asked me to marry him."

Nick laughed. "I went to do my will. It was a lot of messing around, so the solicitor told me to get married and it'd be much easier."

"He's so romantic," Jane said with a laugh.

Nina could tell, that regardless of the reason behind their wedding, they were incredibly in love. As she smiled at them, she caught Warren's eye and he smiled back at her. The doorbell rang.

"Ah, that will be my next customer. Don't rush, you can finish your drinks out here, and go out the back way if you like. I'll hang the dress just inside the door."

"Thanks Nina, can we buy you dinner later to say thank you?" Jane asked.

"Oh, that would have been lovely, but I'm going to a housewarming this evening."

"Tomorrow lunchtime, then?" Jane asked. "What about in that pub? The Eversley Arms, we hear they do a great Sunday roast."

"Jane," Warren said. "Nina's a busy woman." He looked at Nina and mouthed *sorry.*

She smiled back. "I have to spend the weekend sprucing up the house, my fiancé's arriving home next week. He's been away."

"Oh yes, I clean forgot," Jane said with a giggle. "The fiancé."

"I hope your wedding is all you dream it will be," she said as the doorbell chimed for a second time.

CHAPTER 13

*N*ina reached the village green of Eversley. She stopped the car, thinking how beautiful it was in the evening sunshine. She'd so many memories attached to this village. Attending the opening day of Julian's bistro, which was now a favourite with food critics. Bidding at Kelly's Auction House on a few items, none of which she'd won. It was run by Helen Kelly and her son's girlfriend Grace Bunning, whose father was in business with Jaz. She smiled. The village was so interconnected, there was a part of her that envied those who lived there, in the tight-knit community.

She watched children playing catch on the green and wound down her window to take in some deep breaths of fresh air and thought back to the village fairs that used to be held there when she was a child. Her parents often brought her to them. Maybe this would be the ideal place to bring up their child, rather than the remote house in Shepton Mallet. If Ethan would be living between the UK and Qatar, maybe it would be better for her to move to a place with neighbours. And Eversley Village Primary School always had good inspection reports. Living in isolation in the country had always given them a sense of freedom, but it would be more practical to be closer to amenities for family life.

Ethan also loved Eversley. It was where she was when Ethan had asked her out on their first date, having not seen him since college. She'd caught up with him years later at the reopening of Holly's nursery after it had suffered a fire. Initially, Nina had not recognised him at all. This tall and muscular man, with a white smile and fair hair, was nothing like the boy she'd known at college. She'd been waiting to meet the perfect man, and he'd been standing before her, gorgeous and confident. He'd told her he was waiting for a woman to come into his life, who he could love, spoil and treat like a princess. And he'd done just that after they'd hit it off, going to the gym together, off to a yoga retreat together, holidays to the Maldives where they learnt to scuba dive together. She truly believed they were perfect for each other. They'd celebrated all of their wins, taking many city breaks and eating in high-end restaurants.

Her eyes rested on the grocery store. It had been closed since the post office element had been shut down and the postmaster had moved on. It had clearly been taken over by someone new, as there was a bucket of daffodils outside, presumably for sale. She glanced at her phone, realising she had been reminiscing for a good fifteen minutes, and switched the engine back on for the last few yards of her journey.

She turned into the cul-de-sac where Jaz and Julian had bought the largest cottage in the village. It was within the first ever built cul-de-sac where the cottages dated back to the Victorian era and the builders had used stone mined from Somerset quarries. Ashbury Gardens was the most sought after and popular road with incomers to the village, and the locals found it difficult to afford to buy them. Jaz and Julian had been able to snap it up before it even went on the market as they knew the previous owners.

Nina drew up outside the cottage. The front door swung open and Jaz was grinning at her from the doorstep, before Nina had even switched the engine off. Nina opened the car door and gazed at the beautiful cottage with a wisteria in bloom against the front wall with hanging lilac flowers. There was a separate annexe, which Jaz's parents were moving into. It was rendered in a dirty white and Nina imagined it would look pristine once Jaz had finished extending and refurbishing it.

"Congratulations on your new beautiful home," she said to Jaz as she reached the doorstep and handed her a bunch of flowers. With Jaz and Julian owning a pub, she never gave them alcoholic gifts.

"I'll show you around before everyone else arrives."

Nina entered the welcoming family home and felt her throat constrict, wondering whether she would have a family home like this. Would she be a family of two? She paused; she needed to eradicate the negative talk and focus on Ethan coming around. Not to even entertain the thought he would reject her. She also did not want to harbour any resentment towards him which would affect their relationship going forward.

Jaz showed her around the house. It was quirky with a lot of cosy spaces and rooms.

They stepped outside into the rear garden and Jaz pointed to the building next door. "I wish the annex was ready for Mum and Dad to move into."

"It's more than an annex. It's a whole separate house!" Nina said.

Jaz laughed. "I know. Julian's putting a fence up in between our homes, to split it apart from us and we have applied for it to be shown on the land registry as two separate properties. I want Mum and Dad to feel it's theirs, not part of our place. They can grow old there."

"That's so nice."

"The renovation will include an extra bedroom over a new kitchen-diner and a conservatory. It will take a few more months." She sighed. "Mum's been in that house on Eversley Burrows since she was a teenager. It'll be lovely for her to finally move out and to the village. And I'm not gonna lie, I do get the odd flashback to my childhood when I'm over there."

Nina knew that Jaz had had a tough upbringing. "Don't they mind leaving their community behind?"

"They don't need to worry about that, it's only a fifteen-minute walk, or so. The Burrows lot will be over here all the time, I'm sure. It's another reason we want to have a clear divide," she said with a laugh.

"I need some help in the kitchen!" Julian's voice resounded from the house.

"Come on," Jaz said, leading Nina inside and through to the large kitchen-diner which looked out onto the beautiful garden with a huge cherry tree.

The boys came running in. "Hi Nina," they said in unison.

"Hands," Julian said and the boys went to the sink.

"Where's Belle?" Jaz asked.

"Probably upstairs on her phone," Julian grumbled.

Jaz tutted and went to the foot of the stairs. "Belle, didn't you hear Julian? He needs help." She frowned. "Belle!"

"You don't have to shout," Belle said as she stomped down the stairs. "I heard the first time." As she walked towards the dining table, Nina smiled to herself. The scowl on Belle's face reminded her of the way Jaz used to look at her when they were the same age – sixteen. Jaz had been jealous of anyone who went near Holly and that had included Nina.

Nina could not help but cheer up as the family set out the plates and snacks for their guests. Once they'd finished, the boys ran back to the garden and Belle sloped off upstairs.

The doorbell rang.

"Here they come," Jaz said.

The first to arrive were David Bunning and his wife Florrie. David had met Florrie aboard a cruise ship where she worked as a Shirley Bassey tribute act. His daughter Grace followed them in with Helen Kelly, the owner of the auction house.

Nina smiled at David and gave an inner groan as she predicted she'd have to endure another sympathetic chat about losing her seat on the council and how she would gain it back in no time. David had been a councillor at Wells for some time himself before he stood down after meeting Florrie, wanting to spend time abroad with her.

Grace stepped forward and gave Nina a hug. "How are you?"

"I'm fine, really I am." She gave her a squeeze and then

stepped back. "Enforced change is always a time for reflection and signifies a new phase in your life." She didn't elaborate. She was desperate for Ethan to return so she could begin to spread their news, once he'd got a handle on it himself.

"You look well," Helen said with a broad smile. "You're glowing. It'll probably do you good to have more time to yourself. You've been living life at one hundred miles an hour!" Helen wandered off to the kitchen carrying a plastic tub of food.

Florrie stood beside David with her head cocked to one side.

"No need for the 'next election' chat," Nina said quickly to David before he could speak. "I'm fine. I'm simply looking forward and focussing on breathing new life into my business. I've neglected it over recent years, so I'm on it."

"That's the spirit," David said with a smile. He was an attractive man in his mid-fifties and Jaz's business partner.

"I'm glad you're bearing up," Florrie said with a warm smile.

"You're looking tanned, David. Have you two been away again?" Nina said, swiftly shifting the topic of conversation.

Florrie nodded. "We've spent a lot of time at my apartment in Grand Canaria."

"I've come back to see what on earth that daughter of mine is up to."

Grace laughed. "I've been rattling around this past week, as Brendan's away now in California. He'll be gone for months, other than a couple of visits, although hopefully I'll be spending some time there with him for a holiday."

"I thought he was supposed to be building the business here, in the UK?" Nina said, surprised.

"The MD is out of action, so he's been called in to oversee while she gets over back surgery. And he's already got managers in the three UK offices. Further expansion is on hold while they just keep things going in the US."

"So Grace has been in our five-bedroomed house, while we've been living in a pokey two-bed apartment," David said. He owned a house just outside the village.

Florrie laughed. "It's hardly pokey, it has two huge bedrooms with ensuites and a terrace looking out to the sea."

David put his arm around his wife. "True and I miss it already."

The doorbell chimed again and Jaz passed them to answer it.

Florrie glanced at Nina. "We had to come back as Jaz needs an extra hand with the business."

David sighed. "She'll work me into the ground. She's bought in a massive amount of stock from a liquidation deal, so we need to get our skates on and shift it. Mind you, it should raise a chunk towards her buying me out completely."

"Where's Ethan?" David asked.

"He's in Qatar, he has a design going forward over there."

"That's a long way away," Florrie said.

"I know the feeling," Grace added. "You look worried. Is everything okay?" Grace asked as David and Florrie went over to greet the next guests to arrive.

"Yes, although I have a few issues," Nina answered without elaborating. People would find out the full story soon enough when she started growing but she wasn't ready to discuss it until she had Ethan back on side. "But I want to forget about them and have a pleasant evening."

Grace tucked her arm in hers. "Come on then, I'm dying to have a look around. Jaz wouldn't let me in until everything was in its place."

The doorbell rang again and from then on there was a constant stream of arrivals for the next half an hour. After showing Grace and Florrie the house, Nina mingled and got the introductions out of the way and the expected commiserations about her losing her seat on the council. Val, Len, Holly, Mitch and the girls all arrived together. Jaz passed her a champagne flute. "There's only orange and lemonade in yours. Everyone else has Bucks Fizz. You'll be proud to know, I've not said a word. You must feel like you're in limbo waiting for Ethan to come home."

"It hasn't escaped my attention that you've never liked Ethan," Nina said.

"Not originally. I thought you all thought you were better than me as I didn't go to college. I was working."

"You know that's not true."

"Of course. But Ethan, he's too particular about everything, his food, what he wears, his hair, his body. It gets right on my nerves."

Nina smiled. "I think he's always been a bit wary of you."

"He should be now, if he gives you a hard time when he shows his face."

Jaz got called away and Nina found herself chatting to Helen.

"How's business?" Helen asked.

"It's been a tough couple of years and I'm diversifying," Nina said and then explained her plan.

"I'm sure you'll do just fine. *Something Special* has been on the market square for years. I can't imagine it closing. And how's Ethan? I'm sure he'll support you. I hear he's doing very well for himself."

"He's excited about his new project in Qatar," Nina said, not really wanting to discuss him. She needed the bathroom and to escape the constant questions about Ethan. She didn't want to think about him, not knowing what would happen. "You'll have to excuse me for a moment." She went out of the room and up the stairs as the downstairs toilet appeared to be in use.

On the landing she went inside, relieved to be alone. It was bad enough telling people she'd lost her seat and business. How would it be if she had to tell them she was pregnant, if Ethan didn't come around? She felt so out of control when the negative thoughts clouded her mind.

As she exited the bathroom, having remained in there for as long as she could, she saw straight through to Belle's room. The teenager was on the phone to someone.

"I've already said, yes." Belle shut her eyes. "Not yet." She paused. "Look, I have to go." As she ended the call, she spotted Nina and placed her phone on the bed.

"Are you okay?" Nina asked.

"Yeah, someone wants me to help them with their revision." She gave a short laugh. "I told them I can't do it right now. I have to focus on my own grades."

Nina looked around the space from the doorway. "You've a lovely room."

"It's okay. I liked my room at the Eversley." She

pointed to the window. "All I can see outside are other cottages and parked cars. I used to be able to sit and look at the green and the people sitting outside until it went dark and then the lights twinkled. And at Christmas, we could see the big tree, with all the lights on."

"But you'll all be together here, the whole family."

Belle made no comment.

Nina heard footsteps pounding up the stairs and expected to see the boys but it was two girls.

"Where's Belle?" they asked.

Nina stepped aside and Belle jumped off her bed to greet her friends. As Nina reached the bottom of the stairs she heard a baby crying. She stopped and realised, that since she'd found out she was pregnant, she'd not been anywhere near a baby.

"I'll do it," Simon said. "Oh, hi Nina. Have you met Alex?"

The baby began to scream as he crawled towards his mother, his face turning crimson.

"Not yet," she said.

"I'll bring him to you in a mo," Simon said. "He needs changing."

Nina turned around to find Kimberly, Simon's wife, smiling at her.

"Simon's so good. I don't know what I'd do without him." She sighed. "My eldest, Max, didn't have a father around much, as my first husband was married more to his job. Then we split up." She grinned at Nina. "But Simon makes up for it. He spends so much time with Max as well – he was going off the rails but he's been like a different child since Simon came into our lives. Now come on, let me hear your news."

Nina followed Kimberly into the lounge and sat beside her and filled her in on losing her seat and her attempt to bring new life to the shop.

"You're an amazing woman, I know you'll turn it around. Oh, here they are!"

Simon handed over Alex and a bottle.

"Do you want to feed him?" Kimberly asked Nina.

"Oh, yes," she said, cradling the warm baby in her arms.

"I'll get a drink. What are you having?"

"Only orange juice, I'm driving."

Alex stared at her as he sucked hard on the bottle. *Am I really cut out for this?* she asked herself.

CHAPTER 14

ina cleaned the upstairs bathroom of her Shepton Mallet home. As with the lounge downstairs, it had huge windows giving it a bright outlook. This meant they were able to sit in the bathtub with countryside views. With the house being isolated, there was no need for blinds. She decided to take a bath when she'd finished cleaning through. The urge to power through the whole house before Ethan returned was over-whelming. They used to have a cleaner but coincidently she was off on maternity leave and with Ethan away so much, and her being out of the house a lot of the day herself, it was easy to keep on top of, so she'd not appointed a new person.

She wiped over the taps. *Am I nesting already?* she asked herself. Although she knew she was prone to doing housework when she was stressed, as well as reordering her drawers and closet. It was as if reordering her home meant she was ordering her life. She stood back looking at the gleaming room, which now smelled of lemon cleaning product, and breathed out slowly. As much as she knew she would have to move to a more populated area, she'd loved living in the country with Ethan, cocooned in their own slice of paradise, away from the world and their busy lives. *Life moves on,* she told herself, feeling guilty in that moment for hankering after her old life, the time before she found out she was pregnant. Life had been busy, but their personal life had always been so simple. She loved Ethan, he loved her and neither had ever given the other cause for concern. They were going to be together, forever. She felt a warmth enter her body. She still believed that, and yes, this probably was a test to their relationship, when they had not been tested before, but she was convinced they'd pull through.

She hummed as she collected the cleaning products. She had sold most of her stock at the shop and had put a sign up to say she was temporarily closed. That would enable her to source the goods and rearrange the racks in the shop to display the new items. She had seen a sale of bulk items which she intended to attend and hoped to source goods to sell.

As she walked down the stairs she stopped short to find Ethan sitting at the breakfast bar.

"I didn't hear you come in?" She wasn't expecting him until the following morning.

"I just got back. I heard the water running and assumed you were in the shower."

Nina reached the ground floor and put the cleaning fluid on the worktop, feeling she wasn't ready for the conversation she knew she had to have. Not for the big discussion. She wanted that long soak in the bath and to prepare herself. She shot a glance to the coffee table where she'd left the scan picture. *Has he seen it?* "I wasn't expecting you back so soon." She smiled at him but her body tensed.

"I caught an earlier flight. I can't stop worrying about you. I want to hold you. We've always done everything together. And I feel bad, leaving you here to go through all this on your own. I don't want us to be apart. I've come back to talk about our future." He stretched his arms out. "Can we chat about it now?"

She reached out to him for a hug, and breathed in the scent of his aftershave as she felt his arms around her, not realising how much she'd really missed him. "I love you, Ethan." Without warning, she began to sob uncontrollably, releasing the tension that had built up. The strain of having to put on a brave face. Of missing the man who'd been her best friend for five years which to her felt like an eternity. Of not really remembering what it was like not to have him in her life.

"I love you too, babe. And I'm so sorry. I've been an idiot. I should have postponed the meetings I had." He lowered his voice. "I've missed this. Us two, together. I've been so upset by this whole thing. And it's been worse for you. You had to go through it. You mean everything to me." He squeezed her tight.

She leaned back and looked into his eyes. "I can't imagine doing this without you." She had to tell him.

"Doing what?" he asked.

She wiped her eyes with her hands and leaned back looking into his eyes. "I'm sorry Ethan, but I'm too far gone."

"What do you mean? Are you saying you're still pregnant? I thought you had another appointment."

She didn't reply as she stared into his eyes, trying to judge his thoughts and muster up in her mind what it was exactly she planned to say. But instead her mind went blank. "I've been waiting for you to come home, so we can discuss it properly."

"You still haven't decided? Why didn't you tell me? We should have been discussing it together." He ran a hand through his hair. "I shouldn't have gone away." He shook his head. "You've been here, no doubt with your parents putting pressure on you. I take it they know?"

"Yes, they do, but they haven't interfered."

"Who else knows?"

"Holly, Jaz…" She didn't add that Warren knew. He didn't even know who Warren was. She felt a pang of guilt that other people knew her situation, something Ethan was connected to, when he didn't.

"No doubt Holly and Jaz have told Mitch and Julian, for goodness' sake if Jaz knows the whole of Eversley's probably talking about it. Why did you tell them?"

She decided she needed to get straight to the point and went to the coffee table and picked up the picture she'd been carrying around in her purse. It fluttered as her hand shook. She returned to Ethan. "It's too late," she said, trying her best to keep her voice steady. "I'm too pregnant." She handed him the picture. "It's months, not a few weeks."

"What?" Ethan stared at the picture as she held it, not taking it from her, as if he didn't want to accept it. Then looked at her belly and turned away. He walked to the living area and stood in front of the windows. "No, no, no!" he called out, putting his head in his hands.

Watching his natural reaction filled Nina with fear.

Her heart pounded as she felt a chill seep into her veins. It was clear that to Ethan, a child was something he was going to struggle to come to terms with. She didn't expect him to be happy, she knew he'd be fed up, but not this much. Not mortified. She expected him to be more matter-of-fact. He was always so calm, someone who meditated, not someone who cried out in desperation.

He took a breath so deep she heard it, then turned around. "How far exactly are you?"

She didn't want to speak with such a space between them so approached him. "Over three months. It's due at the end of October."

"How did you not know you were pregnant? Isn't it sensible to keep an eye on these things?"

"I've already told you, I was stressed with canvassing. My period often stops when I've a lot going on." Her mouth felt dry so she turned and walked over to the sink. "I thought my period had stopped due to stress." She filled a glass with water.

"You should have taken a test after the first missed period!" he said, having followed her to the kitchen area.

She took a long drink of water, still not facing him. She could not bear to see his face, so disappointed. She already felt a connection with her child, and him rejecting it was giving her a sense of conflict. She took a slow breath, telling herself to stay calm. She turned around. "What I should or shouldn't have done isn't relevant now. It's happened and there's nothing we can do about it. All we can do is discuss what happens next."

"But Nina, I *have* to move to Qatar. I can't manage this project from a distance."

She took his hand. "I want us to be a family. I know

you have to be away at times. Women have children while their husbands are in the forces. It's a way of life for many. If you insist, then of course I'll go to Qatar, but I'm not sure it's the best thing for our child, and I have the shop, and our parents are here to support us."

"Oh, no. You haven't told my mother have you?"

"No. Ma's keeping it to herself, waiting for me to discuss it properly with you. I'm sorry I didn't explain on the call the other day. But we need to talk this out, sensibly in person."

"Agreed. We need to look at the options. Every option." He sighed. "I'll take my case up and take a shower."

"Shall I order in food?" she said. "I've nothing in as I wasn't expecting you." She did have food in, but not vegan, and she'd decided to opt for a diet without supplements for her pregnancy and one that included dairy.

"Sure." He took the stairs.

Nina smiled to herself as Ethan climbed the stairs. As stressed as he was, he'd not said no. He'd not said he was leaving her, he'd not refused to be a father. And he'd said he loved her and missed her. She felt relief wash over her. They'd work it out she knew that. It was bound to have been a shock.

Nina called Ethan once the food had arrived, she'd ordered Indian, the same selection they always had. A vegetable aloo tikki, a vegetable biryani, and chana masala – she loved the chickpeas cooked in a spicy tomato-based sauce. And they had a chapati, ensuring it was not served with ghee. She knew she should eat, even if she didn't always feel like it. The morning sickness had faded but she still always felt better with something in her stomach.

Ethan walked down the stairs with a tired expression. "Can we discuss this tomorrow? I can't think straight."

"Of course, let's enjoy the evening. I missed you so much." She gave him a hug and felt his body shake as she realised he was crying. She squeezed him tighter, feeling acutely close to the man she loved, completely. "We can face anything, Ethan. Together."

Later, after a comforting evening in front of the television, they went to bed and she held him close, feeling such a pure connection, wanting him so much and when he turned around, they made love so sweetly it made her cry.

After, as she laid her head on his chest, she knew he would come around and in that moment, had never felt so in love.

CHAPTER 15

*N*ina rose early and went downstairs as the sun streamed through the windows. She'd left Ethan to sleep in, considering the travelling he'd done the previous day. With it being so sunny outside, she felt much brighter and hoped he would too. Remembering how they'd been the previous evening, how tender it was, she knew in her heart of hearts that they would be together, always.

She soon heard him descending the wide slatted staircase. It would not be safe for a child. A move was most certainly on the cards, but she did not want to discuss that yet, after all they still had to talk through their plans. And she needed to convince him that they should not move their small family home to Qatar.

"It's so nice to have you back," Nina said. "I've felt totally lost without you these past few weeks. Especially losing the seat on top of everything else."

"How's the new guy getting on?" he asked nonchalantly as he flipped on the kettle.

"I've no idea, I haven't had the head space to check in with any of my old colleagues. But when things have settled, I'll ensure I'm as much of a pain in his backside as his father was to me." She laughed, feeling lighter than she had for weeks. "The environmental changes I proposed must go through and I'll be at the public meetings to express my opinion on the matter. I don't think Barry Brent realises just how much waste disposal cuts into the council's budget." It felt good to talk about something else, for a moment, making life appear normal.

"I'll get a shower. I thought we could go out for breakfast?" Ethan said with his green tea in hand. "I need to get out of this place."

"Sure," she said with a smile.

Nina and Ethan arrived at Gradients, a boutique hotel nestled in the countryside which was always their chosen location for an out-of-the-house breakfast. They made their way through the hotel's elegant reception, decorated in a style which fused modern to vintage, and were shown to the orangery. The stunning glass-walled room had a panoramic view of the hotel's manicured gardens and the hills beyond. Ethan had been uncharacteristically quiet during the journey over, giving her the impression that he was mulling over everything in his mind. The maître d' showed them to a table near the glass exterior, offering an unobstructed view of the picturesque landscape. They'd been there many times before and Nina adored it.

They were brought an assortment of freshly baked vegan pastries, including almond croissants and cinnamon rolls, the layers flaking perfectly with each bite.

A selection of breads were served with small pots of vegan friendly homemade preserves. A colourful fruit platter brightened the table, with slices of watermelon, pineapple and mango, as well as various berries. Hot food was also delivered which consisted of tofu scramble mixed with sautéed spinach, cherry tomatoes and mushrooms, drizzled with a truffle-infused oil. Nina's appetite had finally returned as she felt calmer than she had in weeks.

Nina sipped a freshly pressed orange juice, as the aroma of Ethan's herbal tea drifted over. She decided to pick neutral topics to discuss. Nothing that related to their future, not the shop and not where they lived. "The Eversley Arms have set up a darts team. We should go this Friday. Everyone's asking after you." Although she realised that might not be a great idea if Jaz was going to be on Ethan's case.

"How's the arts hub getting on?" he asked, not committing to the date.

"It goes from strength to strength. Holly has all her work slots filled at the hub and a waiting list of people wishing to work from there. And she continues to receive commissions for her own art."

Ethan stared at her intently. "I love taking breakfast here with you."

She smiled at him and touched his hand across the table. "And me you. I've always felt this is our special place. We never bump into anyone we know. It feels private, like our own secret haven."

"I also love the city breaks we've taken. And the holidays to the Maldives, deep sea diving."

"Me too. I love spending time with you."

"Exploring the world and taking adventures has been a big part of our life together." He swallowed. "I always want us to be like this."

"We will, things won't change, Ethan."

He pulled his hand away. "They will with a child. For starters, this place doesn't take children. Can you imagine a pram in here with a screaming kid? It would ruin it. And you can't take a child to the Maldives or on city breaks or to the Grand Prix."

"But we can still do those things together, we have family here who would be only too pleased to babysit. Ma is really excited about being a grandmother."

He grabbed her hand. "Look, I love you Nina, with every atom of my soul."

"And I love you too, I love you more than I ever have."

"Sumitra fits in with the plan I have for us. The compromise."

She gulped. Ethan really was accepting the baby. Tears stung her eyes, but she didn't want to cry, not in public. He'd come around and relief washed over her whole body. *Hold it together,* she told herself. "And what's the compromise? That we take holidays and make sure we come here once a month, just the two of us?"

"No." He pulled his hand away. "I've been thinking. What about if your mother took it on?"

"It?" She sat back in her seat. "Ethan, we're talking about a child, here, not a thing."

"Okay, he or she. Hear me out. Sumitra's at home all day, she'd probably love it. We could live in Qatar and you could come back and visit for a week, every other month or so. Commute back here. Money's no object, we could pay for a nanny to help your parents out if it got too much for them."

"What do you mean?"

"That we can put off being parents until we get back to the UK, after the buildings are completed."

"You said it could take longer than four years."

"I know, but then we could give one hundred percent to the child when we came back."

The fear she'd been carrying around crushed her chest as it returned. She looked into his eyes. *Is he really serious?* "Ma and Dad are retiring next year."

"Exactly, they'll have time on their hands."

"To explore the world, to live their best lives while they still can. Not to spend it looking after *our* child full time. If we were away for five years Dad would be seventy by the time we returned."

"Or there's adoption," Ethan said in a lower voice.

"Ethan," Nina said in a loud whisper across the table. "That's not going to happen. Never!"

He sat back in his chair. "You can't blame me for trying to find a way for us to be together. I love you. I don't want to lose you. I must live in Qatar. I've already signed up to it."

"Have you looked into life in Qatar?" she asked in a small voice, resigning herself to the fact that a move might be her only option.

"Yes. But not with a child. It's going to be work hard and play hard, there's so much networking and constant meetings. Babe…" He looked up as the waiter approached. "The bill please," he said then waited until he was out of earshot. "We'll have to continue this conversation at home. I thought by coming here you'd see what we were giving up. That we can't live our life, the one we've built together, with a child in it."

Nina picked up her bag. "I'll meet you at the car." She made her way to the toilet, the tears already in her eyes. Once inside the cubicle, they fell freely. *I'm so stupid,* she thought. She'd really imagined that Ethan had come around to the idea. She felt faint. What was he going to say back at the house? All she wanted was things to be the same between them. He was the love of her life, her only serious relationship which had now culminated in a child. She grabbed her belly, wishing for a moment that it was not there. *How could you?* she asked herself. What sort of mother was she going to be, already wishing the poor child had not come to be? A precious little being growing inside her. She quickly wiped her cheeks with toilet paper and pushed her hair from her face.

Outside the cubicle, she checked her reflection, deciding she had no option but to wear her sunglasses. There was no point in touching up her make up just for a walk through the hotel reception.

Outside, Ethan switched on the throaty engine of his Maserati as she reached it. She got inside and looked out of the window as he drove them back to the house in silence. When they arrived, he went upstairs and she poured herself a large glass of water, waiting for him to return. She'd negotiated before in other times of her life with wedding dress suppliers, haggled prices with clients and discussed options with stakeholders of the council, but this was one negotiation she felt powerless in. She held no trump card; she felt at his mercy.

After fifteen minutes, Ethan came downstairs. His eyes were red and it was clear he'd also been crying.

"Ethan, I know it's tough and this has been sprung on us."

He looked into her eyes. "I'm going to ask you a question and I need to know the honest answer. Do you promise?"

"Of course. What is it?"

"Did you plan this because you were fed up waiting for a wedding date?"

Nina took a pace back. "I'd never do that and why would I plan to get pregnant when I was running for another term on the council?"

"I just needed to know." He took a deep shuddery breath. "I know for sure, I'm not ready to be a father. You need to compromise. It's only going to work if your mum looks after the kid. I'm sure she won't say no and my mum'll help out. That's the compromise, we just postpone being parents for a few years. Pick up when the kid's four or five years old."

Tears tumbled down Nina's face. "I love this little being inside me. If you can't see that it's a part of us, then how can we ever be a family? Don't you even feel it?" She grabbed his hand and pressed it to her belly.

Ethan looked away and pulled his hand back. He stood with his back to her.

"I don't want you giving me an ultimatum. It's not fair," she sobbed. "Putting it all on me." She grabbed a sheet of kitchen roll and wiped her nose. "It's a shock to me too."

He swung around. "But it's your fault. You should have been more careful and dealt with it in time. You've ruined everything and you're making *me* out to be the bad person? You're unbelievable. Trapping me in this impossible situation then making me out to be irresponsible? *Argh*. I don't want to be trapped in a mundane life. I've worked my butt off for years to get us to this point, where we don't have to worry about money, where we can do whatever we want, whenever we want. The world is our oyster and you've ruined it!" He gestured at her, his eyes red with tears. "You've ruined everything."

"You're lashing out at me, I get it." Nina gulped then put her hand out to his.

He turned away. "I can't do this."

"Ethan, I need you to consider, to think, you love me, you tell me every time we're together. Unexpected things happen. Health issues, family issues, there's more to life than money. I want you to consider having a life with us – me and the baby. We'll come to Qatar with you. This baby needs me. I'm it's mother and you... you're this child's father."

Ethan turned around stared at her, his face crumpling. He slumped to the floor and sobbed.

She rushed over to him, wrapping her arms around the man she loved. "Please Ethan." She'd never begged for anything in her entire life, but she was begging him with every atom of her being. "I can't do this without you."

He shrugged her off then scrambled to standing, sobbing as he spoke, his face crimson, tears running from his eyes and nose. "If you loved me you'd put me first." He left her on the floor and made for the stairs.

.   .   .

Nina took the country lanes at a slow pace. The hedges either side were high and there was only space for one car in most places. She was soon on the road to Wells. She stopped a couple of times to compose herself before finally arriving on her parents' driveway. Her mother's face appeared at the lounge window. Sumitra was expecting her as Nina had texted ahead, explaining, unable to speak on the phone.

The door flung open and Nina shook as she felt her mother's arms wrap around her. "He says it's all my fault and that I'm trying to trap him."

"Everything will be okay," Sumitra said. "We love you more than anything."

Nina could not speak. In the very core of her heart, she'd believed Ethan would come around. It was as if her world was spinning out of control.

"How am I going to be a good mother?" she gasped. "I haven't even been able to get a good father for my child."

"We're a family and we'll pull together," her father said as he joined them. She looked up and seeing tears in her father's eyes crushed her even more.

"But I've let you down, Dad."

"You could never let me down, angel. I'll always be proud of you. You've done the right thing, followed your heart. You could not give up this child, our grandchild living inside you. That's what's in your heart, an unconditional love, and it's the same unconditional love that Ma and I have for you." He opened his arms.

Nina moved to him.

He hugged her. "Honestly, you could have been a tearaway, and we'd still love you the same. But my goodness, you've made us proud, you've achieved so much and if you never did anything from this moment forth, you've done more than most. Caring about the community, serving the members of the public. Making other people's wedding-day dreams come true."

"I'm scared," she whispered as Sumitra joined them and she turned and sobbed into her mother's chest in a way she'd not done since she was a child.

CHAPTER 16

*I*t had been a month since Nina had arrived at her parents' home. She'd not been out since, other than to the garden, which was large with a small wooden cabin at the end which she often sat in, on her own away from the house . She'd helped her mother with the gardening and found it therapeutic. Dr Gupta had visited a few times. Initially, Nina had been reluctant to accept she'd had a breakdown. But she had admitted that she was far from herself. Coming to terms with the abrupt changes in her life, which had imploded with Ethan's final confirmation that he would not be a part of her life going forward, had hit her harder than she'd imagined. She thought she was prepared for his rejection. But she wasn't and had spent a week of the aftermath in bed. And she'd felt like a child, compounded by the fact she was in her childhood bedroom. She had no idea how much her parents were paying for the private care, but decided she would have to reimburse them at some point, even though she guessed they would never accept it.

Having taken a long soak in the bath, Nina put on one of her new looser dresses which she'd ordered online and opened the curtains. It was as if the sun streaming through the window had brought a new phase to her life. She wasn't sure if she was better, but she certainly felt different. Not the same Nina. She wondered whether the old Nina, the business woman, the success driven go-getter, would ever exist again. And whilst her father repeated that she would soon be back to her old self, she knew she never would be. Her old self had died. And now she knew she had to get on with the rest of her life. But that would only happen by carefully putting one foot in front of the other and she had spent enough time isolated.

She'd let the shop go. Her father had dealt with it and sold the remaining few items to an outlet in Taunton. Nina knew his heart was broken, seeing her failures as his own. He was attempting to erase the sorrow from her life. But as Dr Gupta said, 'Only time is a healer', and she'd overheard her telling her father that he would be next if he didn't slow down.

Ethan had packed her belongings together and left their furniture in situ, while he put the Shepton Mallet house on the market. Nina only had sketchy details of his plans, and her parents avoided mentioning him. Although she didn't react to the memory of Ethan now in an emotional way, she simply felt cold. When the therapist who Dr Gupta had arranged asked how she felt about him, she really could not reply. Ethan was now in the recesses of her emotions, and she personally felt she would like to keep him there. She had a new life to live.

Nina smiled at her reflection. She knew she was looking a lot different to how she normally would. Her hair had often been styled in perfect ringlets, which she would spray to keep them in place for the day. She had it tied back. Figure-hugging dresses and suits with clean lines were her signature attire, not the sundress she now wore. She turned to the side. The bump was hardly noticeable unless the observer knew she was pregnant, and she liked the way the soft material graced her curves and the flat shoes were a comfort she thought she could grow to love. She was beginning to feel happy in her own skin, even without the extreme beauty treatments she was used to. And today, she was going out for the first time since she left Shepton Mallet – heading to Eversley village.

NINA KNOCKED on the door of Holly's cottage. It was stone built and set next to Lovelands Garden Nursery and Arts Hub. The sun felt warm on her back as she listened to Trixy's yaps as she waited for a reply.

Holly soon opened the door with her small dog wriggling in her arms.

"Thanks for inviting me over," Nina said.

"I wanted to see how you are, we've not seen you for weeks. I've some quiet time with the girls at school."

Nina followed her into the cottage as Trixy ran ahead of them. "After I left Ethan's, I was in a sorry state."

They reached the kitchen diner. "I'm so sorry he didn't come around to the idea." Holly bit her lip.

"Did he speak to you about it?" Nina knew that Ethan and Holly were close at college and she'd been his confidante at times as an adult.

"Yes, I tried to get him to look at the bigger picture,

but he was so set on those buildings." Holly sat on the sofa which was set by the French windows, away from the dining table.

"He couldn't see past Qatar." Nina sat beside her and Trixy jumped up, settling between them. "Thinking back, he's always had quite an obsessive personality."

"Yes, obsessed with his health, all those vitamins and with the gym, too. And each project."

"He's a perfectionist and amazing at what he does, but everything has to be done in a certain way and order. I guess a child would have created too much disorder in his life."

"I said to him, 'Life throws things at us.' But he didn't seem to be listening. I'm so sorry, Nina."

"There's nothing to be sorry about. It would never have worked, even if he'd tried. I'd hate for him to have resented me and our child. He may still do, but at least we won't have to deal with it day to day."

"Do you think he'll help financially?"

"He said to my parents that he would. But the way I feel at the moment, if he doesn't want anything to do with the baby, then I don't want his money."

"I wouldn't throw it back in his face, though."

"You're right of course, I don't want my baby to go without. But I'm not going to ask him for anything. If his conscience gets the better of him, I can't deny the child that."

"What are you going to do to make ends meet?"

"I've enough in a savings plan to tide me over. I've always had it there as my pension and emergency fund. I won't ever go without as my parents will be there for us. I love them to bits but I still feel like a child there. Especially this past month with me being a mess. Apart from that, it's not fair, Dad's retiring next year, he wants to live a little not spend it as a full-time grandad."

They drank coffee and Holly brought her up to date on her family and the goings-on of the village which Nina enjoyed listening to.

Holly took Nina's empty cup. "Let's go over to the hub. I've something to show you."

Nina stood up and followed Holly out of the cottage and down the path which led to the hub. The old barn was set up with various work stations, some of which were occupied by artists and craft makers, quiet in their work. Nina loved the smell of paints and textiles. It brought back so many memories of her youth. Holly led her to a table in the far corner. On top was a sewing machine and a pile of materials.

"I thought you might like to spend some time in here," Holly said. "You were better at textiles than any of us."

"I haven't been at a sewing machine for years!"

"This space has recently become free as the woman using it decided to give up. She owed me a few weeks rent which she couldn't pay for, so said I could keep the sewing machine and materials. I protested but she's moved to France and wasn't taking them with her." Holly gestured at the seat. "Go on, sit down. I'll leave you to it." Holly walked away.

Nina looked at the craft station as if she'd just been left a gift by Santa Claus. She sat down and threaded the machine, the process coming back to her instantly. She picked up some material and looked through a set of patterns. She found one for a child's pinafore dress, thinking it would be great to start with something easy.

She took a pair of scissors and cut out the shapes of material. As she worked on it, she felt a part of her that had been lost years ago come to the fore. Memories of college and of her original hopes filtered into her mind as she worked. She'd wanted to be a dress designer, rather than a designer dress seller.

Later, Holly returned. "Wow, I didn't expect you to have already made something. That's amazing. You couldn't make a couple of these for the girls could you? If I give you their measurements?"

"Of course! But I have to get off now as I promised Ma I'd be back. She's already been texting me, obviously worried as this is the first time I've been away from her for a month."

"Come back tomorrow, I'm open from nine. You can spend the entire day here if you like."

NINA SPENT much time at the art barn over the following week. It was a good feeling to regularly get out of the house. She felt as if she was going to work, and that made her feel slightly like herself again, although she'd still been keeping herself to herself. The following week, Holly invited her to take lunch in the nursery café as Val was coming in.

"There she is," Val said as Nina walked in. On the counter was a selection of homemade cakes. All were Val's recipes, although she no longer baked for the café – Anne, one of the staff members had taken that on.

Sitting with Val was Len, Joe the groundsman from the nursery and Holly.

"Anne's doing us a selection of sandwiches and then

we'll attack the cake," Holly said as Trixy sat patiently at the table as if waiting for a titbit.

"We always come here for lunch on a Wednesday," Val said.

"Our Holly's been telling us about the dresses you're making," Joe said. "That you've been designing your own."

"Holly's being very generous," Nina said. "I only made the first one of my own design yesterday, and I feel like a new person since I've been here."

"And how are you in yourself, love?" Val asked.

"Healthwise everything's fine, and I've got my next scan coming up soon. Ma can't wait."

"It's nice your mum's excited," Len said.

"They worry about me, too much. But I'm just looking ahead and thinking positive."

"You've got the right attitude, my love," Val said.

Anne brought over the platter of sandwiches and then joined them as they ate and drank tea.

"I was surprised how many clothes you've made so far," Holly said. "You can sell them here and make some money to spend on the baby. I've found a space over by the kids gardening equipment stand that would be ideal. We've so many families coming after school and at the weekend."

"Really?"

"Yes. Test the waters and if they're popular, it could be your new thing."

"And you can go global," Len said.

Nina laughed. "Thanks everyone, you're doing my confidence a world of good."

"Love, you're the most confident woman I've ever met. You'll be back to your old self in no time," Val said.

"Not my old self," Nina said. "But I'm feeling like a new person, that's for sure."

"Oh, and make sure you come to the farmers' market this Saturday," Holly said, "to judge whether you think you could sell them there."

"I think they'd do well," Anne said.

"I was coming anyway. Ma's always raving on about the farmers' market and Dad wants us to get him some sausages."

CHAPTER 17

"*T*hese are the best eggs I've ever had," Harry said, eating them scrambled on buttered toast. "You're such a great cook."

Millie nodded. "I'm glad you were brought up in a café."

Warren laughed. "Best thing that ever happened to me."

"How long is it until Nick and Jane get married?" Millie asked.

"A week today. I'm best man so have a speech written and I need to practise it on you guys."

"What time are we going up to Lovelands?" Harry asked. It was the first West Country Farmers' Market any of them had attended. In the summer months, Holly and Mitch ran a market at Lovelands every other Saturday and they were all helping out.

"As soon as we've finished breakfast. We have to load up both vans, then transport it over," Warren said.

"We've got quite a bit of stuff left over from the boxes

this week which we can take," Harry said. Booth Farms Ltd ran a veg box scheme, filling the boxes with vegetables and additional goods from local farmers and stores. They had a delivery service for Somerset and neighbouring counties. Most of the staff were causal workers coming in for two days, but Millie and Harry monitored it with the help of Mitch's mum who did the accounts and managed orders remotely from one of the Booth Farms in Essex.

"I'm looking forward to it, the market sounds great," Millie said.

"With the three of us I'm sure there'll be slow moments where we can check out the other stalls," Warren said. He wanted to stock up on some items for the following week's meals.

Millie and Harry cleared away the breakfast things and filled the dishwasher, and Warren went to his room to fetch his hoodie in case the weather turned.

Outside, Holly had already arrived and they loaded all the produce onto both vans. He looked up at the nursery as a stream of vendors arrived. They were soon driving the goods over to the nursery. There were many chiller vans there and regular vans with traders filling up the sales sheds which were permanently on the site. Holly milled around making sure everyone was happy.

They set up and the first customers began to drip in. But the drip soon turned to a wave. It appeared that people had come from far and wide. The three of them were working flat out, only leaving the stall for short breaks.

"I think we'll be getting rid of everything," Millie said.

"I wondered why we were bringing so much. I'll get the next box," Harry said.

Around lunch time, things slowed as people congregated around the food trucks. They were all local catering businesses. As the delicious smells drifted over, Warren's stomach rumbled.

"Hi there."

Warren looked up and his heartbeat appeared to stop. It was her, Nina. He hadn't seen her for so long. "Hey, you're looking great," he said before he could stop himself.

She looked down at her middle. "I'm starting to grow."

Warren turned to Millie and Harry. "Hey guys, I'm going to take my break." He washed his hands then removed his apron and left the shed. "Let me get you something, the smell of that food is driving me crazy, I've not eaten since breakfast."

"Oh, sure, yes." Nina smiled at him. "I'm starving too."

They walked around the stalls. He bought a burger and Nina ordered a chicken skewer on rice with Greek salad. They were lucky to find a table which was in the process of being vacated by a family and sat down.

"Is the kebab good?" Warren asked.

"Yes. I haven't eaten meat for over five years, but I've introduced it back into my diet, just for the pregnancy. I've been a bit off-colour and Ma said it was easier to get the iron that way. And anyway, I've so much to think about, it was just simpler to go along with her." She chewed on her food then swallowed. "Ma is loving that I can eat the full range of her dishes." She paused as she smiled, looking around. "It's good being here, I feel like I'm living again."

He'd heard she'd split up with her fiancé – and had felt

guilty at the feeling he'd had, fantasying that she would fall in love with him. Since then, he'd blocked it out, telling himself off as if he'd been pleased that Nina's life was falling apart. Everyone had been so worried about her. Nina had been the topic of discussion at all of the weekly family meals since. Holly had been receiving updates from Nina's parents and had let them know how she had been progressing. At times he'd wanted to contact Nina himself, but it didn't seem appropriate. And he didn't have her number, anyway.

"You've had a bad few months," Warren said.

Nina laughed. "I take it you know what's been going on?"

He nodded as he chewed on his burger then wiped some mustard which escaped with his paper napkin. "How are you?" Warren asked. "In yourself." He didn't add that he knew her fiancé had called time on their relationship. He'd abandoned her.

"I'm fine, it's just all a lot to take in. I had to let the shop go. But I need to find something else. I've got my head around it now. Although it's a bit claustrophobic at times, living with my parents."

"Are you going to continue working when you have the baby?" he said then looked around in case someone overheard,

She laughed. "It's not a secret any more. I asked Holly and Jaz to tell everyone and anyway, it shows." She continued: "Ethan wanted my parents to look after the child while we lived in Qatar and that I should come back every now and again to visit the baby. Even if I was agreeable, it would unfair on my parents. Although, my mother probably would have jumped at the chance, I know Dad wouldn't be pleased and it wouldn't be right for me either." Nina looked to her side. "Oh, my mother's coming this way."

"I wanted to pick your brain, actually. I need to gain support from the council for my silvopasture and the educational events I want to run there. But I've no idea how to go about it or the procedures."

Nina smiled. "Of course. I can go through it with you and there are easier routes."

Warren looked up as the beautiful Indian woman reached their table, dressed in a colourful long-sleeved dress with matching trousers. She didn't look old enough to be Nina's mother. Her eyes were exactly the same. He just stopped himself from saying she looked more like an older sister. He knew that would have sounded crass, even if it was true.

"This is my mother, Sumitra," Nina said. "And Ma, this is Warren, he's a student at Booth Farm. And we were just talking about him gaining interest and support from the council."

Sumitra nodded at him. "I see." She turned back to her daughter. "You worked too hard for years, you deserve a rest instead of getting roped into other people's business. Remember, one step at a time."

"Oh, yes, I'm er…sorry," Warren stuttered, not wanting to upset her mother and realising Nina was supposed to be taking things easy.

"When was the last time you took a holiday?" Sumitra asked Nina.

"I went on the cruise last year!"

"Everyone went on that cruise."

Nina laughed then turned to Warren. "It was Jaz and Julian's wedding."

Sumitra picked up her bags. "We need to go now before the sausages turn. I'll just pop and say hello to Holly because I haven't seen her yet, then I'll meet you at the car." Sumitra turned away.

"I love her to bits but I'm thirty-seven and she still likes to boss me around."

Warren noticed that Nina often mentioned her age. As if she thought he'd forgotten. "Jane bosses me about too."

"When's the wedding?"

"In one week."

Nina wiped her mouth with the napkin and placed it in the empty box. "That was perfect. I'll be huge by the time I have this baby."

"Do you want to leave discussing the council? I feel bad now after what your mum said."

"Don't take any notice of that, I'd love the distraction."

"Shall I meet you tomorrow, at The Eversley? I've been going there for a roast every Sunday."

Her mouth opened and she hesitated, and he immediately regretted asking, but she then smiled. "Yes. That would be nice."

"Shall I book a slot?" The Eversley always liked to know how many customers they were expecting as much of the food was prepared ahead in the bistro's kitchen.

"Yes, one o'clock."

"Great." He felt a surge in his chest as Nina walked away, and an overwhelming sense of excitement. He looked around then noticed the stall and checked the time on his phone. *Oh.* He'd taken a much longer break than the snatched fifteen minutes the other pair had taken. He hurried back.

"You look happy," Millie said. "Did you win the raffle or something?"

"No," he said.

Millie and Harry exchanged a look which Warren pretended not to notice. He knew that every time he met Nina he wanted to spend more time with her. But also he was under no illusion – she was a classy woman. He needed to put thoughts of Nina out of his mind. She had a lot on her plate, but that would not stop him being friends with her.

CHAPTER 18

"What are you doing flirting with young men in your condition?" Sumitra asked as she buckled herself into the passenger seat of Nina's car.

"I was not flirting," Nina said as she put the car into gear and joined a queue to exit the car park.

"You were fluttering your eyelashes, I know when you like a man, my dear, but a student? How old is he, twenty?"

"He's doing a PHD, he's not an undergraduate. He's much older but I've not asked his exact age or whether he's interested in romance. Considering we're just friends."

"Oh, *friends,* is it? That sort of friendship can get you into trouble."

"Ma," Nina said with a laugh as she turned onto the road. "You're being overprotective, and your imagination is running away with you."

"And he's not a man with means." Sumitra looked out

of the window. "Certainly not someone you should be dating. You need a professional man, like a doctor."

"I ate a chicken kebab with him at the farmers' market, it's hardly dating." She didn't tell her that she was meeting Warren in The Eversley Arms the following day. "And dating is far from my mind. You were always obsessed with me marrying a doctor when I was younger. Well, after you stopped trying to convince me I should be one myself."

"It's a good profession. Your cousins in India are doctors."

"Well, I was rubbish at science."

"You've had a very successful career, I wouldn't have changed a thing," Sumitra said in a softer tone.

"Thanks Ma," Nina said as she passed the Eversley village church where many of her customers had wed. She wondered whether she would ever date again. It would feel weird after Ethan. The sound of his name in her mind brought back the feeling of disbelief that they were no longer together. Nina reached the village green. "But Ma. Seriously, I'm in no frame of mind for romance."

"Well maybe you need to tell that to the young man you had lunch with who was gazing at you with puppy dog eyes."

"His name is Warren. And he was not looking at me in any way." *Was he?* She thought, telling herself to be a little bit more observant in future. *He was probably worried about me.*

"You at least need to tell him you are with child."

"He knows. I told him ages ago. We were discussing his project, that was it."

"So he knows you're pregnant and still he pursues you?"

"Ma, stop. He's not pursuing me. You've got it totally wrong."

WITH AN HOUR TO go until Sunday lunch, Nina put on another floral dress which hid her bump. She wasn't sure if she would ever be ready for the tight bump enhancing clothes which she often saw. She picked up her dark glasses. It was a sunny day and she hoped they could find a table outside.

"You look lovely," her father said as she went down the stairs.

"It's a gorgeous day," she said.

"I'm so pleased you're getting out and about, angel."

So was she. Sumitra had been searching through nursery furniture for their spare room and it was getting on Nina's nerves. She wasn't even sure she would be there when the baby was born.

"What about this colour, for the spare room?" Sumitra approached her with a colour pallet in a book from the DIY store and pointed to a pale lemon. "It's called citrus blast."

"Sounds like a mocktail," Tony said.

Nina smiled at her mother. "As lovely as it is here, you know I always crave independence. I'm looking for a place to rent."

"Back in Mumbai four generations live together," Sumitra said.

"And that's lovely, but it's not for me." She looked to

her father. "You've always encouraged me to be independent."

"Yes we have. Ma and I just want you to be happy,
don't we?" He looked at Sumitra with his eyebrows raised.

"Of course. Now make sure you eat with us tomorrow
night."

As Nina drew up alongside the Eversley village green she
spotted Warren immediately, sitting on a bench with a
pint of lager in front of him. She stopped the car and
checked her reflection in the drop-down mirror. *It's not a
date,* she told herself. The guy was being friendly and as
callous as her mother was, it was true, a penniless student
in his twenties was certainly not husband material. But he
made her feel happy and relaxed and that's what she
wanted – a friend. Someone she could help with their
issues and challenges, rather than people constantly
focussing on hers. She was interested in his field and
discussing environmental issues was a serious subject but
a safe one for her. And as nice as he was, she knew deep
down Warren only felt sorry for her and wanted to have
lunch so he could gain some leverage at the council. And
who could blame him? She'd had many meetings and
dinners with people herself in the past, in order to make
contacts and gain information on her way up the ladder.
She sighed. *A ladder I fell from.*

She got out of the car and Warren stood up as she
approached him. His eyes look particularity warm and
dark. She felt a fizzle of attraction shiver down her body
as he smiled at her. *Must be the hormones,* she thought, but
the attraction had shot through her like a bolt. Had she

not looked him directly in the eye before? Yes, she knew he was attractive, but he hadn't made her feel quite this way. She gulped. Maybe it was the smile. *Don't make your life even more complicated.*

"Do you want to go inside? I booked a table." He gestured towards the door.

"I quite like it out here," she said, feeling a little warm. It would mean she could also keep her sunglasses on.

"I hoped you'd say that. What can I get you?"

"Sparkling water with ice and a slice," she said.

"I'll let them know we're ready for our roasts. Is there anything you want excluded from the plate?"

She shook her head. "I'm fine with everything." She touched her stomach as it rumbled. She was pleased the morning sickness had fully passed. She'd skipped breakfast expecting the large meal.

As Warren went inside, she sat down and noticed there were goods outside the corner shop. It didn't used to open on a Sunday. It seemed the new owner meant business.

Warren soon returned with the drinks.

"Tell me what you've been up to," she asked. "Other than the field."

"I've been here a few times. Training the darts team on a Monday then a game here or in another pub every Friday."

"How are the team working out?"

"Hmm," Warren said. "We've a way to go. Carl's getting better. The reverend is the weakest player but no one's got the heart to kick him off, as he's a lovely guy. We've four others that join us and I'm trying to recruit Grace who works at the auction house. But Rob's the star player, he's beaten me a couple of times, now he's sober."

"I'm not sure I've seen him sober," Nina said.

"Jaz has taken him under control. She's got him working here and he loves it. She says he'll get the sack if he drinks on duty, or on training or match days."

"Really?" Nina said. "I thought she was no fan of Rob."

"Even though he can be an idiot, he's still popular. I think she sees him as an asset. And she wants to stick a picture behind the bar of him, with his winner belt on."

"I guess it's like that when you're famous! He'll be dining out on his boxing career forever no doubt. Shame he spent all the money."

"Is it true he went bankrupt?" Warren asked in a low voice.

"Yes, he had to work in the milk factory with his dad while he sat out the three years. Everything had to be kept simple." She took a sip of her drink. "So, if he's working here full time now, what about Simon?"

"Simon's here on and off, but he's earning more as a carpenter and refurbishing properties. He's been doing work over at Jaz's place and helped her dad out on a couple of kitchen fitting jobs. He wants to leave the pub, other than the odd shift for social reasons. He's training Rob up and to be fair, Rob's great. And as I said, he throws good darts. It's often about the mental attitude." He tapped his head. "And he's used to that with the boxing."

"You seem to have fitted in well here. And you've tapped into the village grapevine."

He laughed. "Everyone knows everyone else's business."

"So, what about the field?" she asked.

"It's on track. I've started my application for lottery funding. I want to get support from the council to back it up. And I need a character reference. And checks." He frowned slightly. Nina was going to ask if he was worried about that, but his phone vibrated on the table. He looked at who was calling, but did not answer it.

"Someone you don't want to speak to?" she asked, then took a sip of her sparkling water.

He nodded. "Someone from my past. From one of the foster homes I was in when we were ten. I was a bit of a rogue – we both were. I grew out of it, he didn't."

"I see."

He sat back and sighed. "Without blood family, Scottie's the closest I have to a brother and it's a tough one. Nick and Jane have said I need to let him go. To block him from my phone. But he feels like a brother." He looked down at his hands.

Nina lifted her glasses on top of her head and gazed at Warren. She could see he was a strong man with strong arms and strong body. And yet, he was so vulnerable. She had to take a deep breath to stop herself from reaching out to touch his hand. He looked up at her and caught her gaze and his eyes widened slightly. *Oh no, does he think I fancy him?* She gulped. *Maybe Ma was right?* If so, she needed to get across to Warren that she didn't want romance.

Rob brought their meals out which broke the gaze they'd been holding. "There we are." He placed the filled plates on the table. "Nice to see you here, Nina." He smiled at her.

She raised her eyebrows. Warren was right, Rob was a lot different sober. "Service with a smile?"

Rob chuckled. "That's me!"

Nina smiled back. "I heard you're doing great here."

"It's better than the milk factory, that's for sure. Although having Jaz as my boss is tough. She should have been my boxing trainer, I might have won more fights."

Nina laughed. "You won enough, Rob. Anyway, I hear your darts are good too." She looked at Warren then put her sunglasses back on, not wanting any more intense eye contact with him.

"I doubt we're ready to win a match yet. But this guy here, he's a brilliant trainer. Carl's better too. I reckon if we poached Jaz's old man from the Dogs we'd have a chance." He gestured inside. "We've a home match this week. Come up and watch. And it's great to see you." He nodded at her.

She watched him walk away. "Wow, I see what you mean. It's like he's been possessed by a good spirit." She also noticed that Rob had not mentioned Ethan. She realised that people were probably aware of the situation. The whole village probably pitied her.

After they'd eaten, Nina brought Warren up to speed on the council and took his email address so that she could forward him some contacts.

"The meal was great," Nina said to Rob as he took away the empty plates.

"Today's dessert is sticky toffee pudding."

"I couldn't manage that!" she said.

"Warren? You want some?"

"No thanks, mate."

"I do fancy something sweet though," Nina said after Rob had left them, and looked over to the corner shop. "Maybe a bar of chocolate and then I'd better head back."

Nina wanted to check out the corner shop, to see who'd taken it over.

As they entered, a woman with hair in tight red curls looked up. "Can I help?"

"Hi, I'm Nina." She glanced around the room. It had been rearranged and set out nicely. The previous owners used to stack goods on untidy piles and with the Post Office element gone, there was a lot more space.

"I'm Katie, pleased to meet you. Have you lived here long?"

"I actually live in Wells but have been coming to the village most of my life. I love it here." She gestured at Warren. "We've just had an amazing Sunday lunch at the pub."

Katie smiled at Warren. "You were brilliant at darts on Friday. As per usual. I've never seen you lose. The Kings Arms were gutted when you beat their star player."

"The team are coming along," Warren said.

"Because you're training them!" Katie said. "I can't wait for the home match this Friday. I'll be closing at five if you want to get there earlier?"

"I won't be here as I'm off to Bristol Thursday with family for a few days," Warren said.

Nina was shocked at the level jealousy that shot through her. *Don't be ridiculous.* This was an ideal opportunity for her to get across to Warren that she did not like him in that way. It was embarrassing that he might think she fancied him. Especially with the age difference and her being pregnant. She picked up a chocolate bar.

After paying, Warren walked her to her car.

"I've really enjoyed our lunch. Maybe–"

She cut him off. "She seems nice."

"Who?"

"Katie, and from the way she looked at you, I'd guess you two are an item?"

"No, we're not." He frowned.

"Well, she seemed interested from where I was standing. Maybe you should ask her on a date?"

He stared at her but said nothing.

"Thanks for lunch and for paying, that was generous. My treat next time," she said in a breezy voice. Whilst she needed to impress on him that she wasn't romantically interested, she still wanted to be his friend. "It's been nice." She got into her car knowing Katie, who looked around thirty, was much more Warren's type than a pregnant thirty-seven year old.

As NINA ARRIVED HOME, Sumitra met her at the door. She didn't really want to be quizzed on who she had seen at The Eversley Arms.

"I'm going up to watch television in my room," she said.

"You've a visitor," her mother said in a soft voice.

She followed Sumitra into the lounge, wondering who it was, to find Ethan's mother on the sofa. She had a handkerchief in her hand and Nina could tell she'd been crying.

"I'm so sorry about Ethan," she said then burst into floods of tears. "He told me all about it."

"Don't worry yourself, Christine," Sumitra said as she went to the sofa and comforted her.

"If I can help in any way. Trust me, I begged him to reconsider but he always was so stubborn."

"It's nice of you," Nina said. "But Ethan's made it quite clear."

Sumitra looked up at Nina. "Christine's worried that if Ethan does not come around to the idea that he is a father, she won't get to know her grandchild."

"Of course you will," Nina said. "I'm relieved that you want to and that you've come here. I've been really worried about what to say to you if I bumped into you."

"I feel so awful. As if it's my fault somehow. That I didn't provide him with proper family values."

"Don't worry Christine, we'll always be family," Nina said, sitting the other side of her to her mother. "We are all linked to this baby."

Christine leaned across and gave Nina a hug. "Thank you, that means so much."

CHAPTER 19

*E*arly the following evening, Nina heard the doorbell ring and sighed. It was as if her mother had a constant stream of guests. She assumed that during her month of isolation, her mother had put her friends off visiting and now there was someone visiting every day. She knew she couldn't remain there for much longer. She was someone who appreciated privacy at home and was used to living in the remote Shepton Mallet house, where no one ever just popped by for a cup of tea. Her mother had also been ordering so many things for the baby. Whilst she was grateful, she'd wanted to choose the items herself. She knew that she needed to focus on finding a place soon, before she was swallowed up in her mother's excitement.

A waft of chicken biryani floated up the stairs as she left the room. As she stood at the top, her mother was at the bottom, and she put her hands to her cheeks.

"You look beautiful. So beautiful."

Nina smiled. "I've inherited my looks from you Ma."

She got to the bottom of the stairs and hugged her mum who appeared stiff. Nina stepped back. "Are you okay?"

"Um, yes, we have a guest for dinner."

"Again?" Nina asked nervously.

"Debjani, a friend of the family. Come along we don't want to keep her waiting."

She followed her mother into the living room.

"This is Debjani." Sumitra nodded at her. "She's over from India to visit her son, who's a doctor at the Bristol Royal Infirmary.

"Hello Debjani," Nina said. "You're in for a treat, my mother loves to cook up a storm!"

Sumitra waved her hand at her. "Let's go to the dining room. Nina's father is at a business meeting this evening."

"How long are you in England for?" Nina asked.

"A few weeks. My son Rohan has been working very hard. I am very proud of him and he gets very lonely. So, I am spending some time with him. He's in the respiratory department and has saved many lives. He's also doing a research paper on oxygen therapy." She thrust her hand into her bag. "Here he is."

Nina looked at the picture of Rohan in his graduation robes, realising it must be an outdated photograph.

"What a handsome man," Sumitra said. "Isn't he dear?"

"Um. Yes," Nina said. "And how has he found the UK? He must miss his family in Mumbai. India is such a beautiful country, and a lot warmer."

"He's settled in well." She lowered her voice. "Rohan is shy, he's spent most of his time on his studies and he'll soon be a consultant."

"Let's eat," Sumitra said quickly.

Sumitra was serving up Nina's favourite Indian dish.

163

The rest of the meal consisted of conversation between Sumitra and Debjani and they often diverted into snatches of Hindi. Nina imagined they were speaking of her.

After dessert, they drank coffee and finally their guest prepared to leave.

"I hope to see you again," Debjani said with a grin.

Nina got the impression Debjani wanted her to meet her son, but she would probably change her mind if she knew she was carrying another man's child. Once she'd left and climbed into a taxi, Nina turned to her mother.

"I'm going out this evening." She needed to get away for a while and knew the darts team practised on a Monday.

"Where to?"

"The Eversley Arms."

"To the pub on your own in your condition?"

"I'm pregnant, not sick!"

The front door opened.

"What's the raised voices for?" her father asked as he came through the door.

"She's driving all the way to Eversley village at this time of the day."

"I'll give you a lift, angel."

"So you can keep an eye on me?"

"Look, humour us. I can pop in and see David and Florrie. I want to ask them about a motorhome." He looked at Sumitra. "We might go travelling when I retire."

"Ma in a caravan?" Nina laughed and as she did so, she softened. "Okay, you can drive me. But I'll get a taxi back."

"Nonsense, I'll come into The Eversley Arms and wait."

Nina realised it was not worth protesting. She freshened up and left with her father fifteen minutes later. She was even more determined to find a place of her own.

THE PUB WAS QUIETER than it had been the day before, and only one couple sat outside on a bench, with it being a Monday. When she walked in, she found it was a lot busier in the far corner where the dart board was situated with the team congregated around it.

"That's right," Warren said to Carl. "Much better."

Nina smiled, instantly feeling happier at the sight of him.

"Hi Nina," Grace said as she approached. "Jaz said you messaged to say you were coming in. I'm so pleased, we've all been thinking of you."

Helen Kelly came over as well. "It's great to see you. Are you joining the team?"

Nina laughed. "No! And thanks for the flowers you sent. I went over to the farmers' market on Saturday and was here yesterday for lunch. I'm feeling a lot better."

"Nina," Jaz called out and then approached her, reached up and gave her a hug. "You look amazing!"

"Grace," Warren called out. Then he stopped as he caught Nina's gaze.

Her heart skipped a beat and she gave him a small wave.

Grace turned to her. "Warren seems to think I'm going to make a great darts player and wants me on the team."

"And I agree," Jaz said. "Get over there."

Jaz lifted the bar hatch and went behind it. "I take it you want your usual sparkling water?" she asked.

"Can you put some orange juice into it?" Nina asked smiling. "I need to get my vitamin C up, which apparently will help with the absorption of iron. Dr Gupta has been even more annoying than Ethan was about supplements." She smiled, pleased she could mention his name without an emotional reaction.

"Are you okay?" Jaz asked.

"Yes, that's the first time I've said his name aloud without feeling ill."

"I feel for you, I do. If Julian left me, I'd be done for."

"I've come to terms with everything. It was intense, the way it had happened with all of those emotions tumbling out at once. But I feel lighter, much lighter. In fact, lighter than I have for years."

"You seem bright, and as I said, you look amazing."

"I wouldn't go that far," she said with a laugh. "Ma and Dr Gupta were trying to get me to continue with therapy, but I said I'd see how I go. They said it was burnout from the work I've done over the years, but that's nonsense. I thrive on work."

"Me too, hun! I feel worse when I'm not working."

"You could be right. I probably need a distraction to keep me busy. I'm not sure what the new me wants to do but I'm taking each day as it comes. My most pressing issue is needing to find a place to live as Ma has a constant stream of visitors. There's no way I want to be parading my baby in front of them every single day. I've made it quite clear I'm leaving, but I don't think Ma's listening."

Jaz handed Nina the drinks then came out from behind the bar. "Let's sit this end."

Nina sat down at a table with Jaz. "I'm going to release some of my savings and visit the letting agent tomorrow,

I've enough for a year's rent. But without an income, I'll need a guarantor. Would you mind? I wouldn't put you in the position of having to pay my rent, but I don't want to ask my parents. I'm feeling too much like the dependant adult child at the moment."

"It's simpler for you to be over here, there's no need to be in Wells now with the shop closed."

"You know someone who's letting a place out? Don't tell me it's Holly's caravan. I'm not the camping type."

Jaz laughed. "No, that's her office now and she uses it for meetings. You can live here. Upstairs. For free. While you find somewhere more suitable for you and the baby. Rob will eventually move in here if he works out as manager, but I'm not ready to put my trust in him just yet. He's a lot to prove and he's only been sober for just over a month, although he does drink here on his night off. He's not addicted to the stuff, just really annoying when he's had a few."

"Are you sure? I'd pay you something."

"No. Just focus on finding somewhere to live. You're my friend and we all want to support you in any way we can."

"I don't know what to say." She felt the usual emotion brimming to the top again.

"You just need to say yes." Jaz clinked her glass of cider with Nina's orange and water mix. "Now come over with me, I need to bash that team into shape."

Nina smiled and followed Jaz over to the dart board. Right then the pub felt a warm place and somewhere she could stay. She knew there were separate stairs to the flat above, so she would not have to go through the bar if she was not feeling sociable.

CHAPTER 20

"Brilliant, Grace," Warren said. "Are you sure you haven't played much before?"

"Last week was the first time," she said. "Although I was good at netball!"

"The height helps. Especially as you're able to stand closer to the board, being a woman." He turned around and saw Nina smiling at him as she sipped her drink. "Hi," he said. He didn't want to get over friendly with her, he got the impression that after lunch the day before she thought he was going to ask her out on a date or something, as she'd disappeared in a rush and suggested he ask Katie out. That was something he had no plans to do.

He collected the darts from Grace as Nina approached him. He smiled at her "Are you here to try out for the team?"

"Oh no, I'm useless with spatial awareness!"

"Go on," Jaz said and pulled her arm.

Nina shot him a smile that his body reacted to. She

brushed his hand as she took the darts and handed him her drink. It felt cool in his now warm hand.

He gestured at the board. "Focus on…"

Nina threw the first dart before he could finish. It bounced off the board to the floor. The second was about an inch away from the scoring spaces and the third hit the surround.

"She's better than me," Reverend Stephens said with a laugh.

Nina returned the darts to Warren. "I told you."

"I guess you can't have it all," he said. "Looks, personality, intelligence and be a killer darts player." He gulped; he didn't usually deliver lines like that. It sounded a bit like he was coming on to her.

To his relief Nina grinned at him. "No one's perfect."

"Let's break off," Jaz said, looking at them both with her eyebrows raised. "Then we'll have the practice match. I'll work out who's playing who."

Warren led Nina to a table and they sat down together.

"I didn't expect to see you here this evening," he said.

"I needed to get out. I've stayed at home long enough."

"I guess going back home to your parents is tricky."

"They're amazing to me, I can't fault them, but living with them when I'm thirty-seven is not ideal!"

He clocked again that she had thrown her age into the conversation.

"Jaz has said I can stay here, upstairs."

"You'll be in Eversley?"

"Yes."

"Maybe you can come to the farm for dinner. We have a meal every Monday evening, then I come back here with Jaz for the darts training."

"Ah, so that's where you hear all my gossip?"

He laughed. "I've been fully initiated into village life."

"There are no secrets here."

"No," Warren said, even though he had a few himself – and a big one. He thought about Scottie, hoping he'd got the message that Warren wanted to distance himself by the fact that he never returned his calls.

"That'll be nice, but I'm eating for two, they might not have enough food."

"It won't be a problem, you should see the amount of food dished up! Val and Len usually go home with left-overs for their freezer."

Nina looked around. "Oh, I sensed him," she laughed. "My dad's arrived he's lurking by the bar."

"Nina," Rob said as he approached the table. "Jaz told me you're moving in upstairs?"

"Yes." She shot a glance at her father. "But I've not told Dad yet."

"Oh, okay." Rob lowered his voice. "When are you moving in?"

"At the weekend."

"I'll help you take your stuff up there."

"Thanks."

Rob left as someone called him to the bar.

"I'd help too," Warren said. "But I'm off to Nick and Jane's on Thursday."

"Oh yes, it's their wedding. I hope it goes well, she looked lovely in her dress."

"Come on you lot, it's time for your games, and play it like it matters," Jaz called out.

"Sorry I'm late," Katie said breathlessly as she entered the pub and walked up to Warren at the table.

Warren looked up as she gave him a kiss on the cheek, which was a surprise to him. She didn't usually greet him in that way.

"Oh, hi Nina. Are you here to play?" Katie asked.

"No, just watching."

"I like to encourage the lads." She gave Warren a big grin, and he was worried that it looked as if she was there just to see him and that he had, as Nina suggested, asked her out. He'd certainly picked up the odd signal that Katie liked him. And Nina wasn't the first person to suggest he ask her on a date. He looked across to Nina as she stood up from the table. He knew that every time he spent with her, it felt like a date. He spoke to her in a different way than he spoke to anyone else. But should he shake that off? She'd made it quite clear she wasn't interested and as she mentioned her age repeatedly, she was clearly making a point – he was too young for her.

"I'd better get off," she said. "Dad's waiting." Nina approached the others to say goodbye.

"Can I get you a refill?" Katie asked Warren.

"Um..."

"Your glass is empty. What are you drinking?"

"Stella," he said. As Katie ordered at the bar, he watched Nina walk out of the pub with her father. At least he knew he would be seeing a lot more of her.

AFTER THE PRACTICE match between the team members, Warren noticed Rob staring at Katie a lot. He followed him to the bar with his empty glass.

"Want another?" Rob asked.

"No, I'm off in a minute." He looked over to Katie chatting to Grace. "I see you've got your eye on someone."

"Yeah, that Katie's a sort. Are you gonna ask her out?" Rob asked.

"No. Why are you asking me that?"

"The girl can't keep her eyes off you."

"I'm not interested."

"Well I am. I think she's gorgeous. If I was a bit younger."

"You're not too old."

"I'm battered though," he said. "Oh, she's coming over."

"Hi, can I have a pint of Haze," she said then smiled at Warren. "You're so good and such a great teacher. Rob's improved as well."

"Thanks," Rob said.

"Rob's got the competitive streak, that's why he's my top player." Warren nodded at him. "He's used to competing. He was my idol." He didn't end the sentence with *when I was a kid.*

"What? You played darts before?" she asked Rob.

"No, I used to box."

She screwed up her face. "I hate boxing."

Warren saw Rob's smile falter.

"I love watching darts though. My dad always had the darts on over Christmas. It gives me a warm feeling when I watch. So, Warren, I've got tickets to the rugby this Saturday. Me dad's got a cold. Do you wanna come?"

"I already said, I'm going to a wedding, sorry." He was relieved he had a genuine excuse. "But Rob might be able to."

She looked at Rob. "He'll be working here," she said

then paid for her drink with her phone. "Some other time." She gave Warren a smile then walked away.

"I've no hope with her," Rob said wiping the bar down. "The only thing I've got going for me is that I used to box. And she hates the sport."

"She likes darts players though. All you have to do is win!"

"I don't think she's going to notice me with you here. Can't you hook up with someone else, so she knows you're not interested?"

"I do like someone." Warren took a sip of his pint. "I'm working on it." It was then that he realised that while the timing was not right, he'd wait for as long as it took for Nina.

CHAPTER 21

 ina prepared herself as her father slowed his car to a stop on the drive of the Smith family home.

"Be gentle with Ma, she's going to be upset," Tony said. Nina had already told him that she was moving to Eversley village.

By the time she reached the front door it was already open with her mother in the doorway.

Once in the lounge Nina used a breezy voice. "I've news, I'm moving out this weekend."

Sumitra put her hands to her cheeks. "No, angel. I'm so sorry. I didn't mean to drive you out."

Nina smiled at her mother and gave her a hug. "It's not you. I was always going to leave. I'm too independent to live with you two for more than a few weeks." She leaned back. "You've been a lifeline to me over the past six weeks, you've cared for me at the lowest point of my life, when I thought I couldn't carry on. You've cooked for me. Taken care of my washing. I couldn't be more grateful. I'd have crumbled without you, but now I'm feeling much better, I need my own space."

"Where are you going?" Sumitra wiped her eyes.

"Jaz is letting me live in The Eversley Arms, rent free until I find a place."

"The pub?"

"They used to do bed and breakfast. And there's a separate entrance. I can avoid the customers if I need to." She looked at her father.

"I reacted the same way, Sumitra. But it's apparently nice up there. Julian's parents used to let it out."

"It means I can do more dressmaking. I found it really therapeutic last week and that's what I need, a distraction. And I've so many people to look out for me there, so you needn't worry."

"We can help you move," her father said.

"Yes, of course we can." Sumitra's voice was quiet. Nina knew she was wishing she would live with them with the baby, but her father didn't want that. He wanted to have adventures in his retirement. He'd been talking about the motorhome David Bunning had shown him that evening in a brochure and how it was so posh even Sumitra would love it.

"I'll have people the other end to move me in, if you can help transport my clothes and belongings over."

"You can't bring a child up in the pub!" Sumitra said.

"I'm not, it's just until I find somewhere else."

"I'm sure everything will turn out just fine," Tony said. "Now let's all have a coffee," he said diplomatically. "And I'm so pleased that your entrepreneurial skills are still at the fore, with the dressmaking."

"I'm not sure I'll ever be able to shake them off."

"Just wait until the baby's born," Sumitra said.

"I hope you'll both come to the next farmers' market. I'm going to be selling them there with the other craft stalls."

"I'm sure you'll soon have a new income rolling in." Her father beamed at her.

"It's labour intensive and I only make a few pounds an item but it's a great distraction."

"You could set a website up," Tony said.

"Let the girl be," Sumitra said. "You've treated her like a workhorse since she was old enough to work in your shop."

"I'm enjoying it, Ma. It doesn't feel like work."

THE FOLLOWING DAY, Nina drove into Lovelands' car park and smiled as she saw the art barn. It was time she got back to doing what she loved. She'd not been at the sewing machine since she was in her teens and had been surprised how easily it all came back to her.

As she walked inside, it was a hive of activity. With less than a couple of weeks until the next market, many crafters and artists were being spurred into action. She approached Holly who worked at an easel with Trixy asleep on the ground beside her.

"That's great."

Holly looked away from the colourful chameleon she was edging in gold paint. "Hey, Nina. I heard the news that you're moving into The Eversley this weekend."

"Yes, I'll only be a walk away from here and be able to run up a lot of clothes to sell at the next market."

"Don't work yourself too hard. I know how I felt

carrying the twins. I paid for it in the evenings if I worked too much during the day."

"Trust me, my current life feels sedentary after the last ten years running the boutique *and* being councillor."

"I'm probably beginning to sound like your parents." Holly bit her lip.

"Ma, yes, not Dad. He's already talking of me setting up an online store," she said with a laugh.

"You could do so well at that. And you can fit it around the baby." She gestured around. "It was tough for me, before the girls started school. Luckily, I already had experienced staff."

"And Mitch," Nina said in a lower voice.

"I'm sorry. Look, I always said I never knew how you did it, with all your responsibilities. I'm sure you'll be an amazing mother and an inspiration to us all."

Another artist looked up from her mosaic. "Hey, Nina. Glad to see you're here again. I'd love to buy one of those dresses for my friend's daughter."

"Of course, Jacky. Feel free to come over and pick one!"

Nina loved the camaraderie of the art barn. She settled at her workstation and pulled out the last of her material. She was running low and had already left her father with an order for his supplier. She wanted to make boys clothes and some in neutral styles and colours. The pretty material the previous dressmaker had left was mainly multicoloured pinks and purples. Her father's discount with the supplier would be a lot more favourable than anything she could muster up. Once she was established, she'd be in a position to negotiate reductions for larger orders. She smiled to herself, knowing she could never look at a project without seeing the business opportunity.

The morning flew by and the sun streamed in through the high windows, casting a line of light into the room and bringing warmth with it. She'd designed a pattern for trousers and was looking forward to being able to make soft clothes for small babies. She decided she wanted to make as many of her own baby clothes as she could.

"Hey, Nina," Holly said.

She looked up.

"Do you want lunch over at my caravan? I've some paperwork to sort out for the farmers' market and I'm set up over there."

"Sure," she said and stood up.

"Let's get some sandwiches from the café and take them over."

THEY WERE SOON SEATED outside the caravan. The view across Booth Farm was amazing, with a patchwork of fields in golds and green, laying before the Mendip Hills.

"The silvopasture is coming along. Have you been down to see it yet?" Holly asked.

"No," Nina said scanning the farm. "Is it the one with the trees?"

"Yes. You'll have to go down and take a look, I'm sure Warren would love to show you around." She paused. "He's rather attractive, don't you think?"

"He's not really the usual guy I go for, not that that's got me very far. Most of my relationships were short lived. Apart from…"

"I'm sorry it didn't work out with Ethan. You seemed so suited, liking the same things. Both being ambitious."

"But family wasn't for him," Nina said. "And it's always been something I wanted in my life."

"I know exactly how you felt, I was the same."

Holly's phone rang and she answered it. "Okay." She ended the call. "I've just got to pop to the nursery, the till has frozen in the café and there's a long line of customers. You finish your lunch and hopefully I'll be back soon!" Holly hurried away.

Nina looked back to the field but could not see Warren. She continued to eat her sandwich.

"Hey."

She jumped and looked up.

"Sorry I didn't mean to creep up on you," Warren said.

"Oh, hi, I was looking down at your field, it's much bigger than I imagined."

"It's a pasture and in time, will have animals living there as well. You'll have to come down and take a proper look."

She smiled up at him. "Sit down and have a sandwich. I know I'm eating for two but they've gone overboard."

He took a seat at the table. "This is a great caravan."

"Holly used to live in it. After her place burned down."

"I heard she had a fire years ago. That must have been a shock."

"It would have been a lot worse if Mitch hadn't called the fire service who rescued her from the top floor before the place collapsed." She shuddered at the thought of what could have been, and what wouldn't have been. The hub would not have been built, the twins would never have

179

existed. "Looking at the big picture, the fire brought Mitch and Holly together and her new life."

"Wouldn't life be easier if we could see the big picture when we're going through a rubbish time."

"Have you had difficult times?" Nina asked.

"I had a difficult childhood. Nick and Jane pretty much saved me." He took a deep breath. "Mum died when I was five and then I was brought up in foster homes and never really settled until I met them."

"That's hard."

"So if you are worrying about what sort of mother you'll be, you'll be great. I'm not sure I've met such a passionate woman before." He stared into her eyes.

Nina blushed. "So Nick and Jane really were a lifeline for you?"

"Yes, the three of us seemed to slot together and become a family from nearly the start. They won me over with food," he said with a laugh. His phone dinged with a text and he opened it. "Oh, no."

"What's wrong."

"It's the guy I was telling you about, Scottie. He's texted to say he hears I'm going to be back in Bristol for a wedding."

"Can't you just ignore him?"

"It's difficult. As much as I tell myself to cut him loose, he had a worse start than even me." He rubbed his forehead.

"Warren, if he's taking advantage of you, he's not giving much in return is he? Some people will only learn when you cut them loose. You have to be cruel to be kind." She couldn't imagine what it was like and wondered if she was being too simplistic. He clearly had a bond with Scottie, she could tell that when he was speaking about him before.

"He's been on to me ever since he got out of prison."

"Prison? Hmm, I'm with Nick. It's probably better to block his number. He's not on the same path as you and could drag you into trouble."

"You're very wise," he said.

"Yes *old* and wise."

"You don't look much older than me. And what does age matter? Some people die young. Others live to one hundred. It's more about the ones we have left. My mum was in her early twenties. Younger than I am now." He looked at her intently.

"I guess so."

"You shouldn't stop doing anything you want to do because of age." He looked deep into her eyes.

She gulped. Could he tell, just by looking at her, what she was thinking? "And what is it I might want to do?" Her old self seemed to burst from the depths. She'd been quite flirtatious before she met Ethan. She blushed and looked down at her baby bump, remembering the reality of the situation.

Warren had not answered, as if he was searching for words.

I'm not exactly a catch. Nina said in her head the words that she wanted to say out loud.

"Ah, and there I was, worried about leaving you alone," Holly said. "I see you have company."

Nina looked up.

"I was saying earlier that you should show Nina the field," Holly said to Warren and then gestured at the farm.

Nina felt hot and wanted to collect her thoughts. Had

they really been having a conversation about a potential relationship or was she imagining it? "When you get back from Bristol, I'd love a tour."

Warren stood up. "I look forward to it." He grinned. "See you next week."

"Send Nick and Jane my best wishes and congratulations."

"I will do."

Holly sat down and they watched Warren head back to the farm.

"Hope I didn't interrupt something," Holly said in a quiet voice.

"Like what?"

"Jaz and I think Warren's besotted with you."

"You've been discussing us?" Nina laughed.

"Have you picked it up yourself?" Holly said answering with a question.

"No," Nina lied. "We're hardly a match made in heaven, are we?"

"Why do you say that?"

"He's…and I'm…"

"Exactly, no reason whatsoever. I'll make us a cuppa and then we'll have to get back to the afternoon."

As they drank tea and finished off the sandwiches, she spotted Warren working in his field. Yes, they were a lot different. He'd had a tough upbringing, she'd been spoilt. He was in his twenties, she was in her thirties and he just didn't look like anyone she'd ever dated. Big and muscly with tattoos. She knew he'd never appear on her mother's list of potential matches. But *wow* was he good looking. She felt a flutter of excitement in her stomach. *If he really does like me, maybe I should follow my heart?*

CHAPTER 22

"Come in. Jane's all over the place with nerves." Nick ushered Warren into the flat above the café.

"She's always so laid back."

"Not today she isn't. How was the journey?"

"The van held out, it's only thirty miles. Not sure I'd want to go much further in her and she's not exactly environmentally friendly."

"You're getting use out of something that would otherwise go to the breakers."

"It would be better for the planet if she was recycled. I think Holly's attached to it and doesn't want to let it go." He carried in his holdall and suit bag.

"Where's the memory stick with the pictures on?" Jane entered the room.

Nick was right, Warren thought. *She does look worried.*

"Ah, Warren." Jane stood still and then approached him and gave him a hug. "This is just what I need. It's a shame you couldn't bring Nina."

"Just because she's single, doesn't mean she's going to go out with me. She's got a baby to worry about."

"I'm just going on the way you looked at her!" Jane said.

"In time, son, she could be interested." Nick said. "I mean look at you."

"I'll be seeing more of her because she's moving to the village this weekend. Into The Eversley Arms."

"That's good," Jane said with a smile.

"Right, so what do you need help with?" Warren wanted to change the subject.

"I've a long list," Jane said. "Nick, can you make us all a toasted panini and then we'll plan the next couple of days."

THE FOLLOWING EVENING, Warren grinned as the café filled with Nick and Jane's friends and family. Many he'd known for years. Her sisters from Dominique had brought her mother. Nick's rowdy brothers, including Darius, and their wives and girlfriends were making most of the noise and a few café regulars had been invited. They were having a joint stag and hen do the night before the wedding. It was early on, and the games had ended and the event began to draw to a close. Jane wanted everyone out by nine o'clock so they could have an early night. No one wanted to be tired the following day, although the wedding itself was not until three. Warren was looking forward to it. It was a small but tight-knit and very loud party and there would be further guests at the wedding.

Warren's smile faded as he looked out of the window.

Outside was Scottie. He was shocked, not so much because he was there, when he had messaged him asking him to stay away, but at the state of the man.

Nick put a hand on his shoulder. "You've noticed him then? He's been there a while."

"He looks bad."

"He always has," Nick said.

"Yes, he's always been skinny but he's gaunt." He turned to Nick. "Do you think he's sleeping rough?"

"If he is, it's his own doing. Look, son. He's not your responsibility. As hard as it is, you need to ignore him and if he creates, we'll call the police. I take it you blocked his number?"

Warren looked out to the pavement again. "Every time I go to press block, I stop. I still see him as family."

"He isn't your kin, your family are in this room." Nick gestured out to the street. "Not out there. All he's ever done is get you into trouble. You must have a short memory. I wish Darius was still here, he'd talk some sense into you." Nick's brother had left half an hour before as he was due in work.

Warren thought back to earlier in the evening. Darius had also told him to cut Scottie loose, warning him that he was in something dodgy. He glanced out of the window again and caught Scottie's eye and was instantly transported back to the foster home where he used to look out for him. Scottie had always been a victim, a victim of his parents' abuse, a victim of bullying. He'd consoled him countless times. And he'd been the main victim of the foster parents they'd been lumped with. "I'll have to speak to him." He pulled his hoodie off the back of a chair. "I don't want him ruining tomorrow."

Nick sighed. "If you have to. But be careful, remember we've a wedding tomorrow and I don't want Jane's day ruined."

"Exactly, I don't want Scottie showing up there. It's better for me to deal with him now. I'll make it clear, it's over."

"Okay," Nick said but Warren knew he was not convinced. And he didn't blame him, they'd had similar conversations many times over the years.

Warren stepped onto the pavement and hesitated for a while as they both stared at each other, before Scottie crossed the road.

"You're looking good, War," Scottie said as he approached him.

"You look tired."

"I am tired. Tired of life, tired of trying and not getting anywhere. I'm never gonna be anything, You've got a whole family in there." He scuffed the floor with his shoe. "That never happened for me."

"Nick and Jane tried with you. You didn't accept them." He looked back to the café. "You took advantage of them."

"I was only a kid."

"You were old enough to know right from wrong."

"My life's rubbish and now I'm gonna be homeless if I don't come up with money for rent. The half-way house was a cesspit. And I owe Logan a bit 'cause he paid some rent to help me off the street."

"Logan?" Warren shook his head. Logan was bad news and had got them both into trouble when they were younger.

"Don't start, War. He's better since the long stretch."

"Don't the social pay your rent?" Warren asked, not wanting to know any more about Logan.

"It takes ages to come through and anyway, my new landlord isn't legit. It's also a dump, but it's somewhere to stay without someone breathing down my neck. I was on the streets for a couple of weeks before Logan helped me out. I just need three hundred, to get me through. I'm on a wait list for a warehouse job."

Warren didn't think Scottie looked employable. His face was covered in sores, he wore tatty joggers with a grey stained hoodie and smelled like he hadn't washed for days.

"I can't keep giving you money."

"Just this last time, War. Then that's it I promise. I hear the wedding's tomorrow afternoon?"

Warren didn't want Scottie turning up and spoiling it. If it wasn't for that he wouldn't have given it to him. "If I get you the money, you need to promise you won't bother Nick and Jane tomorrow. You'll steer clear."

"Of course, War. You're a life-saver."

"Come on." Warren walked in the direction of the nearest cashpoint, which was only a few shops along. He hadn't been able to continue and say it was over, to never contact him again.

At the cashpoint Warren covered the screen as he plugged in his pin number. He waited as the machine counted and then dispensed the money which he had to request in two batches.

He held out the cash. "I don't expect you to pay me back. But this is the last handout, Scottie."

"Yeah, I get it." He pocketed the money. "You better get

back." Scottie nodded at him before walking away with his hands thrust in his pockets.

Warren felt flat as he returned to the café. He felt gutted for Scottie – the boy he'd been, and always would be, for he never seemed to grow up, stuck in an endless hell. He took a deep breath. Would anyone ever understand how he felt?

Jane approached him as he re-entered the café. "You gave him money then?"

"I don't want him hanging around tomorrow."

"So that's it?"

"I don't honestly know. Whenever I see him, I get flashbacks and it seems unfair. I've got so much compared to him."

"Because you've made your own life, Warren."

"But I got you."

"Because you took our hand when we offered it to you. Remember, we offered our hand to him too when he came here. But all he took was the tip jar. He's never wanted to work, not here, not anywhere."

"But it's not his fault he had a bad upbringing."

"We all have choices to make. And yes, I'm not belittling his pain, just you ain't helping him by giving him money. Only he can help himself. Now give me a hug. We're chucking the stragglers out and then going up to get some sleep."

All of the guests left the café and they locked up. Warren wondered where Scottie was. He knew he'd have to cut him loose. He didn't want to go to bed, he wanted to walk, to clear his head. He unlocked the door, took the keys and started walking, recognising different houses in the neighbourhood that he'd lived in as a child. He wondered how the other lost children had turned out. It was true some really successful people attributed their harsh upbringing as the reason for their hunger for success, but he was sure many more failed and never pulled themselves out of it.

As he turned the corner, he came to the main pub he used to play darts for and smiled as he remembered The Eversley Arms, wondering how they were getting along with their game. He stepped into the doorway of a closed Chinese takeaway and pulled his phone from his pocket to text Jaz for an update. The Eversley was a whole different pub to the one next door. A world away. As he texted he heard voices.

"Where to now?" a guy said.

"I've two hundred left, let's pick up some vodka and get kebabs."

Warren moved further back as Scottie walked past. He sighed. *Yes, I've been had again.*

CHAPTER 23

"*M*a, if you're going to cry, I won't to let you see the place," Nina said as her mother stood next to her car. Her parents had loaded her father's Mercedes up with a few items as well as filling her own car and he was parking up behind her.

"It's like I'm losing you all over again," Sumitra said. "And you won't even be home tomorrow for Sunday lunch."

Tony reached them. "What's going on here?"

"Ma's upset about me leaving," Nina said.

"Sumitra, she's only been living with us for about six weeks, you cried enough the first time she moved out."

"I'm not crying. Now let's get these things inside."

"You're not lugging anything up the stairs," Nina said.

Rob approached them. "I'll take it up. Carl's coming out to help too."

"I see you're working here now," her father said to him.

Rob nodded. "It's going well."

Sumitra frowned at Rob. "Do you live here as well?"

"No. But hopefully I'll move in if I'm given the manager job. But not while Nina's here. I'll be downstairs if she needs help. There's a special intercom in there, they installed it when the kids were upstairs."

"I'll be safe, I'm sure," Nina said, not particularly liking the way they were speaking about her as if she were still a child.

"Hmm," Sumitra said, staring at Rob. Nina could tell how her mother's mind worked but she was sure she had nothing to worry about.

"IT'S SURPRISINGLY COSY UP HERE," Sumitra said once inside the bedroom. "You'd never know you were above a busy pub."

"It must be the thick stone walls," Tony said.

Sumitra looked out of the window. "A very nice view of the green as well."

"Jaz and Julian loved living here with their family," Nina said. "But it's not big enough for them, now the children have grown."

"I wish you were living on one of the cul-de-sacs instead of here, though."

"Ma, you never know, someone might move out and I might come into a fortune."

Rob brought up the last case and then left them.

"Do you need any help unpacking?" Tony asked.

"No, it'll keep me busy and I'll need to know where everything went. There's the small sitting room I'm using too, as well as the kitchen."

"Can I still come with you to your midwife appointments?" Sumitra asked in a small voice as they prepared to leave.

"Of course you can, I keep telling you. I'm not here because of you, I'm here because of me. I'm a grown woman used to my independence." She smiled at her. "I want you to be a part of my life and the baby's life."

Sumitra threw her arms around her. "I love you so much."

"Come on, let's leave Nina space to settle in," her father said then, too gave her a hug.

HAVING SPENT a couple of hours unpacking, Nina ventured down the stairs to the pub.

"Hey, what are you drinking and how have you settled in?" Rob asked.

"Tap water will be fine and I'm feeling great, with a similar sense of freedom as the first time I left home." She sat on a stool at the bar. "Although back then I really didn't have much to worry about."

"You'll be fine and a great mum. One of those super mums."

Nina laughed. "I don't know about that. Anyway, how did the darts go without your star player and coach?"

"The manager had our backs," he said with a laugh. "It was one of the top teams we played, so it was pretty much a given that we were going to lose. Jaz still pushed for a win though. No wonder she sells so many of those motorhomes, she probably bullies people into buying them."

Julian came into the bar. "Hi Nina, I was just checking in on you."

"I'm doing great, thanks again for letting me live here. It's a lovely room and Ma and Dad were impressed. I was just talking to Rob about the darts."

"Darts, that's all Jaz talks about! She's even been watching it on the TV. And as Rob here's doing so well, I'm having to cover him while he plays."

"What about the bistro?"

"They don't really need me. Natalie does a great job, she's managing the front of house now and Adam's food's always spot on."

"Now I live so close, I won't be able to resist a meal or two in there."

"So," Julian said to Rob. "How's my wife's rising star?"

Rob laughed. "She's on my case, I'll tell you that."

Julian was called over by Reverend Stephens and Rob fetched Nina's tap water.

"Joking apart though," Rob said to Nina when he was back facing her. "That woman saved my life."

"It hasn't gone unnoticed, how much you've changed," Nina said.

"Seems odd. Drink has been the problem, yet it's in here that I've come off it."

"Have you given up altogether?"

"No, I'm lucky. Drink was more of an escape than something I do to cope. I never drank late when I was working in the factory the next day. That would have been plain stupid."

"I guess it was hard for you, going from being a famous boxer to…"

"Total loser. If I'd saved the money instead of spending it all…and then when I stopped fighting, I should have stopped spending, but I carried on. Until there was less than nothing left. Hero to zero… that's me."

"Hey. Don't beat yourself up about it."

"Working in the factory with my dad. That was the worst. I felt like I was doing the walk of shame on my first day. Not that there's anything wrong with the work there. The pay is great. More than here. But I felt like I was going backwards. So then when I came out of an evening, I had a few drinks and felt like I was top dog again."

"You achieved a lot in your career, you've still got the belts and the memories."

"Yeah, messed my face up though."

"You've not been short of female attention."

"I guess not. But no one wants to settle down with me. Look at me. Battered and nothing to show for it."

"You've achieved a lot more than most. It's just the career of a sportsman ends sooner."

"Look at Julian, he was a sportsman and he's got this place."

"But he's still fortunate. Yes, he's doing well and opened the bistro, but don't forget his parents owned this pub, he took it on from them. Like me, yes I had my boutique but my father paid for the lease for the first two years and bought my first stock. So you could say I'm the biggest loser. I've lost my business, lost my council seat and lost my man. Now that's a loser!" she said with a laugh.

"I've never seen you this chill. You on pills?" Rob pushed the tap water across the bar.

"No I'm not! I can't because of the baby."

"Sorry, love. Joking apart, it must be hard." He nodded at her glass of tap water. "It's on the house."

Nina laughed. "I don't actually feel bad, though. A few weeks ago, yes. But you only get one life, we've got to strive to do our best."

"Shame you're so stuck up, I might've fancied you."

Nina threw her head back and laughed again just as Katie came in.

"Hi, can I have a diet cola and a half a lager?" She turned to Nina. "Hi there. How are you?"

"Fine thanks and you?"

"My brother's come to see me, so we're having a drink on the green while his wife minds the shop for me."

Rob smiled at Katie as he passed the drinks over. "There we are, love."

"Thanks, Rob," she said as she paid for them with her phone.

"Are you coming to the practice Monday?" he asked.

"Maybe," she said and then took the drinks and went outside.

"You like her," Nina said.

"Well, she doesn't like me."

"Why not?"

"She hates boxing and she's got her eye on someone else, who's much better looking than me and a whole lot younger."

"Who's that then?" she asked then sipped her water, bringing up the memory of when she'd been in the shop with Warren and the way Katie had greeted at him on the practice night.

"Warren. I mean what woman wouldn't fancy him? With that face. I've no chance."

"Does Warren like her back?" she asked, trying not to catch Rob's eye.

"He says he doesn't but then he knows I got it bad for Katie." He wiped down the bar. "Mind you, Warren did say he had his eye on someone."

"Did he?"

"Yeah, but I've no idea who it was as the only woman I've seen him chatting to is you." He paused and looked her in the eye. "Oh, of course, it's you." He chuckled.

"Me? No, we're not an item."

"Not yet. Warren told me he was working on it."

"Don't be silly, as you say he's much younger and I'm, well…"

"Some men like that. I've a mate who met his wife when she was expecting. He said he liked rescuing her."

"Well, I don't need rescuing," Nina said with a huff.

"Trust me, darling, we all need rescuing."

She looked at his sad eyes. "Why don't you ask Katie out for a meal or something?"

"It'll be too awkward if she says no, with her shop only being up the way and her coming to darts. No, she's not interested. She's out of my league."

Nina felt sorry for Rob, this hard man with such low self-esteem. *Perhaps he's right*, she thought as his words repeated in her head: *we all need rescuing*.

CHAPTER 24

"You look terrified!" Warren said to Nick as they both sipped a whisky in a quiet corner of a swanky riverside bar, a short walk from the registry office.

"I am," Nick said as he gazed into his glass. "It's not every day you get married."

"But you've been together for fifteen years."

Nick turned to look at him and laughed. "I'm not nervous about being married, it's what I've gotta go through to get there." He adjusted his tie and pulled a face as if it was strangling him.

"Here, let me do it," Warren said as he adjusted it for him. "You're going to have a great day. Relax. You'll enjoy it."

Nick picked up his glass and took a gulp of the amber liquid. "I'm glad you agreed to be the best man. I feel better with you here."

"And I'm happy, that out of your family and friends, you chose me."

"You're my closest family. You're my son, even if you don't call me Dad!"

Warren smiled at him. The care shown to him by Nick and Jane had always surprised him. What on earth had possessed them to adopt him, when he was in such a sorry state? They knew everything about him and they still wanted him in their family. Even if the adoption was unofficial, it had always baffled him. He didn't comment on the 'Dad' tag. To him, the terms Mum and Dad had always had negative connotations. A mum that never loved him and an anonymous dad. One thing he was sure about, he'd been someone's mistake.

"Hey, why so glum, son?" Nick said.

"I wasn't glum, just thoughtful." He ran a hand over his dense cropped hair.

"I recognise the look. You always look like that when you think of the past." He slapped him on the back. "You're a good man who's worked against the odds. I'm proud of you." Tears sprung into Nick's eyes.

"Hey, Nick. Don't start crying on me. I need you grinning when we go over there."

Nick shook himself out. "How long have I got?"

"You're not being executed, you're getting married. Now come on, drink up and we'll get some fresh air."

They left the bar and crossed the river using a metal winding footbridge.

Warren handed Nick a mint. "This is for the *you may now kiss the bride* part. Jane hates whisky."

"Do they really say that about kissing the bride?"

"I don't know. I've never been to a wedding."

"Haven't you?" Nick asked.

They reached the park and walked through. Many

people were gathered on the grass, sitting on blankets, some eating picnics, others drinking.

"The only wedding I was invited to, I missed as it was my graduation day."

"I guess there aren't a lot of weddings in my family and of course Jane's are abroad. You know she's after us going over to Dominica."

"I can't go anywhere until my field is established." Now the other side of the park, Warren stopped as they waited for a break in traffic so they could cross the road.

"Her sisters are going to be on at you about Dominica all afternoon and night."

"They mentioned it last night in the café." Warren looked at his phone once they'd crossed the street. "Oh, it's time."

Nick's eyes shot open. "Already?"

Warren put his arm around him. "I'll look after you!"

NICK KISSED Jane to rapturous applause. He faced the congregation and held her hand.

"Meet my wife everyone!"

The family cheered and Warren grinned so hard his cheeks hurt.

Outside, they took photos on the steps and then made their way to The Grand Hotel. They were in a moderate-sized event room with a bar attached. Warren sat with Nick and Jane on the top table and rehearsed his speech in his head as the guests found their tables. Luckily, he was speaking before they ate the meal. He wanted to get it out of the way so he could relax, as now it was his turn to look nervous.

Jane squeezed his hand as he stood up.

He tapped his glass. "Ladies and gentlemen, if I could have your attention for a few moments."

The room quickly fell silent apart from a baby crying at one of the tables.

"I'd like to share a few words about two very special people – Nick and Jane. When I first met them at the café, little did I know that meeting them would change my life forever. The concept of *parents* was something that carried a lot of pain and confusion for me." He took a deep breath as he heard a few whispers around the room. "But from the moment I walked in, there was a warmth and kindness in their eyes that I hadn't experienced before. The same warmth that you all witnessed when they looked at each other as they exchanged their vows."

Jane beamed at him and nodded with encouragement.

"Nick and Jane gave me a place to call home. They offered me not just a roof over my head, but something far more special – a sense of belonging. They taught me what it means to be part of a family." He gestured out to the audience. "And so have all of you."

There was a round of applause.

"I haven't got a list of funny things that happened because when I sat down to write this speech, all I could remember were the good times." He turned to the man he considered to be his father. "Nick, you've always been there with a listening ear. Your patience and understanding have guided me through some of the toughest times. Jane, you've always had sound advice, definitely the sensible one in our family home of three. You've both been my cheerleaders even when I was far from champion."

"You make us so proud, son," Nick said as he put his arm around Jane who pulled a tissue from her silver bag.

"Together, you've shown me that family isn't just about blood – it's about the connections we create. You've not only changed my life but have also shown me that it's never too late to find a family." He coughed, feeling emotion brewing inside, and was surprised by this feeling which appeared to be filling him. He decided to skip the next few lines. He picked up his glass, not wanting to embarrass himself before he reached the last line, which was the most important one. Not the original line on the paper before him. The new one he'd added as he watched them wed. "And now, in front of our wider family, I'd like to say something I've been wanting to say for a long time. Let's raise our glasses and toast the bride and groom. Here's to a lifetime of happiness, for a married couple that I'm proud to call *Mum* and *Dad*."

Jane stood up and hugged him before he could drink any of his champagne.

"Really?" she whispered. "You'll call me Mum?"

"Yes, Mum," he whispered back as he held her while everyone cheered loudly.

"It went well, eh?" Darius said to Warren later after the meal as they stood at the bar drinking lager.

Jane's cousin came over. "Warren, will you dance with me?"

"In a while, sure," he said with a smile.

"You're popular," Darius said. "That's the third girl I've witnessed flirting with you."

"Yeah." He took a sip of his drink.

"Are you not interested in finding someone?"

"Truth is, I'm massively bowled over by someone in Eversley. I can't get her out of my mind."

"I sense from your tone that this isn't a straight forward thing?"

"It's not a thing at all as she's pregnant and until very recently she was also engaged."

"Surely you're not going there? It sounds messy."

"I wasn't, but it seems like it's really over with the ex. She's the sort of woman that if I had her and lost her, it would crush me."

Darius's jaw dropped. "Man, you've got it bad!"

He sipped his pint. "She's all I think about. And on top of that, I'm not even sure she'd let me in."

"Why not?"

"Age difference, she's nearly a decade older."

"Are you sure you like her and you're not going after what seems like the impossible? Hiding from real commitment by chasing an unlikely relationship?"

He looked Darius in the eye. "I'm sure." He took a deep breath. "When I met her it was as if something was unlocked, not fully, but I felt something…new. Hey, I know this sounds pathetic, but I felt a lightness and since then, it's always there and I'm feeling other things, as if this new feeling is creeping into the rest of my life. Like today."

"Wow. You're in love."

Warren paused for a moment. The word love was one which did not pass his lips. The last person he had said he loved had let him down. And romantic love? He wasn't sure what that was. "I only said I like her." He decided to backtrack.

"Hang on, this isn't the woman with the wedding dress shop?"

He nodded.

"Ah, yeah, Jane told me about her. I guess in that case, you need to go for it."

Warren stood for a moment contemplating whether he had really fallen in love. He certainly felt something he'd never experienced before. It was as if in that moment, a door was opened. He smiled to himself.

Before he could consider it further, Jane rushed over and grabbed his hand. "Come on. Dance!"

Warren heard Darius laugh as Jane dragged him onto the dance floor.

CHAPTER 25

"Why are you nervous?" Holly asked Nina. "You've been selling clothes since you left college."

"That's true, but none I actually made myself. Somehow it seems so personal," Nina replied.

Jaz picked up a dress displayed on a small wooden hanger. "They're gorgeous, hun. No one could say otherwise."

"I'm not sure if they're too expensive."

"These are special occasion clothes, a bit like your boutique was! For when the parent wants to show their child off. I'm sure you'll do fine. Holly gets a lot of the rich crowd coming here from all over the county." She gestured behind her. "That's why I always bring a super RV over. Chick, some people still have money to burn! And we need to convince them to part with it."

Nina laughed at Jaz's words. She hoped the clothes would sell; she'd put her heart and soul into them. Dressmaking had been cathartic and it was if she'd thread her own love into every garment. Whether or not she was emotionally ready for the sale, she was certainly ready physically for a long day and had spent the prior evening at her parents having an early night without the distraction of the darts match taking place in the pub. She knew she would not have been able to resist going down to watch.

"Oh, my goodness. These are so sweet!" a young mother said as she held her daughter in her arms.

Jaz gave Nina a thumbs up and moved on.

"I love your stall, what design are they?" the potential customer asked, lifting a top she had made.

Nina pointed to the sign behind her which said *By Nina*. She'd kept it simple without too much thought.

"And are you Nina?" the woman frowned. "I think I know you."

Nina realised she recognised her as well. But then a lot of people were familiar to her, having spent years in the bridal boutique. She assumed this was a previous customer. "I used to have the bridal boutique in Wells." It still hurt her to refer to *Something Special* in the past tense, so she did not call the shop by name.

"Oh, I saw it was closed, but these dresses are amazing. It's great to try something new."

Nina felt a flutter of excitement as she sold her first two pieces and the customer didn't even blink an eye at the price. And more followed. Soon the entrepreneurial fire was reignited.

"I've been watching you."

Nina looked up to find Warren smiling down at her. "You've had loads of customers at your stall." There seemed to be something different about him, but when she looked at him, she couldn't see anything. His hair was the same. He wasn't wearing new clothes and he hadn't suddenly grown facial hair.

"Hi." She hadn't seen him since he'd got back from Bristol. Part of her realised she had been avoiding him, since their last chat in which she thought he was asking her out in a roundabout way. "How was the wedding?"

"Yeah, it was great." He caught her eye. "It brought a few things home to me." He gestured at the children's clothes. "You seem to be doing well."

"Better than I thought. I've enough to cover the new materials I've ordered and more."

"So what's next?" He stepped aside to allow a woman to take a closer look at a dress.

"I've ordered some soft materials so I can put together a baby hamper. I want them for the next market. As there are a lot of repeat visitors here, I'm going to offer something new each time. It's also a good marketing exercise to see what's popular if I go online."

Warren waited as she sold an item.

"Thank you," Nina said as she handed over the dress to the customer. She paused, then turned back to Warren. "I need to get a knitter on board. It's never been my thing, or crochet."

Warren gestured behind. "I have to get back but can you join me for lunch in an hour?"

"Yes, I really fancy another chicken kebab."

Nina smiled to herself as she continued to sell more clothes, wondering what was so different about Warren. She decided that he just had a different energy about him. *A confidence?* She presumed he was feeling elated from having watched his parents marry. Although she also found this confidence made him even more attractive. *Just go with the flow,* she told herself.

ONCE THEY'D ORDERED their lunch from the food carts, Nina and Warren found seats on the end of a long bench after a family had moved along to allow them space. The market was especially busy and she wondered how much busier it would get when the school holidays started. Holly left leaflets with all of the campsites to entice holidaymakers over. Sumitra was covering for Nina at her stall and was in her element telling customers that her daughter designed all of the clothes. If the clothes were not selling themselves, Nina would have considered leaving her mother on the stall all day. She found herself almost apologetic when explaining she designed them herself. Sumitra did a much better job.

"When do your new materials arrive?" Warren asked before taking a bite of his burger.

"I'm picking them up from Dad's shop on Monday. I placed a bulk order, it was more reasonable that way."

He swallowed his food. "I'll take you in the van if you like?"

"That would be great, if you don't mind." She could probably fit all the material in her car if she put the seats down, but at least it would negate the need for a possible double trip.

"Of course I don't mind, I want to." He smiled at her and she looked down at her chicken kebab. *What's got into him?* she thought. His eye contact made her feel as if he was attempting to read her mind.

"I'd like to spend more time with you."

Nina felt the heat rush to her cheeks and she looked up. "Oh, this chilli sauce is quite spicy." She fanned herself with a leaflet she picked up from the bench, not knowing what to say. Had she misheard him? She decided to change the subject, just in case. "So, you said the wedding was great?"

Warren grinned at her. "It was good to catch up with family. Jane said she wished you could have been there."

"That's sweet of her. I've been invited to many customer's weddings but if I'd attended them all, I'd have been going to more than one a day!" She laughed and felt some of her tension release.

"The wedding reminded me of the atmosphere in The Eversley Arms. Joining the darts team's been great." He picked up a chip and ate it. "I guess as a teenager, pubs were like home to me. When I played darts I was appreciated. People suddenly liked me, they wanted me to win. It spurred me on to be better, not just at darts but to be a better person as I realised I liked it when people liked me." He smiled at her.

Nina gulped. The new Warren was a lot more forward and open. Without him actually saying it, she was picking up loud and clear that something had changed. She felt it. And as he smiled at her, she found herself feeling a deeper connection.

"Where are The Eversley in the darts league?" she asked, trying to calm herself down. *What's happening to me?*

"Bottom," he said with a laugh. "But it's a new team. I've told Jaz this summer season is for learning and practice. We'll take it seriously at the start of the winter season. Then we'll have our game on. Not that Jaz is taking any notice of that, she wants a win every week." He popped the last of his burger into his mouth and took a drink from a bottle of water. "She's already building in a bonus scheme as an incentive." He laughed.

"Jaz has always wanted to win," Nina said.

Warren checked his phone. "I'd better get off, but I'll come over and help you pack away when we close. If there's anything left, that is."

"Thanks," she said and looked forward to it. As she returned to the stall, she felt light and had a small smile on her face.

"You seem happy?" Sumitra asked with her eyebrows raised.

"Yes, I'm really enjoying the day. Where's Dad?"

"He's buying more sausages, the pork and apple flavour, before they run out." She pointed to the display. "I've sold two pinafores and a sundress, and here's a number of a woman interested in the baby hamper." She handed her a slip of paper, then lifted her sunglasses so Nina was looking straight into her eyes. "So, how was your lunch?"

"The food was great."

"That's not what I meant. I saw you with that young man."

"I'm not having a romance." It was clear to Nina that Sumitra must have spotted her at the food cart with Warren, even though she'd made sure they were on a bench masked from view of her stall. Nina gave a short laugh. "I'm not going to reject his friendship because he's too young to be my husband... Ma, I'm focussing on the baby."

Sumitra pursed her lips then her face changed to one

of surprise as she looked over Nina's shoulder. "Tony! What on earth?"

"I bought a box."

"That will fill the entire freezer. How many sausages exactly?"

"Not sure, I bought them by the pound. But we'd better go, love, as I'll have to get them frozen as soon as possible." He nodded to Nina. "I'll see you back at our place later. You're doing great."

Sumitra's expression softened. "Yes, well done on the clothes, Nina. They're beautiful and I'm so proud." She rubbed her arm and then kissed her on the cheek. "I'm making your favourite for tea tonight."

Nina sat down and put the money belt above her bump. Her waist had long disappeared.

"Nina?"

She looked up. "Lindsey!" It was someone she used to attend college with. Lindsey had a double buggy with a toddler one side and an older girl in the other.

"You haven't changed a bit," Lindsey said.

Nina instinctively put a hand on her bump.

"And you're expecting?"

"Yes," Nina said. "October."

Lindsey picked up a dress. "I love this. What a great idea to move into children's clothing." She pointed to the *By Nina* sign. "And you've designed them yourself! I keep meaning to get my sewing machine down from the attic. I said to Becky, we should both do textiles again."

"You're still in touch with Becky?"

"Yes, we should all meet up. Is it your first?" she gestured towards Nina's bump.

"Yes."

"Becky can give you some tips, she's on her fourth!"

"I'd love that," Nina said, retrieving her phone so she could take Lindsey's number, although her motive had nothing to do with chats on motherhood.

NINA CARRIED the few unsold items into the art barn. During the farmers' market Jacky, the mosaic artist, had held a workshop there to promote her classes.

"How did it go?" Nina asked as Jacky pulled her car keys out of her bag.

"Great, but tiring, I didn't expect so many people, but I've already had a few sign-ups for my weekly workshops. Which is marvellous. I see you've sold most of your stock. Well done. I'd better be off." She gave a short wave and left the barn leaving Nina in the space, alone.

Over at her corner, Nina placed the unsold items in a drawer. She heard engines from outside as the other vendors drove their vans away.

"Hey."

She turned to see Warren puffing as he came through the doorway. "I'm glad you're still here. Sorry, I thought I'd be free much earlier but both sets of Harry and Millie's parents had come to Somerset for the day, so I felt bad asking them to clear away. I sent them off to spend time with their folks.

"I didn't have much to bring in. It's been a great day and I also made contact with an old college friend who I took textiles classes with and I'm thinking of asking her to run up some of my designs."

"You're the definition of entrepreneur!" Warren said.

"And with all you've got going on." He continued to walk towards her.

"It's because when I'm working my mind is elsewhere, not thinking about where I'll be living or childbirth." She grimaced. "I've not even thought about that one yet. I've booked some antenatal classes and will clear my mind until then, when I really need to think about it."

Warren smiled at her again, his brown eyes a similar shade as her own. His pupils were large and as he smiled at her, it was as if her mind had been rid of all thoughts, and she could find nothing to say.

"I keep waiting for an appropriate moment," he said as he took another step towards her. "I want to ask you…" He broke off as if faltering.

She took a breath, not knowing whether to comment, and then he continued.

"I want you to know that… I… Well. I like…the times we spend together. I feel that you…and me…"

Nina continued to look up at him. "Are you sure about this?" She had no doubt what he was referring to as his eyes appeared to search her face. It was as if the world was melting around them.

"Positive," he said, giving her a smile that made her face heat up.

There was no escaping him this time. He might not have explicitly said it, but she knew for sure that he was clearly asking her for a relationship. "I'm on my way to forty and I've got baggage," she said.

"I've already explained that age doesn't matter." He smiled then looked at her baby bump. "It's not baggage, it's a cute package."

She laughed and took a step back, trying to break the

way she was drawn to him, not knowing what would happen if she remained there. She pushed her hair behind her ears. "You make everything sound so simple, Warren. But it's not."

"It is simple and crystal clear. Being in Bristol, it seemed so obvious to me. I like you, and I think you like me. And nothing about you is going to put me off. I don't care about the decade between us."

"It's actually nine years?" she said with a smile, trying to lighten the thick atmosphere, worried they would be vacuumed together in an intense embrace she wasn't sure she was ready for.

He laughed and took a step closer. Then he looked down at her, his expression suddenly serious. "All I think of is you. From the instant I first saw you. Even when I shouldn't have, as you were engaged. But since then, I've wanted to spend time with you. Can we just..."

As she looked up into his eyes, it was as if something switched inside, and as she took the last step between them, she shut her eyes.

"Are you ready?" Holly called from the doorway. "I'm closing up."

Warren stepped back and ran a hand over his hair.

"Oh," Holly said, looking from Nina and back to Warren. "I didn't interrupt anything did I?"

"No," Nina said quickly. She grabbed her bag and walked around Warren, feeling very warm. "All done and thanks so much for everything Holly, you've really given me a step up. And as from next week I want to start paying for my station."

"There's no need."

"There is for me. I need to feel I'm doing something

viable." Nina paused, very aware of Warren behind her as she exited the barn. "It's more than something therapeutic. I'm serious about the line and I'm going to be recruiting others to help me."

Holly locked the door behind them. "Who are you taking on?"

"Well," Nina said with a laugh, feeling the cool air on her body which had become incredibly warm. "I bumped into Lindsey and she said she's still friends with Becky. Not sure if you remember them from college?"

"Of course I do!"

"I haven't asked them yet but we've arranged to meet up." She checked her phone. "I'm going back home. Dad's got a sausage casserole on the go as he couldn't fit them all in the freezer."

"What time Monday? To collect the material," Warren asked, now at her side.

"Is the morning okay? About ten?" she said and then gulped.

"Perfect. I'll help you with the litter picking," he said to Holly.

"You're a star!" Holly said. "See you Nina, and you're looking great."

Nina watched as Warren followed Holly across to the sales sheds. *I'm always willing to take a punt on a business adventure...why not take a chance on romance?*

arren rolled up at the unloading bay behind Tony's shop. Nina had felt a little awkward when he'd picked her up at The Eversley Arms, after the near kiss they'd had at the weekend. When she'd climbed into his transit, she wondered whether he wanted to carry on where they'd left off. But he'd not mentioned it and they'd chatted away about his field. But still, she was acutely aware of the way he looked at her from time to time.

"Thanks for driving me here," Nina said.

"It's not exactly a chariot."

"But it will fit all of the textiles inside. And I get to buy you brunch as a thank you." She smiled at him. "Anyway, we'd better get out."

As she opened the door, Warren was already around helping her down.

Her father came out of the back door. "The shop's quiet so I can help load up."

Inside the shop there were bundles of fabric and many

rolls as well. As Warren picked up the first roll of cloth, she noticed her father staring at his tattoos.

"I can't wait to get started on this," Nina said, rubbing some material between her thumb and forefinger.

"I'm so pleased you're throwing yourself into it." Tony said. "Would you like a tea?"

"No. I'm taking Warren for brunch up the road, to say thank you for bringing me here."

"Right."

Warren came in for the next roll.

"I'll give you a hand," Tony said.

"No worries, Mr Smith, I'll load them in." Warren lifted another and left the room.

Tony turned to Nina when Warren was out of earshot. "Are you and him...?"

"Dad," Nina said slowly with a warning tone to her voice.

"Your mother says you've got a thing for him and standing here, I'd agree."

"I can't deny we have a connection. He's a great guy…"

"But?"

They heard Warren return and her father passed him the next roll of material, which was a pattern of blue and green. As soon as Warren was gone, they continued their conversation.

"What's going on here, do you think you're not worth much so you are settling for a man not good enough?"

"He's about to get a PHD, is a pioneer in agroforestry in the UK and setting up a silvopasture for future generations. Trust me, if anyone's reaching here, it's me. Baby or no baby." She realised the words had come out a lot more forceful and they both turned to see Warren in the doorway.

Her father's face changed into a broad smile. "I hear you're doing well in agroforestry?"

"I am. It's a passion that's taken over my life."

"Very admirable, although at present there are a lot more pressing issues in our society."

"Exactly," Warren said. "I deal with that in my thesis. You can read it – I published it, if you'd like a copy." He lifted up the last batch of material.

"Oh, right, yes."

Nina sucked in her lips as Warren left the room. He clearly wasn't the type to take a jibe silently.

Alone again her father sighed. "I miss our discussions about the environment since you've stopped sitting on the Environmental Rural Committee."

"Dad, maybe you should go on the committee yourself. I know Jill has wanted out for ages and they're after a community member."

"But I'm not rural. I'm in the High Street. They want young blood, not an old-timer like me."

"I get the impression you miss me being on the council more than I do."

"It's true. I'm ashamed to admit it, but I was rather living it through you. I loved badgering you for the details. I've been bereft since you lost your seat."

"I'm glad you've finally admitted it!" Nina said with a laugh.

He dropped his shoulders. "Yes. I confess."

"And you weren't badgering me, Dad, it was invaluable for me to discuss everything with you. You're discreet and someone I can trust." She rubbed his arm. "You made it so much more interesting. A massive support and help."

"I was?"

"Yes, as I told you many times."

"I thought you were trying to make me feel better about being nosey."

Nina laughed as Warren returned. "We'll be off now."

"Am I all right to leave the van out the back for a while?" Warren asked.

"Of course," Tony said, then beamed at Nina. "I hope you enjoy your brunch.

AS THEY WALKED up the High Street, Nina scuffed the edge of a manhole with her shoe.

She laughed. "If I was still on the council, I'd be sending a rude email to the outside spaces department."

Warren offered his hand to her. "I don't want you to take any chances."

Nina looked at his hand and knew it was nothing to do with a fear of her tripping. She was well aware that he simply wanted to hold her hand. She gave him a sideways smile and then took it. It wasn't like holding Ethan's hand, soft from moisturising. Warren's hand was rough, a hand that was a tool, used to working with soil and rocks. As they reached the square, she led him to the pub on the corner, close to the cathedral and not far from her closed shop. She averted her gaze so that she did not have to see *Something Special,* not knowing how she would react if another business had already taken up occupation.

Once inside, she pulled her hand from Warren's as they squeezed past an elderly couple.

"Have you been in here many times?" Warren asked when they reached the bar.

"More than I could ever recall. The town hall is only a few paces from the back entrance." She sighed. "I avoided looking at the boutique, but I'm in here facing the ghost of the council. I don't want to feel I have to stay away from this place, not when I love their food so much."

"Hi Nina," George said. He was the chef. His partner Adam was the chef in the Eversley Bistro. "I reserved the table you asked for, but you may wish to move."

"Why?" She turned around to see that two tables away was Sam Brent, sitting alone staring at his mobile phone as he ate a full English breakfast one handed, with a fork. "No, that's fine." She was after all in there to face her demons, and there was one of them now taking a sip of his tea.

"Is that Hedgehog Sam?" Warren said to her in a quiet voice as they approached their table.

"It certainly is."

They sat down next to the window and checked the menu. She looked down the list of options. "I'm having a full English, what would you like?" she asked Warren.

"I'll join you and have the same."

At the bar where the food orders were taken, she looked back at Sam. He hadn't noticed her. He was too busy staring at his phone with a frown upon his face. After ordering, she passed his table and he looked up.

"It's you!"

"Yes, it is." She carried on but when she sat down, she found that Sam had followed her.

"I need to speak to you," he said.

"Sam, we're here for a private brunch," Warren said.

"Oh, yeah, sorry." Sam turned and sloped away.

Nina tutted at herself, then called him back. "Sam."

He turned around and she beckoned him over. He pulled a seat out and sat down.

Warren raised his eyebrows at her.

She mouthed back at him that it was okay.

"How can I help?" she asked, realising the intrigue had got the better of her.

"I need to go over the recycling initiative. I've been to the meetings and it's a great idea."

"I'm surprised to hear you say that. Does your father feel the same way?"

He groaned. "No!"

"You do realise that's why he wanted you on there, to do his bidding."

"I do now. But I can't. It goes against my vlog. I'm supposed to be next to nature guy, saving wildlife, not encouraging people to pollute the planet. But Dad's on my case. He says he's getting himself on the committee as Jill's leaving and he'll take the community member space."

Nina thought back to her own father's comment. "He's not very rural, is he?"

"I can't get anyone else interested. I don't know those types of people. What I was thinking is that you could do it. Come back on, as a community member."

"I'd rather not, I'm expecting a child." She also felt uneasy with the idea, baby or no baby.

"Oh yeah, I remember they mentioned it at the last meeting." He smiled at her and then at Warren. "Congratulations you guys."

Nina blushed but did not explain that Warren was not the father.

"I'm not getting on good, at the council," Sam said.

Nina wasn't surprised. "It's a lot of hard work."

"All they go on about is you and what a mess it's been without you there. Everyone hates me."

"You seem to care, Sam. They probably think you're like your father. And well, you've a lot to learn."

"Tell me about it."

"As far as the committee's concerned, you only need an interest from someone else and your father won't get a look in. What you need is someone who's passionate about the environment and who lives out in one of the villages." She grinned at Warren.

"What am I getting roped in to?" he asked with a laugh.

"This is what you wanted. A connection to the council to help your application. All you have to do is discuss the environment and impart information."

"I guess I'm more than qualified."

"Are you?" Sam asked him.

"I'm in the last stages of a PHD on agroforestry and the environment is what leads my work."

"Oh, mate, please."

"Okay, sure," Warren said.

"I've someone else to introduce you to as well," Nina said to Sam, "who can help. Give us some privacy while we have our brunch *date* and I'll take you to them when we're finished."

"Oh…right…yeah. Thanks so much, Nina." He made a praying sign with his hands and then went to finish his food.

Warren smiled at her and spoke in a low voice. "You're generous to Sam, many people would have blanked him."

"I still care about the initiative. I was the one who

proposed it and I've been gutted that I lost, knowing it would be shelved once Barry Brent got Sam to object."

"That's blown up in his face then?"

"Sam's coming into his own by the looks of it."

"You told Sam we were on a brunch *date?*" Warren said with a smile.

"To make sure he left us alone," she said.

"It feels like a date." He sat back in his seat as their food was delivered to the table.

Nina made no further comment, but she had a smile on her face she was battling to control and changed the subject, bringing Warren up to date on the matters the Environment and Rural Committee had been working on. "So it'll be a breeze for you."

"I'm not worried about feeling out of my depth knowledge-wise, but I'm guessing there may be some difficult personalities." He stood up as they prepared to leave.

"You'll get on fine," Nina said, then waved at Sam who was now at the bar to indicate they'd finished.

The young man followed them down the street until they reached her father's shop. They waited while a customer left.

"He may look a little surprised to see you," Nina said to Sam, and she was not wrong.

"What's he doing here?" her father said, gesturing at Sam as they entered the shop.

"Sam's having difficulty pushing the recycling initiative through."

"I thought you were going to oppose it?" Tony said.

"He's getting some backlash, close to home," Nina added.

"Ah." Tony's face softened.

"He needs a mentor and I told him, I know the best."

"Let's talk," Tony said to Sam with a smile.

CHAPTER 27

*W*arren waited at the front door of the farmhouse. They rarely used it, mainly opting for the back entrance to the house, through the business side, via the kitchen. But he wanted to be the one to greet Nina in private. He'd invited her to the Monday meal. It wasn't a long walk from The Eversley Arms, but it was a tricky one, either along a road with no footpath or across the field. With Nina being pregnant and not knowing the land as well as himself, Holly and Mitch, she was driving over.

As soon as he saw her white car, he stopped leaning on the door frame and greeted her at her car.

"You look good in black," she said to him as she got out.

"Oh, thanks." She'd caught him off guard. There seemed to be two different Ninas – the one who was shy and reserved, and also a flirtatious one. He liked them both. He knew she liked him but guessed the sensible side in her was wary of letting go and allowing him into her life. He felt that every time he looked into her eyes, they were telling him she liked him, even if she didn't say so herself.

He took her hand. "Come on. You're not going to be disappointed. I've made a Caribbean stew, one of Jane's recipes." He'd not only taken the morning off, he'd ended up taking the whole day off to include a trip out for ingredients.

"I thought you loved these meals because it was the one day a week you didn't cook."

"We're having a week off from darts practice and I'm trying to impress someone this evening."

"Oh yeah? Who's that?" She gave him another one of her flirtatious looks.

"Hmmm." He looked into her eyes and had to look away as he had an overwhelming urge to kiss her.

"Here she is," Jaz said. "We can dish up now."

Warren sat Nina between himself and Jaz. At the end were Val and Len with the five children. Belle was absorbed in her phone, the twins were colouring at the table and the boys were chatting. Holly and Mitch were serving up and Millie and Harry were at the other end. Greg was down at the sheds waiting for the vet as they had a sick cow.

"Belle, get off the phone," Jaz said. "Look, Holly's handing you a plate."

"What is it?" Belle said, turning her nose up.

"It's a Caribbean stew, my mother's recipe," Warren said, realising it might not be something Belle would like.

"You can have sausages with the girls if you don't like it," Holly said. "Warren did extra just in case anyone wasn't keen."

"I love curry, it smells like curry," Noah said.

"I won't take it personally if you don't like it," Warren added.

Belle smiled at him. "It's okay, it smells really nice."

They had an enjoyable meal. Warren loved the mildly spiced and fruity stew which he'd served with brown rice. And with Nina sitting next to him, he considered this the best family meal they'd had since he'd been at the farm.

"Belle, not at the table," Jaz said to her sister who had finished her food and was now back on her phone.

"You're not my mum!" Belle stood up and stormed out of the room.

Jaz sighed and looked to Holly. "Enjoy the girls now, you've got that to come, times two!"

"I can't wait!" Mitch said.

Warren watched Belle storm out. "I'll check she's okay."

He passed through the working kitchen where Trixy looked up from her bed.

Outside, he found Belle sitting on a tree stump tapping away at her phone.

"Hey," he said.

She put the phone to her chest. "All right?"

"Yes, how about you?" he asked.

"Just the usual. Jaz. She's always on my back. She's my sister but thinks she's my mum, moaning at me the whole time. I don't see why I have to come up here and sit with the kids and get treated the same. I'm sixteen not six."

Warren could see she was genuinely fed up and didn't want to alienate her. "It's hard for adults, there's pressure on us to set a good example."

"You should try being me." Her bottom lip trembled.

She angrily brushed a tear from her cheek, clearly embarrassed.

"Hey, it doesn't matter. You're allowed to be upset."

"It does matter." She stood up and stormed off.

"Hey, don't go," he called after her.

"Tell Jaz I'm going home."

Warren paused as he watched Belle stomp towards the field. At least she wasn't going along the road. He returned to the house.

"Belle's left," he said as he reached the dining table. "She said she's going home. She probably needs some space."

"That girl has enough space," Jaz said. "She spends all her time on her own in her room, on her phone." She began to rise from her chair. "I'll have to go after her."

"Finish your dessert first," Holly said. "Call her in a while and check she got back okay."

"You had your moments yourself when you were that age," Val added. "A bit of space can do wonders."

After they'd eaten a dessert of tropical fruit salad, Nina helped Warren clear the plates away after Jaz had left to check on Belle. "You look concerned."

"I sense something's up with Belle. I wanted to go after her, but it would have been awkward and I'm not sure she's going to open up to me." Warren left the pile of bowls which Millie and Harry loaded in the dishwasher.

"I was supposed to have a word with her myself a few weeks back," Nina said as they returned to the table. "But I forgot. Jaz said she was worried about her."

"I think you've enough going on," he said. "Are you going to hang back here after the others have left?" he asked.

"If you like," she said with a smile that sent his heart racing.

"I do like." His mind was becoming clouded with memories of their near kiss. All he could think about was holding her close.

They drank coffee at the table as Val and Len finished off a noisy boardgame which all four children were playing, and Mitch and Holly told them about a film they had seen.

"Come on girls, it's nearly bedtime," Holly said.

"But I like it here," Poppy said.

"Can we stay five more minutes?" Daisy added.

Nina smiled as Holly struggled to get the girls to put their shoes on.

"I won for the first time," Len said.

"Well done Uncle Len," Mikey said giving him a hug.

Jaz entered the room, scowling. "She's not there."

"When she said home, she might have meant Eversley Burrows, love," Val said. "Have you called your mum?"

"Yes. Look let's be quick and I'll drop you back, then go to the Burrows to look for her. She may have stopped at a friend's house on the way."

Warren considered offering his help as he felt guilty that Belle had left and he had not stopped her. "If you can't find her, give me a call."

"Thanks, Warren."

The house was now quiet. Millie and Harry went to their rooms, leaving Warren and Nina alone. Away from the long dining table, they could sit much closer on the sofa.

"Shall we put a film on?" he asked, whilst longing to pull her close for the kiss he desperately wanted.

"I'd love that. Have you any snacks?"

"Sure." He went to the kitchen cupboards and found some popcorn and brought it back to the sofa, with a six pack of cans of sparkling orange. He picked up the remote control and switched the television on. Once they'd found a film they both fancied, he looked down at her. The tension between them was electric and he knew he would not concentrate on a film. He wanted to lay it out, the way he felt.

"Nina…I…"

He was interrupted by his mobile ringing. *Typical,* he thought. It was Holly calling.

"Warren. You couldn't help could you? Jaz can't find Belle and she's going mad. Mitch is out too looking, but I've got the girls."

"Of course I can. I'll retrace her steps by foot, through the field." He ended the call and then puffed out, feeling a little guilty that he resented having to go out. "Belle hasn't turned up. Holly's asked me to go looking for her."

"Don't worry, I'm sure she's fine." Nina sat up as if preparing to leave.

"Would you wait here?" he asked. "Hopefully I won't be long. I'm sure she'll turn up and we can still watch that film. I'll be as quick as I can." He was desperate to keep her there.

She smiled at him. "Okay. I'm looking forward to it."

He hesitated. Her expression was telling him she wanted to be close to him as well. *Should I kiss her now?* he thought, then decided against it. He knew that as soon as he held her in his arms, he wouldn't be able to tear himself away.

CHAPTER 28

*A*fter tramping through the field, then taking the path through Lovelands, Warren reached the green, with no sighting of Belle. As she'd not gone to Ashbury Gardens, he decided to trace the steps she would have taken to Eversley Burrows, where her mother lived. He'd been over to the estate when they'd played an away match at The Dog and Horn. He hoped nothing had happened to her and began to feel nerves stabbing at his gut. He knew that not everyone in the world was good, he'd had a taster of that himself. His phone dinged with a text from Jaz:

Any sight of Belle?

No, I'm going to the estate. What is your parents' address?

Once Jaz had texted the address, he plugged it into the map app on his phone. As he rounded the bend into the estate, he narrowed his eyes in the fading light. He saw two young people sitting on a bench within the play area. One had dark brown hair, just like Belle. He didn't want to call out and scare them off.

He slowly approached, overhearing their conversation.

"You promised." It was a blond boy seated next to her.

"But I'm not ready." He recognised Belle's voice and relaxed, at least he'd found her.

"You're sixteen, it's time. It's the law."

"Doesn't mean I have to!"

"You do, unless you want the world to see those pictures."

Warren was done listening. He grabbed the boy's shoulders from over the bench. The lad shouted out and struggled, then swore as Warren swiftly moved around the bench and pinned him to it.

"What are you doing here?" Belle said with fear in her eyes.

"I'm stopping you from making a big mistake with this little creep." He turned to the lad. "She said she wasn't ready. That means no!"

Belle stood up. "Urgh. You're making it worse. Can you just leave?"

"No, I can't. Now, can you tell me what he's black-mailing you with?"

"Nothing."

"You can tell the police then," Warren said.

"No, Warren, please," Belle begged as she burst into tears.

The boy cried out. "Just let me go. I'll leave her alone!"

Warren pointed in the lad's face. "What's your name?"

"Cole."

"Get your phone out, Cole."

"No."

"Now!"

The boy took his phone from his pocket.

"Not to me. Give it to Belle and unlock it first."

He handed it to Belle.

"Find whatever pictures he was talking about and then delete them and delete them from the trash folder." As Belle tapped at the phone, he looked back to the lad. "If I hear one mention of your name, you'll have me to deal with." He released him. He knew he wouldn't scarper while Belle still had his phone. Warren stood with his arms crossed blocking Cole from Belle.

"I don't believe it," Belle said. "He's got loads and they're not all of me. On no!" She lifted the phone. "This is really bad."

"Don't show it to me, Belle," Warren said. "I don't want to see."

Cole lunged forward for the phone.

Warren grabbed him. "You're going nowhere. Belle, call the police, 999, now!"

Cole struggled to get away. "No!"

Belle cried. "Are you going to tell Jaz?"

"Call the police," Warren repeated.

She called as he'd asked and put the phone on speaker. Warren spoke to the operator.

"I've performed a citizen's arrest on a minor, he has a phone with inappropriate pictures on it and I'm also here with one of his victims. Can you send someone as soon as possible."

"Let me go!" Cole screamed. "He's a pervert."

Warren groaned as Belle gave them the location, realising he might have a struggle when the police arrived.

They soon heard the sirens and as the police pulled up, Belle met them.

"That boy has pictures of girls on his phone and was blackmailing me to do things with him. My friend, that man, is helping me."

One of the police officers put her arm around Belle. "I'm Erin, calm down. You're safe now."

"Here's his phone." Belle handed it over to her.

Warren released Cole into a policeman's custody as a second car drew up.

"Thanks, Belle. You're doing the right thing," Erin said as they reached Warren.

"Who exactly is this man?" Erin asked Belle.

"Warren. A family friend."

"I was out looking for Belle who went missing earlier," Warren said.

"We'll have to speak to you both, but I can see you're upset at the moment, Belle."

"I'll get her home," Warren said.

"How old are you?" Erin asked Belle.

"Sixteen."

She took her notebook out. "And can I have your address?"

Belle gave her the Eversley Burrows address.

"Thank you, we'll be over soon," Erin said. "Hopefully within an hour."

They watched both police cars drive further into the estate, he assumed to visit Cole's parents.

"Sit down, and take a breath," Warren said, pointing to the bench.

She cried as he messaged Jaz to let her know he'd found Belle but to give her time. That he would take her back home to her parents' house.

They took a slow walk back.

"I sent him a picture," Belle volunteered without Warren asking. "It wasn't bad, it was only of me in a bikini."

"You don't have to tell me this."

"I want to, in case when we get back, I can't tell Mum." She sobbed then composed herself. "Then he said if I didn't send him another one, a bit worse than that, he would show the bikini one to everyone when we start at college in September."

"How long has this been going on?" he asked.

"Since exam time. I'd taken some cider from the bar and got a bit tipsy, that's why I did the first...I'm stupid, I know that."

"We all make mistakes. I've made a tonne. It's what we do next that matters. You need to be brave now, Belle. Not just for you, but for the other girls."

"I know a few of them and their pictures were worse. Tonnes worse. Will you stay with me when I tell Mum and Dad?"

"Of course." They were now nearing her parents' house.

Warren sent a quick text Nina to apologise and said he would hopefully be back within an hour. He was desperate to return, but knew he couldn't abandon Belle when she'd put her trust in him. And he couldn't tell the details to Nina, not before Jaz had found out. He hoped he could get away soon.

WARREN MADE tea for Belle's parents as they sat with her in the lounge. He'd broken the news to them, then left them to discuss it with Belle. He was trying to blot out Darren's face. The man had looked broken, no doubt thinking of his little girl being taken advantage of. Warren had offered to make tea as the parents blamed themselves. As the kettle boiled, Belle was reassuring them it was nothing to do with them and from what he'd overheard, the pictures Belle had sent were more to do with suggestive poses than anything revealing.

There was a break in the conversation and he carried in a couple of mugs of tea.

"Thank you so much, Warren," Darren said. He knew the man quite well, having met him over at The Eversley Arms and The Dog and Horn when he'd played darts against the Dogs. "Belle's lucky you got there. Cole comes from a rough family."

"His dad's a right creep," Stacey added. "Oh, someone's here."

Darren stood up and opened the door.

A woman followed him in. "Hi, Stacey."

"Hi Donna."

"What are you here for?" Belle said and clutched onto her mum. "You're not going to take me away to a foster family again are you?"

"No," Donna said. "I heard what had happened and have just come over to see how you are, nothing official." She looked around the room and back at Stacey and Darren. "It's so nice to see you all back as a family."

Warren looked at Belle, not realising she'd been in the care system, not knowing the history of the family.

"So how are you, Belle?" Donna asked.

"I'm pleased it's all over," she said. "I was feeling so

stupid but when I saw the other pictures on there, I realised I'm not the only idiot."

"And that was all happening around exam time too," Stacey said. "It's disgusting."

"I hope I haven't failed," Belle said.

"I'm sure you'll do just fine. And you've got your college place anyway," Stacey added.

"That lad's got it coming to him," Darren said.

"Let the police deal with it," Donna said. "I'm glad you're coping well. I'll leave you in peace," Donna said and then left.

"Are you going to tell Jaz or shall I?" Stacey asked Belle.

Belle looked at her. "Mum, there's more that's been worrying me."

"What else?" Darren said as he sat down having seen Donna out.

"Shall I go?" Warren began to rise from the chair.

"No, stay. I want you to tell me what you think about it." Belle took a deep breath. "I don't like it at the cul-de-sac."

"Why not?" Stacey said. "It's a beautiful house and you couldn't stay in the pub. The boys needed their own space too."

"I don't mind it for a few days a week, but I don't want to leave here." She gestured around the room. "I love coming back at the weekend, it's quieter and…you're here." Her bottom lip trembled.

"Oh love, we'll only be next door."

"But I don't want you to get rid of this house. I love being here with you. And you're the best mum in the world." Belle hugged her. "I prefer it here and the thought that I can't come back to see you both, just us... And my friends are close by, too."

Darren smiled at his wife and daughter. "Your mum feels the same way."

"Daz, don't say that. I don't wanna upset Jaz after all she's done." She pulled a hanky from her pocket.

Belle turned to Warren. "What do you think?"

Warren suddenly felt as if Belle expected him to have all the answers.

"We can't pull out now," Stacey said. "She's been refurbishing that annex,"

"My advice is to be truthful," Warren said.

"I'm sure she's going to be angry." Stacey wrung her hands together.

"She won't be angry, love," Darren said. "But she might be upset. The kitchen she asked me to install is top notch as well. But we haven't ended our tenancy with the council. Look, she can sell it on. If you two want to stay here, that's what we'll do."

"My advice is to tell her sooner rather than later!" Warren yawned and looked at his phone. "I really should go now."

"Thank you so much, Warren, for what you did today," Darren said.

"Thanks," Belle said. "No wonder Nina's in love with you."

He laughed. "I'd be so lucky."

"Jaz and Holly say she is."

"Young lady, you're as bad as your big sister at keeping secrets," Stacey said with a laugh as Warren felt the mood lighten. Or was it him feeling light at the thought of Nina having feelings for him?

Warren got up to leave, now really wanting to get back to Nina as soon as possible, when he saw the police drawing up.

Once inside, the police asked him to stay to take a short statement. He knew he'd have to text Nina again.

CHAPTER 29

*N*ina sat in the quiet living room at Booth Farm. She had been there years before, when it was decorated in an old style. The whole room had been Sydney Booth's sitting room, with dated furniture and furnishings. Since then, it had been transformed into a clean living area with kitchen. But while it was modern, it looked very sterile in her opinion, with wipeable sofas and furniture. At the end of the room was a conservatory full of plants, which were kept watered and looked after by the rotation of students living there. This area of the house had been specifically set up to accommodate those who came to the farm as part of their studies. Some like Harry and Millie taking an entire year out to work there.

Am I being foolish? Nina thought as she checked the clock. It was half an hour since Warren had texted her to say he'd found Belle. She looked down at the coffee table, upon which was a six pack of cans of fizzy drink, one of which she'd drunk already. and a packet of toffee popcorn. She flushed; it felt like a teenage date, certainly not something she was used to. On a night spent in with Ethan, they would have shared a flavoured water with vegetable snacks, like parsnip crisps. *What are you doing?* she asked herself. When she was with Warren, everything seemed simple. It was as if they were in their own little bubble. She liked him and he definitely liked her – he'd made that clear and he wasn't worried about the age gap. And he made her feel special. *Is that it?* she asked herself. *Am I just flattered?*

She pulled at her top as the heat rose from her chest, and then her phone dinged with a text. Hoping it was from him to say he was on his way, she lifted her phone from the table. It was from Lindsey:

I've got a few issues with this pattern. I've tried it twice and I'm getting into a right mess.

She'd been messaging Lindsey since Saturday at the farmers' market. Lindsey had brought her sewing machine down from her attic and had popped into the hub that afternoon to pick up a pattern. They'd chatted briefly and Lindsey was enthusiastic about helping Nina run up the clothes. Following her text was a picture. Nina saw immediately where Lindsey had gone wrong and decided to tell her she would visit the following day. It would be easier to explain it at her own sewing machine. As she began to type, another text came in, this time from Warren. She switched to it.

Sorry, the police have just arrived. They want to take a statement. Will get there asap feel free to start the film and popcorn xx

She returned to the text she was sending to Lindsey.

I'm free now, if you want me to pop over?

Lindsey replied immediately:

That would be amazing, the kids are in bed.

Nina didn't send Warren a return text. She took a pen from her bag and ripped a page out of the small notebook she carried with her.

Called out by Lindsey the seamstress. Hope Belle is okay. I guess it wasn't meant to be. Let's keep it as friends. Nina x

It seemed cowardly to say that in a note. But it was far simpler that way. She felt foolish and life was way too complicated to add a relationship into the mix. She was going to be a mother, with a huge responsibility. She had to think with her head and not her heart.

LINDSEY ANSWERED the door before Nina knocked, clearly waiting for her to arrive. Nina guessed she didn't want to risk the doorbell waking the kids up.

"Hey, come in. Tea or coffee?"

"No thanks, I've just had a can of fizzy orange. I'll only be wanting the loo again."

Lindsey laughed. "I remember the feeling."

Nina spotted Lindsey's sewing machine as they entered the lounge, which was set up in the corner, sectioned off by a child gate.

"I've set up this space, away from the kids. I've been loving doing this, Nina. Thanks so much for the opportunity."

"The thanks goes to you for supporting me in this venture. Especially when I'm not sure it'll work out!"

"Of course it will. What's next?"

"Setting up an online store, which I know how to do as I had one with…the bridal boutique. I took a few email addresses at the farmers' market so will invite them to my new mailing list, once I've set it up. And Jaz is seeing Tyrone and Crystal for a party in a couple of weeks." Jaz was friends with a football player and his influencer wife, having sold him a car and a motorhome. "She's taking one of my dresses for their daughter."

"Crystal? I love her! And she's expecting again. That Jaz knows all sorts. It's so exciting, Nina. I know you'll do amazing, you always do."

Nina sat on the sofa. "Not so lucky at relationships, though."

"They're never easy, I've had my moments with Sean. But you're gorgeous. I've lots of friends with children who find new relationships. Once you've got used to motherhood, I'm sure you can find someone."

"I'll worry about that in a couple of years." She rubbed her bump. "I'm just looking forward to being a mother now." But all she saw was Warren's image in her mind.

"You're so positive."

"Right, show me this dress then." Nina stood up and went to the sewing machine and helped Lindsey, all the time wondering what Warren would say when he saw the note she'd left, feeling a sickness inside, wishing she'd not written it and that she was still there, waiting for him to arrive home. Wondering what would have happened if they'd had the kiss at the weekend, rather than it being interrupted.

The dress was soon completed.

"Thanks Nina, and it looks so good."

"I think with a few more people on board, this could turn into a profitable business."

"I'm seeing Becky tomorrow, I'll ask if she's up for it.

Why don't you see how many more of us from college are still available?"

"I don't remember their names, do you?"

"Go on the socials. There's a page for our old college."

"Is there?"

"Yeah, look I'll get us some tea, biscuits and my laptop and we can have a look who's about and if we can remember any of them."

Nina sat down as Lindsey made them drinks, imaging Warren's face when he saw the note she'd left. She reached for her phone to text him then put it back in her bag. *No, it's for the best.*

CHAPTER 30

*W*arren admired the huge cottage pie Holly had made. It was six weeks since the incident with Belle. He still felt gutted about Nina cooling it off. Not that their friendship had ever heated up, but it had certainly been warming. After chatting to Holly about it, he understood that Nina was not in the right place. But he certainly was going to wait. It was only a matter of weeks now until her due date. However long it took, he decided not to give up hope. They'd seen each other in The Eversley Arms, but never one on one.

"That's my favourite," Noah said, gesturing at the pie.

"Mine too," Belle said. The teenager had been in much better spirits, especially since she received her exam results, as she had exceeded her predicted grades. He'd also had good news and been awarded his doctorate.

"How's your annex coming along?" Val asked Jaz.

Jaz sighed. "It's nearly finished. We've split it off completely from the house with a fence now, especially as Mum and Dad aren't moving in."

"No point in them moving, if they're happy where they are, love," Val said. "I was born in me house, I'd hate to leave it."

"Sorry, Jaz," Belle said.

Jaz laughed. "I keep telling you to stop apologising, I get it. As Holly points out, I tend to take over."

"But we all love you for it," Holly said.

Jaz sat up straight. "But on the plus side, the rent will bring money in."

"So, you're letting it out?" Mitch asked.

"In the short term. I sold the Wells flat to buy the cottage, so can't make another capital gain this year else I'll get slaughtered by the tax man. I was thinking of taking a mortgage on it as Dave wants me to release him from the business and totally buy him out."

"Are you actually going to allow him to retire?" Holly asked.

"Yes, he's got two more RVs to shift. But he can go at any time. He's putting pressure on himself. And he knows the better the sales, the bigger dividend and more chance that I can buy him out. He'll be free of me," she added with a laugh.

"Lucky man," Len said.

"I love Uncle Dave, I'm gonna miss him," Mikey said.

"Yeah me too," Noah added.

"He's not going anywhere. He's still spending the summers here and the winters in the Canaries. And he always comes back for Christmas with Grace and Brendan living here."

"When's Brendan due back?" Val asked after Grace's boyfriend.

"He'll be back in the UK full-time in a few weeks. He

was already supposed to be here. It keeps being extended," Jaz said.

Warren listened to them in silence as the family ate and discussed the first day of the new term with the children. He dug into the cottage pie. With it were freshly shelled and blanched peas and a smooth gravy. August had flown by. He'd been busy with the project and the committee he'd joined. He'd spent a lot of time with Sam after the meetings. The guy seemed genuinely interested in environmental issues. And Nina's father had met with them a few times as well. He was definitely making a difference to Sam. Tony had even been telling his protégé that he had a big future in politics and should start preparing for a career in government. Warren smiled. Tony was certainly someone who liked to push people to do their very best and he could understand why Nina was so ambitious – where she'd inherited it from.

He gave an inward sigh as a picture of Nina came into his mind. He could not contemplate that she didn't feel the same way about him as he did about her. But if only he could get her alone, for a chat. He'd seen her at the home darts games, but Katie from the store did seem to monopolise him. He was forever trying to egg Rob on to ask the woman out as he knew Rob was keen on her. He was brought out of his thoughts by Jaz.

"Oh no!" she said as her phone dinged. "The computer's gone down at work and Dave's stuck trying to put a contract through for an RV. We can't let this sale fail, it's worth forty K to us." She stared at Warren. "You can't do me a massive favour, can you?"

"Sure," he said.

Holly looked over at Jaz and lowered her eyes.

"I was supposed to be giving Nina a lift to her antenatal class. It starts at seven. It's being held in the primary school hall."

Warren nodded. "Of course, I'll drop her." This was his opportunity to spend a short while with Nina. Even if it was for a five-minute drive. He shovelled the cottage pie in.

"Hey, slow down, you'll get indigestion." Jaz said. "You've still got twenty minutes. It takes me ten to get to the showroom, that's why I need you to step in. You've enough time to eat that and your cherry cobbler."

"Yeah, the cherries are from our garden," Mikey said.

"Me freezer's bursting with them," Val added.

WARREN WAITED FOR NINA, wondering whether she would mind arriving at the school in the old van. He got out and opened the door for her as she appeared.

"Thanks," she said. "I hear Jaz has an emergency."

"Thousands of pounds at stake, apparently." He put his hand out to help her up.

"She sells such high-ticket items." She took his hand. "I used to get nervous selling a dress for a couple of thousand, let alone an item worth six figures." She settled down on the seat and he closed the door.

Inside the van, Nina continued: "I would have driven myself but my car's still having its service. Jaz was sorting it for me. She's been ever so good. I've been well and truly taken under her wing."

"Does it need work?" He started the engine.

"She arranged a full service so it's in tip top condition before the baby comes. And she's taking off the tired stickers with my old business logo on. It's not finished yet."

Warren thought back to the look Holly gave Jaz across the dinner table. Surely she hadn't concocted the two stories to get them together? *No, she wouldn't do that,* he thought, especially when Holly had told him to give it time.

It was only a short trip to the school and the gates were open. He drew up beside a car and jumped from the van and went around to help Nina out. The baby bump was now prominent, but he thought it suited Nina. He realised he would think anything suited Nina.

"Oh, my goodness. It's not Nina, is it?" A woman said who was getting out of the car parked beside them.

"Hi, Chloe," Nina said. "Long time no see."

"Not since I closed my shop. I saw Something Special folded too."

"It didn't fold, as such. I decided not to renew my lease. As I've new priorities."

"Nina's started a new line in children's clothing," Warren said, feeling as if he wanted to cheer her on.

"That's nice," Chloe said with a smile. "And you must be her husband. Pleased to meet you."

"Erm…well…" Nina said.

"We're not married," Warren said, stepping in for her.

"Neither are we," Chloe giggled. "I'd only known Christoph for a matter of months and well…this happened." She rubbed her bump as Christoph came around the Mercedes.

"My car's having a service," Nina said. "Warren's leading a project over at Booth Farm. He's just been awarded his doctorate and is overseeing a silvopasture."

"Wow, pleased to meet you Dr…?"

"It's Dr Hunter," Warren said with a laugh. "But I'm not planning on having people call me that. Warren will do."

"Well, if any of us ladies need a doctor…"

"I don't think a knowledge of crops will be much help there," he said.

"Come along and tell me all about this silver thing, it's intriguing." She hooked her arm in Warren's and led him away.

Warren shot a look back to Nina and she opened her eyes wide and nodded. It appeared she was happy for him to go in.

Once inside the hall, they found it set out with chairs, bean bags and mats.

A woman who was not pregnant welcomed them and gestured around the room. "Take a seat, on a chair, bag or the floor. Wherever you feel most comfortable."

He waited for Nina as Chloe sat on a chair and Christoph took the one beside her. Nina smiled at Warren and gestured towards the chairs.

"Look around the room. Many people make lifelong friends at these groups," the leader said. "Right, if we can go around the room and introduce ourselves."

Nina appeared nervous. "Just go along with it," she whispered to Warren. "Do you mind?"

He smiled. "Of course not." He listened to the introductions.

"And Nina and…"

"Warren," he said.

"Just like Chloe and John," Nina said. "The baby was a complete surprise."

"Yes, we can't wait," Warren added.

"Great. Now that we're all acquainted, let's talk about your birth plans. Take these notebooks and between you, write down the things that are important to you. And any things that would upset you."

Warren felt Nina breathe a sigh of relief and she began to make notes as she chatted to him about her plans for the birth. After the discussion that followed, they focussed on breathing exercises.

WARREN CUT the van's engine outside The Eversley. "I'm coming in as it's training day for the darts team."

"Oh no! It's Monday, I forgot about that. I'm so sorry to have taken you away."

"I messaged Rob to say that both Jaz and I might be late. But they don't actually start until half eight so we're only ten minutes late. Are you going to come in or are you going straight upstairs? Has your mind been bombarded with all that information?"

She smiled. "I knew most of it anyway, I've been reading up on it."

"I learned a lot. It was a real eye-opener!"

"I'm sorry for not telling them you weren't the father. It's just I saw Chloe... I didn't even realise she lived in the area any more and I never specifically said you were the father, just that it was a similar situation to Chloe and a surprise. Luckily she didn't ask me about Ethan."

"I enjoyed it. Hey, I'm happy to come every week."

She paused.

He realised this was his opportunity to speak. "I don't expect anything from you, Nina. You know how I feel. But if you want me there, I'll come along next week and if it gets awkward, we'll say I've been called away or something."

Nina looked at him for a while before speaking. "I did enjoy it a lot more than if I was on my own."

"Great." He wanted to say more but realised he'd have time alone with her over coming weeks and didn't want her to change her mind. "Come on, let's get inside." He jumped out and then helped her down.

"Ah, here they are," Jaz called out as they entered the pub.

"I'll just go upstairs and change," Nina said.

"Be sure to come back down," Jaz said, then when Nina was out of earshot she approached Warren. "How did it go? You stayed then?"

"Yes."

She clapped her hands. "I love it when a plan comes together."

"You didn't!"

"She just needs a little push!" She turned and shouted. "Right, you lot, who's next?"

CHAPTER 31

ina had finally given in and bought clothes designed for maternity. She'd been avoiding it, wearing regular baggy dresses and stretchy lounge wear, but all she wanted now was total comfort. She'd purchased some over-the-bump jeans in a soft material and a selection of bump-hugging tops which would not let a draft in. Autumn had arrived. She was still living at the pub. She'd grown to like the room and it was big enough for the cot to go at the end of the bed, if she failed to secure a rental. She'd been so tied up with the new children's clothing line that she'd not dedicated herself to the home hunt. She knew she was throwing herself into the baby clothes business so she didn't have to think about anything else. She'd heard nothing from Ethan and whenever she'd met his mother, he was never the topic of conversation.

She looked out of the window. The few trees on the green were shedding their brown and gold leaves. It was already turning dark and the lights were on in some of the cottages in the cul-de-sacs. Nina wondered whether she would still be in The Eversley Arms when the Christmas lights were switched on. A fir tree not far from the pub was usually decorated during December.

She smiled as she thought of Warren. It was the first darts match of the winter league that evening and he was excited about the first game. They'd become closer, having attended five antenatal classes together. While there, she felt as if he was her real partner. But she could not let herself go and allow herself to explore their connection. What if he let her down? And it wasn't just her, he would be letting the baby down too. She heard a cheer coming from the pub below and made her way down the stairs, through to the bar.

"Right guys, stay off the booze until you've played you individual games," Jaz shouted. "Do you hear me?"

Reverend Stephens took a quick sip of his pint then placed his glass on a table.

"I feel a pint loosens me up," Carl said.

"I said no! If Rob can stay off the booze while he works here, you lot can go without it for an hour or so."

Carl muttered something under his breath.

They'd finished bottom of the summer season, but only by one point. Since then, the practice nights had continued and they also met on a Friday to play against each other.

"I want A-game, people." Jaz gestured at them.

"I feel nervous," Grace said.

"The blokes playing you will be the nervous ones," Rob assured her. "Worrying you'll beat them. You've won a lot more games than a few others in the team."

"That's because they put their worse players against me."

"Don't put yourself down," Helen said. "You're a great player."

"I agree," Reverend Stephens said. "Warren's always saying you'll be one of our best if you focus on your confidence."

"Surprise!"

Helen turned and grinned at her son as he entered the pub.

Jaz spun around and groaned. "What are you doing here?"

"That's no way to greet a man who's been away."

"Brendan!" Grace called out.

Nina smiled at the couple as Grace's boyfriend scooped her up. He had a healthy-looking tan.

"Put her down!" Jaz said scowling. "She has to be focussed for her game."

"I can't wait,' Brendan said then released her and gave Helen a hug. "Hi, Ma." He gestured towards the dart board. "Who're you playing against?"

"The Dog and Horn," Reverend Stephens said. "Nice to see you back."

"They always thrash us," Carl said. "So don't expect much."

Jaz had her hands on her hips. "Stop the negative talk! We can win."

"Don't tell me you've drugged your dad?" Rob asked.

"Hmm, that's a good idea for the cup match!" she added.

Everyone laughed.

Nina caught Warren's eye as he entered the pub and approached her.

"You look nice," he said.

She looked down at her bump. "I feel huge."

"Well not long to go, then there'll be two of you."

She leaned up and gave him a kiss on the cheek, then whispered in his ear. "Good luck."

His face filled with a smile, which lasted as the team warmed up at the dart board.

Katie sat next to Nina as she took a stool at a poseur table.

"You seem to be getting on with Warren. He's so excited about the baby being born, it's all he talks about."

"Really?" Nina asked.

"Yes. Have you found somewhere else to live? It's only a few weeks away, isn't it?"

"Jaz says her letting agent has the perfect place for me and it'll be ready to view tomorrow afternoon." Jaz had invited her to her place for lunch the next day and said she would drive her to see it. "Although, I quite like it in Eversley," Nina added.

Katie sighed. "The village is so tight-knit. I'm happy living above my shop, but the thing I can't find is a man. I did like Warren, but apart from the fact that he's so into you, he wasn't what I expecting."

"What were you expecting?" Nina asked, interested to hear what it was someone could possibly not like about Warren.

"Well, he looks hard, with the tattoos and everything. And the muscles. But he's all brains and well…too *nice*."

Nina laughed. "When you get to my age, all you want is nice."

255

"Everyone knows he's besotted with you, but that he's not your type. So you do like him?"

"It's not down to type," Nina said, not surprised she was the subject of the village gossip. "He's young and has so much to achieve. He's just got his doctorate and I can't see him wanting to stick with me, and it's not just me, is it?" She realised she was oversharing, especially as Katie wasn't that close to her. "I don't want to hold him back and ruin his life."

"You're so sensible, someone who thinks with their head. That's what I should do. But age difference doesn't matter. I've often gone for an age gap, in both directions."

Nina looked across at Rob. That was an age gap and it seemed Katie was not bothered. "Rob's single and he's a hard man. He was a boxer."

"I guess. I've never been a fan of boxing. He does slip me a few free drinks."

"I doubt they're free. Jaz would come down on him like a tonne of bricks if he gave drinks away. He'll be paying for those himself!"

"Really?"

"Yes. Have you chatted to him much?"

"No, not really." She laughed. "Other than thanking him for the free drinks."

"I think you'd like him if you got to know him."

They turned around as the Dogs filed in, and the pub became extremely busy. Nina found herself a seat, away from the noise at the other end of the bar, and stayed there until the matches were over and the team were eating food. Warren approached her with two sausage-filled rolls.

"Want one?"

"Yes, please. I shouldn't really eat before bed, but I can't say no. I heard the Dogs celebrating."

Warren sat beside her. "It was close."

"You've come so far," Nina said.

"And the Dogs are the top team," Jaz said as she passed them on the way back from the toilets. "We might have a decent chance in the league and we're still learning and developing, whereas they've reached their peak." She turned and shouted to the team. "Right, you lot. We need to beat the Dogs in the cup match at the end of the season. If we win the cup, I'll take you all on a bender to Newquay."

There was a collective cheer to which the Dogs shouted out that they had no chance. Nina laughed at Jaz. She made a good manager.

CHAPTER 32

*I*t was a chilly morning as Nina sat in the arts hub at the sewing machine, wearing fingerless gloves and a huge woollen cardigan belonging to her mother. As she cut the thread from the machine, she yawned. She'd not had a great night's sleep after the late evening hot dog and had slept sitting up due to indigestion. She'd come to the conclusion that overeating was not a good idea when her stomach was being squashed by the baby.

She wondered what the rental was that Jaz's letting agent had found. Part of her decided she wasn't going to like it. There was something homely about living in Eversley, and while the pub was not ideal, she was used to it and with all her things inside, it felt like so much longer than three months that she had lived there. Far from rushing by, her pregnancy had felt as if it was stretching out endlessly, as if she'd always been this way.

She placed the dress with the others she had made in that style, wondering whether Jaz had heard from Crystal.

The influencer was planning a social media video featuring her dresses and the new baby hamper. Crystal was backed up with paid-for promotions and said it would take a while to get to, as she was fitting it in as an extra. Nina did not complain considering Crystal was promoting her clothes for free. With that in mind, Nina had sent, via Jaz, clothes suitable for a variety of seasons.

Nina had a lot of stock saved up now since the farmers' markets had stopped. She now had five people at their sewing machines and a knitter working for her, being paid per item and at that stage she was only just about breaking even but knew if she managed to sell the stock she had so far, she would be into a decent profit. It was time she knew to focus more on her website and sales, and she didn't need to also make the clothes, but she found it so calming. For her it had come full circle and again was therapeutic.

She shivered; it was getting too cold in the arts hub for her to work on a day when it was officially closed. And there wasn't space at The Eversley Arms to sew. She pulled her coat on over the cardigan, scanning the room which had more of a barn feeling without other bodies in there, or the heating on. She was the only person working there that day. In the winter, Holly only opened three days a week, but Nina longed to sit at the sewing machine and also was fine with being the only person there. She wasn't sure how often she would be able to get to the sewing machine after the baby was born. She looked down at her bump, which made it trickier as she was not as close to the machine as she used to be thanks to the obstruction. She took in a sharp intake of breath as the baby kicked and smiled, massaging her bump where the foot had been.

She glanced to the side, assessing whether there would be enough space for the pram next to her station – she had no idea how she would cope after the birth. But knew that at least she had enough other people able to make clothes for her.

"How can you stand the cold in here?" Holly called out to her as she entered the barn. "You won't be working in here throughout the winter. I'm arranging for you to be set up somewhere else."

"Where?" Nina asked, quite pleased as her hands felt as if they were going to seize up.

"I'm still sorting it. But no worries, as from tomorrow you'll be able to work in the warm."

"Thank you," Nina said. Lovelands Nursery had all sorts of spaces.

"Jaz asked me to give you a lift over, I'm joining you both for lunch.

"Great." Nina tidied her work station then stood up and followed Holly out of the barn and waited as she locked the door.

She headed for Holly's van.

"No, we're taking the car," she said with a laugh. "I remember climbing into my old transit when I was as pregnant as you. It was awful."

"You were carrying twins. I climb into your old transit every Monday night when Warren takes me to the ante-natal classes."

Nina got into Holly and Mitch's family car and had to agree that it was indeed more comfortable than a van. She noticed the children's seats in the back. She'd already bought a whole baby travel system with a car seat and had practised fixing it into her car, which was tricky with her bump so large. She was looking forward to feeling a lot more mobile again. *Not long now,* she thought.

They drove the short distance to the village green and then into Ashbury Gardens and drew up at Jaz's place.

"They've finished the annex off then!" Nina said, looking at the freshly painted property and the new separate path that had been laid to the pavement.

"Yes, as you can see it's not an annex any more!" Holly said.

"All that work when she hoped her parents would move in. At least it'll sell for a good price."

Jaz appeared on the threshold of the annex and gestured behind. "Do you want to come in and take a look before we have lunch?"

"Yes please." Nina said and walked up the path. As she stepped over the threshold, she smelled the freshness of the place. "It's beautiful," she said, wishing she could afford a place like it and wondering who was buying it. Nina wasn't in a position to raise a mortgage. Her savings would be enough for a deposit, but without an income, no bank would agree to lend her the required funds. But she'd stopped thinking about all the things she couldn't have.

"Come through to the lounge," Jaz said.

"It's so nice." Nina looked out to the end where there were French windows leading to a garden with a stone wall one side, and new fencing the other, separating it from the larger cottage. From the living room was a door leading to a kitchen, also with French windows. "Who's buying this place?" she asked.

"Wait until you see upstairs," Jaz said.

She walked into the master bedroom, looking out to

the garden. "If only I was in a position to buy. I would have snapped it off you."

"Jaz, stop it," Holly said. "I can't take it any more."

Jaz laughed then approached Nina. "I want you to move in here."

"I can't afford it."

"Not yet, but I can't sell it this year anyway. You can rent it, until you can afford it. You'll be close to the hub."

Nina blinked, imagining herself living there.

"Look at the other two bedrooms," Holly said.

Nina felt overwhelmed. Could she really live in this perfect home? "Are you sure?" she whispered.

"Trust me, chick, you'll be doing me a favour. A woman from the PTA wants to move here and she'll do my head in as a neighbour!"

Holly put an arm around Nina. "Jaz means it, she wouldn't offer it otherwise. So is it a yes? You'll move here?"

Nina nodded and then descended into tears.

Jaz pulled her phone from her suit jacket pocket and made a call. "She said yes!"

Holly laughed. "Your parents are up the road with a hire van full of your baby stuff. We would have filled the place up but held off just in case you didn't want to live next door to Jaz."

Nina went to Jaz and gave her a hug. "Thank you so much."

THE REST of the day was taken with arranging the items her father brought in with Julian's help. Holly collected her sewing machine from the hub and they'd placed it in the third bedroom. They'd also brought the bed from her room back in Wells. It had originated from the flat she lived in before she met Ethan, along with a sofa which was originally hers also. Her parents had bought her a folding table and chairs for the kitchen. When finished, they ordered a fish and chip supper.

Nina raised her glass of water as a toast. "Thanks everyone. I don't know what to say, other than thanks."

"We're all here for you, chick," Jaz said.

CHAPTER 33

*W*arren entered the living room of Booth Farm. Millie and Harry were seated at the table eating take away Chinese.

"Wow, you've dressed to impress," Millie said as he approached them.

"Who are you off out with?" Harry asked.

"His girlfriend," Millie said.

"She's not my girlfriend," Warren answered.

"She won't be, will she? Unless you ask her to be," Millie said with a laugh.

Warren smiled as Millie teased him. She was always asking him when he was going to make his relationship with Nina 'exclusive' as she liked to call it. That term was irrelevant to him as he'd never been one to see more than one woman at a time. But even though he was only friends with Nina, he'd never felt so close to a woman. Sharing her journey, listening to her plans with her business and the baby. Never had he felt he wanted to be with someone this much, to make them smile, to make them happy.

"She must be mad not to want to be your girlfriend," Millie said. "Anyway, we've bought you a present."

Harry pushed a wrapped package across the table. "Happy birthday, Warren."

"Thanks guys." He opened it to find a soft khaki beanie hat.

"It matches those cargos you always wear," Millie said.

He laughed. "Yeah, it does. I needed a new one, it's freezing first thing." He'd also received a card and a gift from Nick and Jane and cards and gifts from Holly and Mitch at the family meal the day before. Val had also made him a cake and they'd sung happy birthday and all the kids joined in and the twins had made him a card. He was feeling well and truly spoilt, but his best present was from Nina – an invitation to dinner.

He left through the front door as the back had become muddy and he didn't want to get his shoes in a mess. He'd spent ages soaking in the bath, scrubbing his nails, trying to look like someone who would normally eat at an award-winning bistro and not like someone who worked all day in a field.

He took the road, and kept close to the hedge, turning on the torch app on his phone in case a car passed. He smiled to himself as the village green came into view and the buildings looked inviting, emitting a yellow glow from their signs and the windows. It was a real treat to see Nina on a Tuesday. To see her two days running. Mondays had become his favourite day of the week. Nina ate with them at Booth Farm, then they both attended the antenatal class to spend time with a group of people who thought they were a couple. *Calm down man,* he told himself. The classes would soon come to an end. One couple had already had their child and Nina's was due in only two weeks and they said that at thirty-eight weeks, the baby would be considered full term. So it could really be any day. Warren wondered whether Nina would keep up with the friendships she'd made at the classes. He felt sick at the thought of her telling people they'd split up if she had to explain his absence in her life at future meet ups. What would they think of him? It made him even more determined to win her over. His main goal was to be the full support she needed over the coming weeks and he hoped that when the baby was born she would let him into her life, completely.

When he reached the bistro, he opened the door. Nina was already there. She smiled at him from a table and a young woman approached him.

"Hi, I'm Natalie, welcome to the Eversley Bistro. Shall I take your coat?"

Nina smiled at him as he reached the table and he kissed her on the cheek. "Thanks for bringing me here, I always wondered what this place looked like on the inside." It was an intimate setting with a mixture of stone and plastered walls, displaying a few pictures of the village.

They were seated in the corner.

"It's popular in here," he said, looking around. Every table was filled.

"It's booked up months in advance," Nina said. "But Julian blocks out a couple of tables every week for locals. I hope you like it. Adam's an amazing chef."

Warren studied the menu. "Is there anything you recommend?"

"The menu changes every week," Nina said. "But I'm having the salmon pasta."

"That sounds good, and so does the Thai pork belly. I'll have that." Warren put the menu down. "You look…" All he could hear was the word *beautiful* in his head and his mind momentarily went blank.

Nina looked at him expectantly.

"…happy," he said.

"I am. I didn't realise how tense I was, not having a place suitable for the baby, until I got it. After being in the pub for months, the cottage feels like a haven."

"What's it like living next door to Jaz?"

"No one bothers me and Jaz is really busy negotiating her motorhome stock for next year. And she's been filling in at the pub with Julian, now Simon has left completely, to give Rob his days off. He's moved into The Eversley now I've left. But moving to Ashbury Gardens has made me feel so settled and if things keep going as they are with my business, in a year or so when I've some solid accounts, I might be able to raise a mortgage to buy it."

Warren stopped himself from saying he'd love to go back there with her and see the place. He was becoming increasingly self-conscious about his feelings for Nina, maybe it was because it appeared he couldn't hide them from the rest of the world. He found it confusing with the mixed signals she gave him, feeling she liked him, yet her words always suggested they were just friends. He didn't want to overstep the mark and ruin their friendship, especially at a time when she needed a friend most.

"Have you had a nice birthday?" she asked.

"It's been a good day on the field and the evening's even better."

She took a sip of her water. "How's your lottery application going?"

He felt a dull sickness seep into his gut. "I'm in the latter stages. Although I'm worried about the vetting process."

"Why would that make you nervous?"

He lowered his voice. "As you know, I've a troubled past."

"You were a wayward child, not a wayward adult."

Warren nodded. "But there's still a record of it. Even if I was fifteen." He wasn't sure how far back checks were made but the form specifically asked for any convictions, so he'd had no choice but to add it, because if he didn't and it was flagged up, he would be considered to be lying and that would be an instant no to funding.

"There's something you've kept back, isn't there?" she said, looking at him over her glass of water. When he didn't reply she continued, "You can tell me about it later, if it's worrying you this much."

He smiled back. It would be good to tell someone, he'd carried it with him for so long. But on the other hand, he didn't want Nina to be put off. But it was also delaying him posting the form, which was still in his room, in the envelope. Everything had been completed with supporting documents. All he needed was the stamp.

"Stop looking so worried. It's your birthday." Nina touched his hand.

He smiled back at her and pushed his thoughts aside, appreciating the feel of her touch.

The meal was delicious, the pork belly had been slow-cooked until tender and then crisped and glazed with a tangy and aromatic sauce with jasmine rice. They chatted about the bistro and the chef, Adam, came out for a short chat with them. Then Julian and Jaz came through from the back holding a chocolate birthday cake, just big enough for two with a candle atop as the rest of the diners joined in and sang *Happy Birthday*.

"Thanks guys," Warren said, having blown out the candle, thoroughly embarrassed but also touched at the same time.

Warren sipped his coffee, feeling completely satisfied having shared the decadent birthday cake with Nina, which was a warm chocolate fudge. Adam had brought out salted caramel ice cream to accompany it.

"Did you have a nice evening?" Nina asked.

"I did and thank you."

"I have something else for you," Nina said. "At my place."

"Okay," he said. Being alone with Nina would be the best birthday present of all. He didn't add that but wondered what it was she had got him.

They took the short stroll back. It had rained so they walked around the periphery of the green rather than across it and Nina slipped her arm into his. He slowed, wanting to savour walking along with her like that, feeling so close to her, as if she was his and they were together, as a couple.

Once at her new home of 5a Ashbury Gardens, he followed her inside and removed his shoes. "This is great," he said, feeling instantly at home.

Warren knew cottages in Eversley sold at a premium. He wished he'd the money to support her. *Slow down,* he told himself. He knew with the weekly antenatal classes he'd been getting carried away. As much as he wanted her, the reality was that Nina belonged in a different class to him. He'd never lived in a home this sleek. He'd often been in crowded homes, and then in the small second bedroom in the flat above the café back in Bristol. Or tiny rooms in student accommodation. The room he had at Booth Farm was the largest he'd ever had, but that was not his either, he was a tenant. He realised their backgrounds couldn't be more different.

"Are you okay?" Nina asked. "Is it because I asked you earlier about your past?"

No, it wasn't that. It was that he felt he would never be good enough to take care of a woman who had spent a lifetime living in comfort. But how could he tell her that?

She grabbed his hand which felt so soft in his. "Come on, tell me all about the thing you're worried about, the thing that you don't want the lottery funding to find out about. Get it off your chest and out of the way."

He'd not told anyone, other than Nick and Jane, and that was only because Darius had forced him to after he'd found out about it through his job as a police officer.

Nina motioned for him to take a seat on the sofa and then sat beside him. All he could think of was holding her, of kissing her, as he looked into her warm brown eyes.

"So, what happened?" she asked.

He took a deep breath, realising it was best to get straight to the point, with no preamble, no excuses. "There was this guy, Logan. He was older than Scottie and me. We were still kids, fifteen, Logan was nearly twenty."

"Scottie, he's the one always pestering you for money, who you grew up with?"

"Yes. Logan asked us to help him with a house clearance, he called it. He said there would be fifty pounds for each for us. When we got to the house, in a van he told us he'd borrowed from a mate, we went around to the back door which wasn't locked. It didn't strike me as odd at the time."

"He was breaking in?" Nina asked.

"Yes. He started pulling open drawers then ordered us to do the same and take anything that looked valuable. I asked him what was going on and he said an old lady had died and we were doing a house clearance of anything valuable with the rest of it going to Staple Hill tip the next day. Scottie was a lot more gullible than me and carried on, but I could tell Logan was lying – he was twitchy and pulled the curtains closed, so no one could see us. I challenged him. He came up to me." Warren stopped, remembering the vile look on Logan's face, the way he'd stuck his finger right up to his nose. "He told me to shut up, that we were in it together and if he got caught, so would we."

Nina rubbed his arm. "Go on."

"An elderly lady appeared at the lounge door, in her nightgown. 'Who are you?' she asked. Logan was surprised and asked why she wasn't at bingo and she said she had a cold, then asked whether he was Betty's grandson."

"He was robbing his grandmother's friend?"

"Yes, then he went for her. She screamed and he kicked her then grabbed the bag he had and ran out. He called us to follow him and Scottie went, but I couldn't leave the woman. She had blood on her face and was sobbing. It was bad. Scottie came back and called me from the door. Then I heard the sirens – I guess one of the neighbours had called the police. Scottie ran off and I heard the van screech away. I felt paralysed, as if I couldn't leave. I slumped down to the carpet and waited with the lady, telling her help was coming. It felt like it was only seconds until the police got there."

"What did you tell them?"

"I couldn't snitch on Logan. I was petrified of him and I considered Scottie to be my brother. So I was taken in."

"You took the blame for breaking in and assaulting an old lady?"

Warren hung his head. "I had no choice."

"What happened to her?"

"Thankfully she only had cuts and bruises, but they reported it in the local press, that a youth had broken in and beaten her up and showed a photo of her face swollen with black eyes. But the police knew it wasn't me as the neighbour who called them described Logan and Scottie running from the scene and driving off. They knew it was Logan, they'd been after him for a while, they told me so, saying that I'd have no record if I agreed to be a witness against him, but if I didn't, I would go down on record as having committed a crime. But I wouldn't rat on them. They even had him in for questioning, but couldn't pin it on him. Logan always got away with it. They found no evidence. The van he'd used was stolen so wasn't traced back to him. The old lady wasn't able to identify Logan in a line up and picked the wrong guy and said she couldn't be sure it was Logan as she hadn't been wearing her glasses. That he probably just looked like him. The police were easy on me in the end, and said I did a good thing, waiting with the poor lady, but I was still charged with being an accessory to burglary and received a reprimand.

I was told if I slipped up again I would be punished." He took in a deep breath. He remembered, six months later, when Darius had shown him his police badge in the café for attempting to steal his bike. At the time he'd thought that was it.

He looked into Nina's eyes. "I've had to disclose it, and I'm worried it'll ruin my chances. I've not told anyone before and didn't disclose it on my university application. So I feel a bit awkward, as if I should mention it to Mitch. I need the funding so he can be compensated for me taking the field."

"And you've been carrying this around with you?"

He looked into her eyes as she placed her hand on his forearm and in that moment felt so close to her. He moved an inch forward. *What are you doing?* he asked himself, then leaned back, thinking of something to say to diffuse the situation. He'd told himself not to come on to her, that wasn't what a friend did. "Are you going to show me the place?"

"In a minute." Nina leaned forward until he felt her lips upon his. It was a brief kiss. She leaned back and smiled at him. "You look stunned."

"I…"

She leaned forward again and this time it was not a quick brush of the lips. He wrapped his arms around her, gently pulling her close as he felt the warmth of her lips, pressing his harder against hers as his mind swam and body reacted, so much so that he wanted to cocoon her and stay that way. She put her hands around his neck and brought him closer and ran her hand over his hair, setting his body on fire. As the kiss became deeper and passionate his whole being wanted her.

She pulled away. "The baby's kicking," she said with a laugh. "It's saying no, Ma let me out."

He smiled at her as her eyes seemed to glisten, reflecting the warm light of the nearby lamp. "Nina. I've wanted to do that so much, for months," he said gazing at her, his vision slightly blurred.

"Me too," she said. "And if you were wondering, that was your birthday present."

"You planned it?" He chuckled then gazed again into her warm eyes. "You're the most beautiful woman I've ever set eyes on and each time I see you I have to battle with myself not to tell you." Now that he'd spoken, it was as if he could not stop himself. "All I think of is you, all I want is to be with you. To hold you, to care for you, to protect you. Sorry." He paused and rubbed a hand over his head. "I'm saying too much."

She pulled him close for another kiss, which told him she was far from put off by his expression of emotion.

After a while she leaned her head on his shoulder.

"I wish I could provide for you," Warren said. "To buy this place for you two and everything you wish for."

"Hey, Warren. Ethan could afford buy me anything and where's he? Thousands of miles away. He may as well be on the moon. You want me for me, at a time when I've been feeling lost and uncertain. Whereas he just ran away from it. You're the perfect man. My worry has been that you'll wake up one day and wonder where your life went, throwing opportunities away to be bogged down with me."

"Nina, my life has been hard. But you've opened something inside me, a feeling I've never experienced. You've given me hope. Even though you've pushed me away at times."

"I'm sorry. I've been scared."

"I know what it's like to be let down," he said. "Starting with my mother."

Nina softened her voice. "She died. I'm sure she loved you."

Warren felt a rush of emotion he wasn't expecting, so strong he couldn't control it and his eyes brimmed with tears. His mother was the only woman, the only person he had ever uttered the words to – *I love you.* He swallowed. "Sorry, I don't know where that came from," he said, his voice gruff.

"Hey, oh my goodness, I didn't mean to upset you on your birthday!" Nina put her arms around him and squeezed him.

He needed to explain and then never to mention it again. He had to get this out of the way, before he could allow himself to move forward. "I was the one who found her." The picture rushed into his mind, a picture he never allowed himself to see, a picture which snuck into his nightmares. He stared at it in his mind, as if allowing it to be seen, his mother lying there, lifeless. "She didn't love me enough, she didn't want me, because she ended it, herself."

Nina pulled away and her chin trembled, then she held him tightly. "I'm so sorry, I didn't realise."

"Because I didn't say. To anyone. Not even Nick and Jane." He took a deep breath. "All I want is to take care of you. And I know we need to take it slow. But at least let's say we're together. Will you allow me to call you my girl-friend and take it from there?"

"I'm scared of being let down," she said and then looked into his eyes. She appeared so fragile.

"I promise you, Nina. I'll never let you down and I'll always be here for you."

"Honestly? Even when I'm in labour?"

"Especially that day, I've already had all the training." He chuckled. "I promise that I'll be there for you."

After a coffee, she showed him the house. In the bedroom, she pulled him to the bed and he lay down beside her and held her close, feeling closer to her than he'd ever felt to anyone in his life since the day his mother left him, and they remained that way, fully clothed, until the early hours of the morning.

CHAPTER 34

When Warren woke in his bed at Booth Farm, he was buzzing and felt completely alive, even though he hadn't arrived home until gone two in the morning.

The autumn sun did it's best to warm him as he took a slow walk to his silvopasture, eating a slice of toast, with his coffee-filled travel mug in his other hand. His phone dinged with a text, so he popped the last of the toast in his mouth and pulled the phone from his pocket. It was from Nina:

Morning. Don't go too far, I'm having regular twinges, this could be the start!

Do you want me to come over? he replied.

Not yet but get anything you want doing done. I'll keep you updated. Can't wait to see you xx

Warren grinned as he neared his field, glancing at the willow he'd planted in the spring, imagining it growing into a fully fledged tree and wondered what the pasture would look like when Nina's child was an adult. He couldn't ever remember feeling this happy. He kept replaying their kisses in his head, how it felt to lie beside her, holding her, relishing the romantic feelings, the type he'd never felt before. Yes, he'd been with women before but that had been a physical thing, not this all-encompassing emotion. He knew in his heart that this must be love, but he still would find that declaration too hard to express verbally. *I don't want to jinx it,* he thought. The child within him was scared of telling someone he loved them, because of what had happened to his mother. He took a deep breath in of the fresh air, his heart swelling at the thought of becoming a stepfather, because that's what he wanted. He couldn't quite believe how lucky he was that she had finally come around to the idea that they could be together, to possibly become a family.

He arrived at the greenhouse and opened the door, breathing in the thick aroma of the plants. He looked for the bulbs he wanted to plant that day, and picked out some garlic and wild leeks which should go in sooner rather than later. He placed his phone on the wooden slats which ran along the length of the greenhouse, as he removed his coat. It was always warm in the greenhouse. Picking up the bulbs, he headed to the door when his mobile phone rang. Realising he should carry his phone with him at all times, considering Nina could go into labour at any moment, he picked it up and frowned – it was Scottie.

He shook his head. *Why didn't I block his number?* Everyone had told him to. To his surprise, it was a video call rather than a voice call. He felt strong now. He had other responsibilities he wanted to take on. He was strong enough to tell Scottie straight – it was over. After hesitating and taking a moment to compose himself, he answered. Scottie's face appeared on the screen.

"Before you start," Warren said. "I'm sorry, mate, but I've a new life and responsibilities, which I can't afford to mess up. I need every penny I have. All our conversations involve you asking me for money. We're done." The night before had cemented that for him. A baby was coming into the world, and he already felt protective of it, as protective as he felt of Nina.

"But you've got to help me!" Scottie cried.

"I saw you, Scottie," Warren said. "Last time I gave you that money, drunk at the Raven on your way to the kebab house. You never gave that money to Logan or your landlord."

He was about to end the call when another face appeared on the screen. One that sent an instant shot of fear to his gut – Logan. He looked much older and had a beard, but Warren would recognise his eyes anywhere, the eyes that had terrified him as a youth.

"Long time no see, grass."

"I never grassed on you. I took the heat." Warren's voice had come out as a growl which surprised him. It was lucky for Logan that he was not face to face. He knew he would now tower over the man. He was the bigger man, not just as far as human nature was concerned.

"You're cosied up with that pig Darius Christou, he knows about the old dear, he told me. But now your brother needs you."

"Scottie isn't my brother," Warren said and meant it.

Logan ignored the comment. "And you're right, he never gave me the money he owed me. Listen to what he has to say, and you listen clear." The picture went back to Scottie.

Warren felt cold and rooted to the spot as his heart thudded.

Scottie's face reappeared. "Logan says he's gonna finish me off if I don't give him what I owe," Scottie pleaded.

Warren heard Logan in the background. "With interest he owes me two grand. I need it by ten tonight."

"Two thousand?" Warren asked.

Scottie's eyes widened. "Please, Warren, this is the last time. I promise."

Logan called out, "If you don't get here with it, you'll never see him again."

Warren never wanted to see Scottie again anyway, but neither did he want him dead. However, he had new responsibilities – there was Nina and the child to think of. The last thing he could do was get mixed up with Logan, who was into just about any dodgy deal going.

"Where are you?" Warren asked.

"Unit 5, Tickton Industrial Estate. Please, mate, please." Scottie's eyes were bloodshot, but wide open. The video call ended.

Warren swore under his breath. He had no intention of giving any of his money to Logan. But what he could do was call Darius. Scottie had brought this on himself and he couldn't help him. He called Darius, but there was no reply. So he texted him, asking him to call immediately as it was an emergency. He returned the phone to his back pocket and picked up the saplings, taking them across the field.

His phone dinged with a text and he grabbed it, thinking it was Darius, but it was Nina.

The contractions are now regular, but really mild. May be a false alarm. Pop over for lunch if you can, I might need to start those breathing exercises. She added a screaming emoji.

Warren smiled, feeling a surge of emotion. He decided to hurry, tidy away and tell Mitch he was signing off, possibly for a day or so. *This could be it,* he thought. He knew enough about the birth process from all of the meetings they'd attended and that there was no telling how long it would take. He texted Nina back to say he would be there. She replied:

See you soon xx

Warren felt excited and needed, realising he'd never felt needed before in his entire life.

After about twenty minutes of planting he left everything neat and tidy as he realised he might not be back to the field for some time. As he made his way towards the farmhouse, he saw a black 4x4 SUV roll into the drive. Two men got out, dressed in dark clothing, and scanned the area until they spotted him. His senses twinged with a pang of fear, inherent from his youth, being able to sniff out what he used to refer to as 'the pigs'. He squinted, thinking it might be Darius, but as the men walked towards him, he realised it wasn't him, but they definitely resembled police.

He walked towards the men as they were clearly headed in his direction. "Can I help you?" he called out.

"Are you Warren Hunter?" one of the men asked.

"Yes. Have you spoken to Sergeant Christou?"

"We'd appreciate it if you accompanied us," the man said, flashing his police badge.

"I've called Sergeant Christou. I can't come now."

"We'll discuss it when we get back to the station."

"Is this about Scott Jackman? Because I've already contacted the police, well, Darius, myself." He wished he'd left a more detailed message rather than *call me.*

"We can't discuss it until we reach the station."

"I'll have to send a text." Warren pulled his phone from his pocket, fear shooting through his chest.

The policeman swiped the phone from him and in no time they'd cuffed him.

"Hey, I have to call my girlfriend."

The other detective placed his hand on his shoulder. "Warren Hunter, I'm arresting you on suspicion of conspiracy to commit a crime. Anything you do say may be used against you."

"Just let me call my girlfriend," he said as they bundled him into the back of the SUV. Panic took over. He heard himself calling out to them to let him go while they strapped him in, as if it was another person crying out. Memories flooded back from his youth, but this time it was worse, he had somewhere to be and someone depending on him and something to lose.

They quickly drove off, the wheels spinning in the gravel.

Warren took deep breaths to calm himself, as he heard the sound of his heart thudding in his ears. He knew shouting out had been a wrong move. He shut his eyes and counted to ten then leaned forward, the cuffs digging into his wrists as the seat belt restricted him. "Can we discuss this and you not treat me like a criminal?" he asked through the grill which separated the back seat from the front. "As I've said, I called Sergeant Christou and you can tell that from my phone, if you want to check it."

The policemen remained silent. For a moment he panicked. Were they really policeman? Or was this some sort of set up by Logan?

"Could I have my phone back, please? I need to call my girlfriend – she's pregnant, and I'm waiting for a call from Darius Christou."

The policemen exchanged a glance. "What's your connection to Christou?"

"He's family. I know we don't look alike – I was adopted by his brother."

The two policemen spoke in hushed tones, but all they did was turn on the siren of the unmarked car and speed around the traffic.

Warren groaned as he looked at the road signs, realising it wasn't the local police station they were taking him to. It was likely to be Bristol – he assumed to the main station. But at least that was where Darius was located. Fear ripped through his chest, a pain he'd not experienced before, the pain at not being able to contact Nina.

As they arrived at Bridewell Police Station, in the centre of Bristol, he asked again, "Could you please call Sergeant Christou?"

"We're taking you to an interview room."

As they entered the building they took him to the desk.

"I'm emptying your pockets," the detective beside him said.

Warren felt panicked. He knew the drill, remembering the last time he was brought to that same station, after the bungled burglary.

"Can I have my phone back? To make my call?"

The duty sergeant ignored him as he took a note of the items, calling them out as he did so. His wallet, his keys and a packet of mints. He guessed his phone had already been whisked away by one of the detectives who had already left.

"Come this way," the remaining detective who still held his arm said. "I'm Detective Bestow." He gestured for him to walk ahead.

After taking his prints and mugshots, Bestow directed him to the corridor. "It's the second on the left."

A uniformed officer followed them into the interview room and stood by the door. Warren was shown to a seat opposite the second detective who was already in place, at a table.

"Can you tell me what this is in connection with?" Warren asked.

Detective Bestow switched on the recording device and recorded the date and who was present.

"I'm Detective Sergeant Shaw. We're following up on an investigation. Could you please explain your relationship with Scott Jackman."

"He's been abducted."

"From the beginning. The details of your relationship."

Warren breathed out and sat back in his chair. The sooner he got this over with, the sooner he could get back to Nina. He had his credit card in his wallet. A taxi would be expensive, but he had to get back. "We grew up together in foster care."

Bestow stared at him. "And your present day relationship?"

"I've nothing to do with Scottie, I've moved on, but he called me today."

The other detective leafed through the papers on the table. "You are telling us that you no longer have a relationship with him at all?"

"That's correct, I've moved on with my life, he hasn't. I've recently obtained a doctorate and am working and living in Eversley village."

"We're aware of that." The detective pulled a photograph from the pile. "For the record, I'm showing Warren Hunter item reference MH343." He pushed the picture towards Warren. "A photograph taken from the security camera at 625 Fishponds Road." He paused. "Can you explain this?"

Warren stared at the grainy picture of himself and Scottie. "That was the day before my parents' wedding."

"Your parents?" Detective Bestow looked at the file. "We have you as an orphan as from the twenty-ninth of October 2001 when Judy Hunter died, and that you spent the rest of your childhood in foster care."

"The couple who became my unofficial parents at age sixteen are Nick and Jane Christou. Look, you can check this with Darius. Can I make a telephone call? I'm allowed one."

"To your solicitor? We'll make it for you."

"No, to my girlfriend."

"I must warn you again that you should call a solicitor. We can arrange for the duty solicitor should you require one."

"My girlfriend's pregnant."

"You're due to be a father?" he asked.

"It's not mine but…" He shook his head not wishing to go into the details, after all officially Nina had been his girlfriend for less than twenty-four hours. And what if they then went after Nina, interviewing her when she was in labour? *Please let it be a false alarm.* No, he couldn't drag her into this, he didn't want her tainted by his past.

"Let's continue." Detective Sergeant Shaw moved the picture closer to Warren. "Why were you pictured with Scott Jackman on Fishponds Road on the third of August?"

"He was in trouble."

"You've been funding his operation?" Detective Bestow handed over another photograph. "For the recording I am passing Warren Hunter item MH344 at 633 Fishponds Road."

Warren looked down at another grainy black and white picture of himself. It was close-up and he presumed it was of him at the cashpoint. His heart beat a little faster, hoping that Darius would arrive soon. He was pleased that he'd already explained the position to him at the wedding, and that Darius knew he'd met Scottie the day before to give him the money in the hope he would stay away while Nick and Jane tied the knot.

"He came to me wanting money. It was my parents' wedding the following day and I didn't want him bugging me. He knew where and when it was taking place."

"And what's your relationship with Frank Logan?" Detective Sergeant Shaw stared at him.

Warren shut his eyes. *Is this really happening?* "The last time I spoke to him was the day of the robbery in 2012, which you must have on your file."

"Maybe you will enlighten us, Dr Hunter?"

"Please, can you call Sergeant Darius Christou. He'll back me up."

"If you don't co-operate we'll have to place you in a holding cell until we make alternative enquiries."

"Logan committed a burglary in 2012 and took myself and Scottie along, telling us we were doing a house clearance job. It's on your records, I was charged with accessory to a burglary but refused to name Logan at the time. I was fifteen and scared of him. As a grown man I can sit here and tell you, he did it and he's abducted Scottie and wants me to pay up. Look, I don't want to have to be here any longer than I have to. My…friend needs me."

"Why did Logan call you today?"

"It was Scottie who called me, he said he owed Logan."

"The phone is registered to Frank Logan."

Warren gulped. Was Scottie working with Logan? A feeling of dread seeped into his veins.

"Logan came on the phone while I was speaking to Scottie…"

"You said the last time you spoke to him was 2012."

"I meant, before today." He shook his head.

"What did Logan say to you?" Detective Sergeant Shaw asked.

"He demanded that I pay him two thousand pounds, otherwise I'd never see Scottie again."

The detectives exchanged a glance.

"So where are you planning to deliver this?"

"I'm not. I called Darius to report it to him, so he can deal with it. But Logan said to drop it at Unit 5 Tickton Industrial estate."

Detective Sergeant Shaw put his hands together. "That's not where the call was made from."

"If you know about the call, I presume you were listening in! Why are you playing games with me?"

"I can assure you, Dr Hunter, we are not playing games. We did not tap the phone, we just know a call was made to you and a rough location of where it originated from and it was nowhere near Tickton. What time are you to drop the funds?"

"By ten o'clock tonight."

"Recording ended at ten fifty-five." Bestow switched the recording device off.

"Can I go now?" Warren asked.

"We need to verify the information you've given us and strongly advise you to contact a solicitor."

"I don't need a solicitor, I need you to contact Darius. Have you?"

"As soon as he arrives at the station, we'll alert him." The detectives both stood up and the officer who had been guarding the door approached him and unclipped his cuffs from the table.

Warren panicked as the uniformed officer led him to a cell. "You can't just put me in here? I'm entitled to a call, I know that. Let me make the call." His heart pounded and his vision became blurred.

"We're able to hold you for twenty-four hours." The officer uncuffed him then shut the door behind him.

Warren paced the room like a wild animal, looking around, remembering his youth, as fresh in his mind as it had ever been. He thumped on the door in frustration.

An officer flipped the window open. "Yes?"

"I need to get out of here!"

The man just flipped it shut again. Warren slumped to the bench and put his head in his hands. "Stay calm," he whispered to himself as he waited to hear from Darius. "He'll sort it out."

CHAPTER 35

ina sat in her new conservatory. The sunny weather they'd been having was interrupted by rain. She listened to droplets of water upon the glass roof, it calmed her as her parents were in the kitchen preparing lunch and she needed to explain to them that Warren would be over to join them and that he would be a part of her and her baby's lives. Which was awkward since she'd spent months convincing them they were just friends.

She smiled. She was sure that when they saw them together, they'd know it was love. Even if they had not uttered those three words to each other. Her bump tightened again and she took a deep breath in and closed her eyes. It was unlikely that she was having practice contractions as although they were mild, they'd been constant since she'd woken up. She was excited about seeing Warren, he was always so interested at the antenatal classes. It seemed only right that they experience this process together. She put the final push out of her mind. She needed to stay calm.

She wondered how to tell her parents. In a way she felt she'd always known that she wanted to be with Warren and the only reason she'd held back was that that she was being sensible. Even though they'd decided to take it slow, she felt she wanted him to move in with them, from the start of family life, to be the father from the very first moment. The contraction came to an end. It was similar to period pain – at least it only lasted for a minute at a time. She knew this early stage of labour could last some time, even days. In her mind she pushed out thoughts of the pain she knew she would endure over the coming hours and focussed on holding her baby in her arms, with Warren by her side.

Her parents entered the room carrying a tray each, one with toasted teacakes, the sweet, yeasty fragrance filling the small conservatory. The other was laden with a pot of tea and cups, a service that Sumitra had bought her. They sat on the new rattan suite, another gift her parents could not resist buying her. She had told them to hold off but they said they had taken it out of the wedding fund which they were going to spend on her anyway.

"You look deep in thought," Sumitra said as she passed Nina a cup of tea. "Are you having another contraction?"

"One has just finished," Nina said, picking up a notebook where she was recording the length and their frequency. She glanced at her parents as they settled on the opposite sofa. "I wanted us to have a chat."

"Are you worried about the future, angel?" Tony asked.

"No, in fact I am feeling really positive about it."

"That's a relief," Sumitra said. "You'll be an amazing mother. An inspiration to any child."

"You know Warren has been a real support to me?"

"Yes, I admit, I was worried about him to start with. But he's been a good friend," Sumitra said with a sniff. "Even if I thought you two were romantically attached. You've reassured me, you're just friends."

"Yes, he's been a great friend," she said. "And the warmest, most loving man I've met. Well apart from you, Dad," she added with a laugh.

"Loving?" Sumitra said and Nina noticed her father watching her intently. He clearly sensed she was about to make an announcement.

"He's going to be with me at the hospital."

"For the birth?" Sumitra asked. "Isn't that a bit… well…personal?"

"Yes, it is. But he's been at all of the antenatal classes."

"You never mentioned that?" Sumitra said.

"And he's going to be around a lot after the baby's born," Nina added quickly.

Tony returned his toasted teacake to his plate. "Are you trying to tell us you're having a serious relationship with this young man?"

Nina paused. Her father was making Warren sound like a boy, not the man he was.

"How on earth is he going to provide for you both?" Sumitra continued.

"He doesn't have to, Ma. He wants to be a part of our lives, we get along so well, he's been so good, he's been my best friend."

"Well, he's certainly landed on his feet if he is moving

in with you here," Sumitra grumbled, wiping her hands on a napkin.

"We only decided to be officially girlfriend and boyfriend yesterday. And to take it slowly. We have not discussed him moving in." She didn't add that she wanted him to.

"Do you love him?" Tony asked.

"I do. And I want you to be pleased for me."

Sumitra smiled but this juxtaposed her eyes, which emitted a concern she was clearly trying to hide. "Of course we are, aren't we Tony."

Her father gave a silent nod and she knew neither of them were convinced, but at least they did not challenge her. She smiled to herself, knowing how amazing Warren was and that he would prove them wrong in time. It was clear to everyone else around them that they were suited. Whilst her parents cleaned up the elevenses things, she messaged Warren.

I've told Ma and Dad that we're together. See you when you get here.

LATER, Nina put her head back as she sat on her sofa, still listening to the pitter-patter of rain. She took in a deep breath as she felt her bump tighten. The pain was becoming more intense and she knew this was the real deal, the baby had started its journey. She'd messaged Warren twice more and she'd not heard back from him. He was two hours late. After trying his phone, which went straight to voicemail, she called Holly, who checked with Mitch. No one had seen Warren since breakfast.

Where is he? She hadn't felt like eating lunch. She hadn't eaten since elevenses. Her bump tightened again. She opened her eyes, the pains increasing in intensity. She began the breathing exercises she'd been taught to manage the pain.

Ten minutes later, she felt another. She took a sharp breath and picked up her phone. Still nothing from Warren. "Where are you?" she said aloud and then called his number but again, it went straight to voicemail. Her lips trembled and she battled away tears. *Where's he got to?* It wasn't like she hadn't warned him.

An hour later, in the kitchen, she leaned with her palms face down on the cool worktop. She looked up as she saw Jaz arrive home. She rapped on the window and gestured to her then made her way slowly to the front door.

"Are you okay chick?" Jaz asked.

"My labour's started," she said in a forced voice.

"Really? Who do you want me to call? Where's your hospital bag?"

"In my bedroom," she said in a small voice.

"Have you managed to contact Warren?" Jaz asked. "Holly messaged earlier to ask if I knew where he was."

Nina shook her head as a contraction set in.

"How were you going to get to the hospital, surely you weren't going up in that old van of his?"

"I planned to add him to my car insurance. I didn't expect it to start today. I wasn't due for two weeks." She stopped and leaned against the door frame and moaned as a stronger contraction ripped through her lower body. "I'm worried about Warren."

"I'll just change then take you in," Jaz said.

"I can't go yet. I called the hospital," she said. "The contractions need to be closer together."

"Where are your parents?"

"I sent them away, thinking Warren would be here. I told them to rest in case I needed Ma at the hospital tonight. And they'll be asking questions about Warren. I told them we're together." She cried out as a sob escaped. "I wish I'd never said."

"You're together officially? When did that happen?"

"Yesterday. But now he's nowhere to be found. Maybe he got scared."

"Never, he's not that type."

"So why isn't he answering his calls?" She began to pant.

Jaz pulled her phone out of her suit pocket. "Get back inside, you'll catch a chill. I'll call Holly."

Jaz followed Nina in and helped her to settle on the sofa and then went out of the room to call Holly.

She returned with a frown upon her face. "No one knows where he is. He hasn't taken the van. They presumed he must have bussed it into Wells, but he's not come back. Mitch has called Warren's parents and they've not heard from him either and Holly called the council in case he had a meeting there, but he didn't."

Nina felt her chin tremble. He'd promised to be there for her. Another contraction took her breath away and she gasped as she battled to calm herself down.

"Hun, I think maybe we need to get you to the hospital, as soon as," Jaz said.

"I want to wait for Warren."

Jaz went over to the sofa and knelt beside her. "The

most important thing is that you're in the right place to have this baby that seems to be well and truly on its way."

Nina panted until she could speak. "We can't go yet."

"Well, I'm staying with you until it's time. Or until Warren gets here."

Jaz left briefly to update Julian on what was going on and came back with a plate of food which she ate.

The contractions ebbed for a while giving Nina a break and, she hoped, time for Warren to appear again. It gave her time to have a bath and Jaz helped her in. The warm water relaxed her and seemed to slow everything down, allowing her to breathe.

By the time she'd dried and dressed, it was gone ten and the contractions returned, this time even stronger.

"Can you put the television on?" she asked Jaz. "It might take my mind off it."

Jaz switched on the television which was showing the local news. "Oh my goodness, there's been some sort of hold up with the armed police in Bristol."

Nina sighed as she saw the footage being shown from the news station's helicopter. "What's the world coming to?" Then she switched to a deep moan as the pain ripped through her, feeling as if her lower frame was being pulled in two different directions. She cried out.

"Right, that's it. We're going to the hospital," Jaz said. "It's going to take at least half an hour to get there. We can't wait any longer."

Nina looked at the notebook she'd been using to record the contractions. "Can you help me to the loo?"

Inside the confines of the downstairs bathroom, she tried ringing Warren one last time, but there was no answer. She gasped as another contraction started, tears streaming down her face. She moaned loudly, knowing she'd left it later than she really should have. She now felt an urgency to get to the maternity unit as soon as possible.

"I've put your bag in the people carrier," Jaz called through the door.

"Better put some plastic on the seats, in case my waters break." Nina felt bad about leaving it so long, but Warren had promised. She burst into tears as the pain surged through her. "I wanted him with me," she sobbed as Jaz opened the toilet door.

"I know, hun, hopefully he'll get the message and make it."

As Jaz drove, she panted, practising her breathing techniques between contractions. It was half ten and Warren still had not replied. *Maybe there's something wrong?* She didn't want him to have been harmed, but neither did she want him to have purposefully left her when he'd promised to always be there.

WHEN THEY ARRIVED at the hospital, she was in pure agony and crying out with the pain. The maternity unit were expecting her as Jaz had called ahead and read out the record Holly had been keeping of the contractions.

"We'll just check you over," the midwife said in a calm voice. "Are you the birthing partner?" she asked Jaz.

"Er...yes," Jaz said, then smiled at Nina. "I'm here, chick. I was with Holly for a lot of the time when she was having the twins, it'll be a breeze."

Nina laid back on the bed.

The nurse examined her. "You're already eight

centimetres dilated. Well done for managing this so far. You can go straight through to the birthing suite."

She helped her off the bed as Nina moaned and Jaz carried her bag.

Inside the room, the nurse helped her into a gown and took her blood pressure. The contractions were coming harder and so close together she barely had time to breathe between them.

Jaz held her hand. "You just need to concentrate on the baby now."

"I know," she said. "I can't wait to see her." She'd blotted everything out. The baby was the most important thing. She felt the determined Nina come to the fore, the woman who always reached her goals. The one who didn't need help. The independent woman.

"You're going to be the best mum ever."

Nina cried out as the pains became acutely intense.

"Would you like some gas and air?" the midwife asked.

Nina nodded, trying to remember her breathing exercises.

"Let me know if you want me to stay, or if I should fetch Sumitra," Jaz said. "Your Dad brought her here. They're in the waiting room."

Nina nodded. "Thanks."

Half an hour later her waters broke. She initially felt relief but then the contractions dragged through her body. She called out to Jaz. "Can you get Ma?"

Sumitra soon came in, her eyes open wide, rushing over to her and holding her hand.

She smiled and pulled the gas and air mask from her face. "I'm fine Ma. But I wanted you with me."

Tears fell down Sumitra's cheeks as she sat beside her

and took her hand. "I'm always here for you, angel. And I'm so proud of you and you've done so well."

She burst into tears and gasped. "Ma, he promised he'd be here for me."

"Ma's here. Just stay calm."

Then Nina felt an overwhelming urge to push.

CHAPTER 36

Warren sat staring at the cell door, wondering what time it was. There were no windows and he'd also been asleep at some point, although he didn't know how long for. He was disorientated, feeling as if he'd been there for an eternity. Finally, the door opened and Darius entered wearing his uniform.

"At last," he said feeling as if he could cry.

"I only just found out you were here! They had to keep it all under wraps until the op. I got your message and called back, but of course it went to voicemail, as they had it."

"Why won't they let me go?"

"You can go now. They had an op on."

"What, to do with Logan?"

"Yes, a big one. They couldn't allow the possibility of you contacting Scottie or Logan, that's why you weren't permitted a call. They pulled the SIM and battery out of your phone as soon as they took it off you, so it couldn't be tracked."

"I'd never have phoned Scottie, you know that."

"Yes, I do. I gave them the background, that you've distanced yourself from him and have had nothing to do with Logan since the robbery. I also explained about you giving Scottie money to keep him away from the wedding and showed them your message to me which proved you called me straight after the video call."

"So they believe you?"

"Yes, they apologised but there was nothing they could do. I can't give the details but as well as seizing an illegal consignment, they caught not only Logan but another gang leader. Sorry you've gone through this, mate. But you helped by giving them the address. So, no real harm done."

Warren shut his eyes. *I hope she hasn't had the baby.* "I need to get back to Eversley, When I left, Nina was having contractions. I don't even know what time it is."

"It's just gone two in the morning." Darius stood up. "I'll give you a lift back. It's the least I can do for the help you've given the force."

"I need my phone."

"I'm sorry, but they're keeping it as evidence."

"I have to contact Nina." He gulped hoping she was okay.

"You can borrow my phone."

"I don't know her number off the top of my head. Look, let's head straight to Eversley village. I need to explain it face to face, not in a message. I just hope it was practice contractions and she's at home." He didn't want to disturb her, so he decided to somehow rouse Jaz, she would know how Nina was.

"Let's collect your things from the desk and get going."

· · ·

As THEY SPED through the quiet streets of the city in the panda car, Warren turned to Darius.

"So what happened with Scottie and Logan? Can you tell me anything?"

"Scottie's been working for him for years. Since before he went inside. They were doing a deal and it sounds to me as if they wanted to put your money towards a purchase, then to make you the fall guy if it went wrong. Good job you called me and didn't go along."

"I told Scottie on the phone I was done with him. If I'd blocked his number, he'd not have got through."

"Don't beat yourself up. He could have phoned from another number."

"But an anonymous number wouldn't have been tapped by your guys."

"What's done is done. At least you didn't get involved. It could have had repercussions. The chief says it's the most successful operation of the year. It wouldn't have happened without your input. You might be in for a Chief Constable Commendation. He's not given one out for a while and has been under pressure."

"They treated me like a criminal." Warren shuddered and rubbed his wrists, still sore from the hand cuffs.

"No real harm done. Now let's get you back to Nina. I can see you're worried. I take it you're an official item now?"

"We were, but I may have just ruined it." He felt sick to his gut but prayed hard that she was fine and that she would understand once he'd explained.

They drove into the village, which was completely quiet, lit only by the soft amber streetlamps.

"I've not been here before, it's a far cry from where we live," Darius said followed by a low whistle. "You've gone up in the world."

"It's the second turning on the right. Ashbury Gardens."

Darius slowed the police car.

"Thanks for bringing me. I'll be okay and can walk back to the farm from here."

"Don't be a stranger," Darius said. "Bring Nina over and meet us. And the baby. You've turned into a good, solid man. Don't ever forget that."

Warren nodded then got out of the police car, his heart beating, wanting to know that everything was fine.

"Warren," Jaz called in a loud whisper from her open front door. "What happened?" She approached him. "Where've you been?"

"It's a long story."

The police car moved slowly out of the cul-de-sac.

"Well, it better be a good one." She crossed her arms.

"I was helping the police with an investigation."

"What?" She uncrossed her arms and gestured at him. "You were arrested?"

"Yes. They thought I was caught up in a dodgy deal my foster brother was involved in. They took my phone in case I was going to alert him. They still haven't given it back to me." He gestured towards the door. "Look, is Nina okay? I've been beating myself up over it."

Jaz took a step forward and placed her hand on his arm. "Sorry Warren, she had the baby a couple of hours ago. I've just got back, myself."

Warren felt as if he had been punched in the stomach. "I missed it?" he whispered, feeling hot. He turned away, not wanting her to witness his reaction.

Jaz's voice softened even more. "Hey, there was clearly nothing you could do. I'm sure once she's had time, she'll understand."

"But she thinks I just left her to do it alone." He turned around. "What was she saying? Was she upset?" He stared into Jaz's eyes.

"She was worried about you," Jaz said but he could tell she was being tactful. "Just give her time."

"It's all my fault." Warren's whole face quivered, there wasn't any point in him trying not to cry. "Everyone told me to cut Scottie off. To block his number. If I'd listened, it wouldn't have happened." He wiped his eyes. "I promised her, Jaz." His voice cracked, not being able to imagine Nina going through that whole process, the intense pain, when he was supposed to be with her. All he could hear in his head were his own words. *I'll always be there for you, I'll never let you down.* "And how's the baby?" Warren slumped the low wall in front of Jaz's cottage.

"She's perfect. Seven pounds exactly and healthy." Jaz put a hand on his shoulder. "The most important thing is that Nina and the baby are okay. She had me there and her mum. She wasn't alone."

"I need to see her to explain face to face." He looked up at her. He was shaking and wiped his face with the back of his hand.

Jaz sat beside him, her voice gentle but firm. "Warren, listen to me. Nina needs to focus on the baby right now. You can't go upsetting her. Give her some space. I'll call

303

you when she gets back. And of course I'll tell her exactly what happened."

AFTER TEA with Jaz in her kitchen, Warren refused her offer of a lift and trudged back to the farm, hating himself, repeating in his head, *Why didn't I block him?*

As he approached the farmhouse, he spotted Nick's car on the drive. Inside, he was waiting for him with Jane.

"Darius called us," Nick said, pulling Warren into a tight hug. "We're here for you, son."

Warren clung to his adoptive father and his voice cracked as he spoke. "I've messed up."

Jane joined them and they both held him as he sobbed.

CHAPTER 37

ina gazed at Ruby as she slept in the car seat beside her in the middle row of Jaz's people carrier. She found it difficult to drag her eyes away from her. Ruby had a shock of dark hair and a cute little mouth that quivered every now and again.

Belle turned around from the front passenger seat as Jaz backed onto her driveway. "I'm so excited to see her in her nursery."

"Me too," Nina said as she unclipped the seat belt, longing to feel her precious baby in her arms again. "But it's all got to be put together yet."

She glanced across at her new home. "I'm so grateful, Jaz, for you letting me live here."

"Hun, you're paying me rent."

"But you could have let it to that woman at the school. Take the thanks."

"Okay," Jaz said with a laugh. "But I still feel like you're the one doing me a massive favour. Now, we'll let you settle in peace."

"Thanks. Ma and Dad will be over in an hour."

"And Nina, I don't want to interfere, but as I said, Warren was totally broken by the fact he couldn't be here."

Nina just nodded. She'd listened in silence to what Jaz had relayed to her, about Warren being detained by the police, but had blocked it from her mind. She didn't want to spoil the moment and memories of bringing her perfect daughter home. A child that had been let down before she was even born, not by one dad, but by two! Although she knew that was unfair. Warren had only been her boyfriend for a matter of hours. Again, she pushed thoughts of him aside, although it wasn't easy.

She walked into her home with Ruby. It was just the two of them. She felt grounded. It wasn't just her now, she couldn't mess around with romantic feelings. She was responsible for another life and had to be strong for this little person who depended on her and her alone.

"Welcome home little one," she said with a smile. She'd never felt so centred in her life. As if being Ruby's mother was her sole purpose.

She removed Ruby from the car seat, held her in her arms and took her to the sofa to feed her. Ruby soon woke from the journey and began to make noises until she latched on, Nina smiled at her as she fed. Once she had burped her she felt sleepy herself and placed Ruby in her Moses basket and drifted off.

She woke to the sound of gentle knocking on the door. She rose from the sofa and answered it to find her mother and father there.

"We're here to help. Just tell us what to do," Sumitra said, her face beaming.

"Thanks. I need the nursery to be made up. The cot, the chest of drawers and the wardrobe. Sorry, I can get someone in to do it. You don't have to."

"There's no need to apologise," Tony said. "We've done enough flat packs in our time. I'm sure we'll manage."

"And make sure you rest," Sumitra said. "We'll sort it all. You can't do any heavy lifting."

Nina wished she hadn't ordered flat pack furniture, but it was so much cheaper. Ethan's mother had suggested she took furniture from the Shepton Mallet house which was still up for sale, but she didn't want anything from that part of her life.

She made teas and coffees as she heard her mother and father bickering.

"Let me read the instructions first!" Sumitra hissed at Tony.

Nina grinned. It reminded her of her childhood. She checked Ruby was sound asleep and then took the stairs, with a slight dragging pain present. She didn't want to risk spilling the teas on the way up but she wanted to go up and let them know that maybe they should put a hold on building the furniture.

As she reached the top, the doorbell rang.

"I'll get it," Sumitra said. "And check on the baby, in case she's stirred. I take it you're not up for visitors yet?"

"Oh, I don't know. It depends on who it is." Nina looked out of the window. There was no car, so she assumed it must be Jaz.

"Ah," her father said as he turned the instructions up the other way. "That's how it goes."

"Look, Dad, I can last a week without these being

made up. I'll get someone else to do it. I don't want you two falling out over it."

Sumitra returned. "It was that young man." She huffed. "I told him he's a day too late."

Nina looked out of the window to see Warren with his back to the house and she instantly wanted to follow him. She shut her eyes and took a deep breath, then reopened them to see him slowly walk away. The block she'd applied to the feelings she had for him instantly melted. She'd previously decided to give it a couple of days before she approached him, knowing Jaz had told him to give her time. But a flutter of excitement settled in her stomach, pleased he'd come over. Realising she would have felt let down if he'd actually stayed away considering how close they were.

She turned to Sumitra. "I need to speak to him," she said as a growing warmth covered her body. "It's unfair of me, not to hear him out." She felt a smile spread over her face, unable to contain it. "Can you keep an eye on Ruby?"

As she left the room, she felt the animosity fizzle away. After all, Jaz had said it was out of his control. She hadn't really listened to the full details, she'd not been in the mood, but as soon as she'd set eyes on him, she wanted to hear his voice, to hold him tight.

She held the rail, taking the stairs as quickly as she could considering the after effects of giving birth, then reached the bottom and walked to the door. She threw it open and called out to him. He turned and paused. She could see clearly from where she was standing that he exhaled, as if with relief. He paused for a moment, as if composing himself. She beckoned him and he ran towards her until he was only a couple of feet away.

"I'm so sorry." His voice cracked.

She stepped towards him and pulled him close, feeling his body shudder in her arms. "I know you are. What exactly happened? Jaz said Scottie caused trouble with the police."

He took a deep breath. "He was trying to drag me into a deal, I'm not aware of the actual items being dealt, but by the scale of the police operation, it was serious." He leaned back and gazed into her eyes. "It was my fault I got dragged into it. You were right. Mum and Dad were right, Darius was right. I should have cut Scottie off years ago. I had months when I could have blocked his number and this wouldn't have happened. I would have been … at the hospital, with you."

As she took in his gaze she knew he was hurting and could not bear to witness his remorse. She pulled him close and squeezed him tight. "You're a caring person." She leaned back. "Why was it that you didn't block him?"

"Because I'm an idiot. But yesterday, I told him as soon as he called, we're done, it's over." He paused. "Because of you. But it was too late, the police had already traced the call to my phone and assumed I was involved."

"But why, really, did you not block him sooner?"

He took a breath. "Because he was like a brother to me, I felt responsible for him."

She smiled at him, now feeling tears running down her cheeks as she witnessed the pure emotion he showed in his face. "You cared about him, he was all you had from your childhood." She swallowed as a lump formed in her throat. "You loved him, Warren." She watched his face quiver as he battled to control his emotions. "And I know why you told him yesterday that it was over." She pulled him close, not wanting to force him to say it, knowing that it wouldn't be easy for him to declare his feelings and there was time enough in the future. "You're a loyal man. I know you'd never have let me down and can't imagine how awful you felt locked in a cell, powerless."

"All I was thinking of was you. All I want in the whole world…" He took a deep breath. "All I want is for us to be a family."

Nina felt so close to this complicated man who had so much love to give. "It's what I want too. Come in. There's someone special I want you to meet."

"Wait." He pulled her hand. "I have to tell you. I love you, Nina."

She grinned up at him. "I know you do." She kissed him on the cheek. "And I love you too. Let's go inside."

As Nina watched Warren gaze at Ruby for the first time and lift her into his arms, she knew in her heart that her daughter would grow up to call this man Daddy.

CHAPTER 38

"Come on angel, you can do it." Tony laid on the floor with his granddaughter before him and a toy just out of her reach.

Ruby stretched her arm out and then made a squeaking noise before she cried in frustration.

"Dad, you're not her personal trainer," Nina said. "Stop tormenting her."

"I wanted her to crawl before Ma and I go on holiday. She's so close and we'll miss it."

Nina picked Ruby up and gave her the toy. "It seems a little cruel, she'll crawl when she's ready."

"I did it with you!" Tony said as he stood up and brushed himself down.

"You know what? That explains a lot!" Nina said with a laugh.

"You crawled at five months."

"I'm sure I did," she said as she kissed Ruby on the forehead. "Grandad will have you training for the England women's football team at this rate."

"Nothing wrong with a little parental encouragement."

"I know, Dad, I've had a lifetime of it, and it never ends."

"Now, are you going to cope with us gone for a couple of weeks? I know you're busy." They were staying with Florrie and David at their apartment in Gran Canaria.

"Yes, I'll be busy, but I'll take Ruby with me."

"We're so proud of you, darling."

Nina had noticed that Ruby had taken on the name *angel*, and she'd been promoted to *darling*. "All I ask is for you to babysit tonight so I can watch the darts."

Nina went up to her room to get ready. She smiled at the pictures she had collected on her dressing table. There was one of Warren in his robes at his graduation ceremony for his doctorate. He was now nicknamed *Doc Hunter* in The Eversley. There was another of them all at the farmhouse at Christmas with both sets of parents. Then a third picture of Warren with his award at the Avon and Somerset Police event where he'd won a Chief Constable Commendation for helping the police put two gang leaders behind bars. Nina felt it was part compensation for him missing Ruby's birth.

They'd been taking their relationship slowly, not wanting to take it too quick and fizzle out. Although the couple of days a week they'd started with soon became most of the week and in recent weeks, there hadn't been a day when they'd not seen each other. But it had developed over time and being with Warren was so easy and Ruby loved him already. He always got a giggle out of her. It was as if they both knew they'd be together, but the timing had to be right.

Ethan had finally received an offer on the Shepton

Mallet property which was waiting to complete. His mother said that he was going to make a settlement with Nina, but she decided she'd worry about that once the property had gone through. Her business was still in its early days and even though she had enough capital to put a down payment on the cottage, she couldn't raise a mortgage without proving she had a regular income. She guessed that would take time. Any spare cash, after paying her team who made her designs, was reinvested.

Nina was looking forward to the darts – it was the cup match as a finale to the winter season. Warren had asked her to join him beforehand for a quiet meal in the Eversley Bistro.

Once ready for her evening out, there was a knock on the door and she opened it to find Warren on the doorstep, looking exceptionally smart.

"I guess you won't be playing darts in that?"

He lifted a rucksack. "I've my team shirt in here. But as we're going to the bistro, I thought should make an effort." He wrung his hands together.

"Are you nervous about the game? she asked.

"No?"

"You seem it," she said. "You're making me nervous too." She turned around and took her coat from the stand just inside her door. "See you later," she called out to her dad. She'd already kissed Ruby goodnight, who was in the nursery with Sumitra.

"Have a nice time, darling," Tony called after her.

Nina stepped out and took Warren's hand as they walked the short distance around the green. She loved the feeling of being next to Warren but something was still stopping her from inviting him to live with them. It was as if she was waiting for something solid to hold onto before she made a commitment, before she allowed them to get super close. Before they spent the night together.

He opened the door of the bistro for her and they went inside. They were shown to the only laid table in the centre of the room, upon which was a small vase of red roses.

"This is lovely," she said. "They're quiet tonight."

"Would you like me to take your coat?" Natalie asked, beaming at her.

She removed her coat and passed it to her.

Warren waited until she was seated and then sat opposite her.

"You look stunning," he said. "You always look stunning. You're the most beautiful woman I've set eyes on. And you get more beautiful with every moment that passes."

She grinned at him. "Are you after a big favour or something?"

"Yes, I am." He looked nervous.

"What is it?" she asked. "Just tell me."

He took a deep breath. "I've a new job."

She frowned. "A job? What about your field? It's your passion, your life's work!"

He laughed. "I'm not giving it up. I've got the job I've always had my heart set on. As a professor."

"Oh my goodness, where?" She put a hand to her throat hoping this wasn't going to turn into bad news. "You're not moving, are you?"

"Of course not! It's commutable. The university is opening up a new centre in Taunton, for agricultural science. They're taking a long-term lease of the silvopasture so Mitch is compensated. And my salary, well it's more than I'd ever dreamed I could earn. It solves the endless wait for lottery funding."

"Oh my goodness, Warren, I'm so proud." She touched his hand across the table. "How did you find that job?"

"One of the deans was at the police awards night. I got chatting to her and then she contacted me out of the blue with the proposal! I'll have a regular income."

She smiled at him. "So what's the big favour?"

He retrieved a box from his pocket and looked at it as if summoning up the courage to lift the lid.

Nina stared at the box then up at him, her heart pounding.

He opened it and lifted out a ring with one large ruby, and two smaller rubies each side. "The favour is that I want you to marry me."

Nina put her hand to her mouth which was widening to a grin. "Yes, I'd love to."

Warren took the ring out and put his hand out for hers. "It's not like the rock you wore when I met you," he said.

"It's a ruby and a ruby has so much more meaning," she said.

"And there's more. I want you to allow me to buy the cottage with you. I've more than enough to raise a mortgage."

She laughed. "Of course you can."

He slid the ring onto her finger. "I love you, Nina."

She lifted her hand up to admire her ring. "I love it. And I love you too."

Warren called over to Natalie. "She said yes!"

"Let's go next door," he said. "Sorry, but there's no dinner."

She laughed as he led her out of the back entrance of the restaurant which took them into the main bar.

"It's a yes!" he called out.

Everyone cheered as she looked around the pub. All her friends were there. "You must have been pretty confident I'd say yes!"

"I took a punt on myself," he laughed. "Crack open the champagne," he shouted to Rob who had the bottles lined up.

"Calm down everyone," Jaz shouted. "We've got the match in an hour and only one glass of champagne each!" She scowled at Warren. "Why did you have to ask her today?"

Warren laughed. "Come on, the game will go great. Rob's overtaken me as the best player. We'll walk it."

"I can't wait to watch it," Nina said. "I feel like it's England in the football finals." She looked at Warren and then back to Jaz. "The women's team, of course." They all laughed.

The Dogs soon arrived.

"Ready for another thrashing?" Digger asked.

Jaz narrowed her large eyes. "I can see the nerves written all over your face. And you know we're going to take your crown when the summer season starts. We haven't lost a match in weeks."

"Whatever. We've won the league, why do you think you can take the cup?"

"Because my guys are hungry for it, that's why!"

Digger called out to Darren. "Daz, tell your kid to back down."

Nina laughed as she stood by her friend.

"Oi, she's no kid," Darren said. "She'll make mincemeat of us if you speak to her like that!" He winked at Jaz.

"Carl, you're on first!" Jaz called out as Warren put his arm around Nina.

"Digger you can start, mate," Darren said.

Nina smiled at Jaz. "Calm down. You're so tense. You need to enjoy it."

"You're right. Julian says I'm obsessed."

Carl threw his darts and then shook his head as he pulled them out of the board. "Sorry Jaz." He only made eighty-two.

"One hundred and eighty," the Dogs' crowd shouted in unison when Digger had taken his turn.

"Don't let them get to you," Jaz said in Carl's ear then pushed him towards the oche.

Carl tried his best but failed to claw it back with Digger finishing on a double twenty.

"Sorry, guys." He returned his darts to their case.

"It's not the end," Warren said. "Come on Eversley." He winked at Nina.

"Go on Rob, do your best!" Jaz said.

Nina had never seen Rob so focussed. She guessed he had his boxing head on as he looked fearsome. Every dart he threw went exactly where he wanted it to.

"You should go pro!" Warren shouted then turned to Nina. "I've been trying to convince him, he's good enough."

Rob won and ended with cheers and Katie threw her arms around his neck, giving him a kiss that was a lot more than a peck, which received an extra round of applause.

"Settle down," Jaz shouted. "Grace, you're on next!"

"Spud, it's your go," Darren said.

Grace beat him and everyone cheered although Reverend Stephens lost his game.

It was equal until the last game.

"Warren versus Daz," Rob shouted out. "Come on Doc Hunter!"

Everyone cheered as the last dart flew in and Warren took the game. He shook hands with Darren. "Sorry, Daz."

"No worries, you deserve the cup. And congratulations on your engagement."

"Well done," Digger said to Jaz. "Seriously, I'm impressed. It's gonna be a tough summer season for us."

"Newquay here we come," Carl shouted. They picked Jaz up and carried her outside onto the green to celebrate while she screamed at them to put her down.

AFTER THE FOOD which Adam had prepared, which was a selection of his speciality pies, Jaz sipped a well-earned cider at the bar with Nina and Holly and sighed. "I tell you, I needed this."

"Take some time off from darts," Holly said.

"I think I'll have to, I'm busy at the showroom with Dave gone."

"Looks like we're off to Newquay, then!" Nina said to her.

"Julian was threatening to make me go on my own! But I've convinced Simon to cover the pub for us."

Nina's phone began to ding with repeated notifications.

"You're popular," Jaz said.

"Has word got around about the engagement?" Holly asked.

"Most people I know are here." Nina pulled her phone out of her pocket. "It's my website. The app must be glitching." Her phone continued to ping.

"Oh, hun. I forgot to say, what with the game and Warren's proposal. Crystal said she was doing a reel this evening, on social media, showing off your clothes."

Nina blinked then logged into her store. "Oh my goodness, it's going crazy!" I'd better text Lindsey and co to make sure they've nothing planned for the next few weeks, we've a tonne of work to do." She laughed then noticed her parents approaching.

"Congratulations on your engagement," Tony said. "Warren told us his professor news and that he was proposing earlier tonight."

"Thanks. Where's Ruby?"

"Don't worry, she's sound asleep and Belle's watching her," Sumitra said then lifted her hand and admired her ring. "It's beautiful. Give me a hug."

"Thanks Ma," she said as she held her mother close.

Sumitra spoke into her ear. "I always said you'd marry a doctor."

CHAPTER 39

ina looked around the shop. It was different to how it used to be over a year before, when she'd closed it. Instead of rows of taffeta and lace, the shop was bursting with colourful cotton and wool. And the previous bridesmaid area was now a display of the baby hampers. They were her biggest seller with the largest margin – grandparents were her main target. They were also popular with workplace baby showers. She also catered for older children on her website but was keeping to the early years in her shop. Then there were her upsells – shelves of soft toys which she knew shoppers would find too cute to resist. She'd already taken a couple home herself.

She gazed at her logo which Holly had painted on the far wall – *By Nina,* with butterflies around it. The plan was to open further shops, as the internet sales had rocketed over the past few months, making her more money than the wedding dresses ever had. It seemed that whilst people liked life-hacks when it came to weddings, the sky was the limit when it came to showing off their children.

She moved a soft toy which had toppled onto its side.

"Ma," Ruby called to her from her pushchair, having just woken up.

Nina unstrapped her and perched her on her hip, then turned to a rapping at the door.

Holly smiled through the glass at her. Nina unlocked the door and let her in.

"Oh my goodness it looks lovely here. And you're all set for the reopening."

"I know, I can't believe it. I feel like I've really come home." Nina took in a deep breath. It had been an emotional rollercoaster for over a year. "Can you hold Ruby for me, I just need to use the loo."

She reached the toilet just in time. Even though she'd been sick, she smiled as she flushed the chain, then brushed her teeth with the toothbrush she kept in her cabinet. She'd been here before and knew it was only part of the process.

Back in the shop, she smiled at Holly bobbing Ruby up and down, singing a nursery rhyme. "Here she is," she said to Ruby.

"Ma," Ruby held her arms out.

"You're lucky this place was still available," Holly said as she passed Ruby to her.

"Connor nearly bit my hand off when I said I was interested in a new lease. All he'd had here were pop up shops. He's had no long-term interest at all."

"I bet you negotiated a good rate."

"You bet I did," she said with a laugh.

"I've heard your other news, that you and Warren completed on the cottage."

"Yes, once we received planning permission to extend it to the side. It's lucky there's so much land around the cottages. We want another bedroom and a playroom downstairs."

"It's always handy to have an extra guest room. We haven't got one at all, but we just stick the relatives over at the farm when they come in from Essex."

Nina smiled, her extra room wasn't intended for guests.

"How's Warren getting along at the university?"

"He's loving it. He's still writing the course and will oversee the delivery in October."

There was another rap at the door and Holly went over and let Warren in.

"How are my girls?" he asked.

"Daddy." Ruby outstretched her arms to him.

Nina passed Ruby over and smiled as Warren kissed Ruby on the cheek. "It's clear who her favourite is."

"Don't worry, you'll be favourite next time," he said.

"Next time?" Holly asked, looking at them both in turn.

Nina raised her eyebrows at Warren.

"You're not?" Holly grinned.

"I am! But only Ma and Dad know, so far. We're telling Nick and Jane today."

"Congratulations, how lovely," Holly said.

"There's a crowd forming outside," Warren said.

Nina looked out. "Are all these people here for the shop opening? I thought it was a coach party arriving for a trip around the cathedral."

"I think Jaz got the whole village here."

"Who's she rustled up for the ribbon cutting? She said it was a *local* celebrity, rather than a *national* one," Nina said.

"It's actually your dad who arranged it," Holly said with a laugh. "Oh, here he comes."

Nina went to the door. Outside, the life-sized mascot Hoggy and Sam Brent came into view. She laughed. "At least he always draws in a big crowd." She stepped outside.

Jaz started off the applause as Nina looked around. The bus from Eversley village must have been full, as it seemed that Holly saying that Jaz brought the entire village wasn't that much of an exaggeration.

"Don't worry," her father said. "We've booked a room at the town hall for the drinks and nibbles after everyone's had a chance to look inside the shop. We can't fit this many inside."

Nina stood in the doorway with Warren by her side as he held Ruby, who tucked her head against his chest, shy at being faced with so many people. Sumitra stood at the front of the crowd with a collection of her friends including Dr Gupta. Val and Len were also at the front, sitting, having brought folding chairs. The entire darts team had made it and she guessed they'd already been in the pub for a lunchtime drink, as they had their arms around each other. Grace and Brendan beamed at her. Mitch stood with the twins, who were enjoying an ice cream each. Next to them was Julian with his and Jaz's clan. Nick and Jane also had ice creams and waved at her.

Sam came over and smiled as Jaz held one end of the ribbon and Tony held the other end. Sam turned around to address the crowd. "It's an honour to be here for the opening of this new childrenswear shop, run by the super businesswoman Nina Hunter."

She smiled up at Warren. Every time she heard her married name, she thought back to their wedding day at Eversley village church. It had been such a special day.

Sam continued: "Please let's give a big cheer for..." He paused. "Sorry, Nina, what are you calling the new shop?"

"Something Special," Nina said with a laugh, pointing to the original sign which has been spruced up.

"Three cheers for *Something Special*," Sam called out and then cut the ribbon as the hip-hip-hoorays came from the crowd. Nina looked up at Warren as he gazed down at her with Ruby in his arms, and knew she simply couldn't be happier.

I HOPE you enjoyed this series if you want to read my new series *Escape to Lake Blue* set in an alpine village then you can start with *New Beginnings at Lake Blue*:

Heartbroken and lost, she decides to spend the summer at her late father's birthplace. Little does she know – this trip will change her life forever.

Isabelle is suffering with empty nest syndrome after her youngest takes a job on a cruise ship. She hopes to cross a few things off the bucket list she wrote with her husband, but her life is blown apart when he leaves her high and dry.

With the family home sold, she decides to do something she has always dreamed of, to visit the birthplace of her late father.

Against the wishes of her mother, Isabelle heads to Lac Bleu, to research her family history and connect with relatives she has never met. There, she meets Jacques who runs a boat hire business and dips her feet into the waters of a fresh romance.

But when a secret kept for decades knocks her for six, Isabelle questions her place in the world. Can she forgive the lies she has been fed her entire life? Or will the past ruin her chance for a new beginning?

ACKNOWLEDGMENTS

I'd like to thank my creative writing tutor Rosemary Dun, both inside the OU and out! You encouraged me to pursue novel writing and gave me so much information and guidance, I'm still reading the handouts! You are amazing. Thanks also goes to my brilliant mentors Alison Knight and Jenny Kane of Imagine Creative Writing and their Novel in a Year course, which gave me lots of help and kept me on track and for continuing to be dear friends.

Thanks to the inspirational friends I met through the Romantic Novelists' Association, and the Bristol writing community (I'm too scared to list everyone in case I miss someone off!) And to my Beta readers, Tara Starling, Cinnomen Matthews McGuigan, and Michelle Armitage. Thanks also to Helen Blenkinsop who is a guru on the 'hook' and amazon ads. And thanks to my best writing friends – Callie Hill, Claire O'Conner and Jenny Treasure, for also being beta readers and for sharing the journey with me. And to my Cozy mastermind, especially Scarlett and my accountability partners Soraya, Halana, Kari, Wendy and Mary. My Editor Becky Halls who is more than an editor and also an inspiration. My final proofreader Liz Lane who hunts for the last pesky typos. And not forgetting my mates Andy and Laura who make life fun!

Thank you to my advance reader team who are really supportive and there for me, even from the first book.

Thank you to those on my mailing list who interact with me.

And thank you to Victoria Tait for helping me out so much when I need it most.

Thanks to my family for supporting me, especially Gary for putting up with me tapping away at the keyboard 24/7.

Made in United States
North Haven, CT
26 September 2025

80142014R00196